When
Nighttime
Shadows
Fall

When Nighttime Shadows Fall

a novel

Diane Michael Cantor

The University of South Carolina Press

© 2017 Diane Michael Cantor

Published by the University of South Carolina Press
Columbia, South Carolina 29208

www.sc.edu/uscpress

Manufactured in the United States of America

26 25 24 23 22 21 20 19 18 17
10 9 8 7 6 5 4 3 2 1

Library of Congress Cataloging-in-Publication Data
can be found at http://catalog.loc.gov/

ISBN 978-1-61117-832-6 (paperback)
ISBN 978-1-61117-833-3 (ebook)

This book was printed on recycled paper with
30 percent postconsumer waste content.

In Memory of
Grace Paley
1922–2007

Who inspired a generation of writers to tell the stories of those
all around them, and by honestly expressing such stories,
learn better how to tell their own.

In Honor of
Constance M. Park, M.D.

Who encouraged a generation of medical students to see in each
patient a unique personality and brave story rather than only
the manifestations of illness.

When Nighttime Shadows Fall

I need someone to love me most every time of day,
Someone who truly loves me, no matter what folks say,
Just like a tiny baby when nighttime shadows fall,
I need someone to love me more than anyone at all.

Someone who cares about me
Who'll always take my side
Won't let nobody curse me
'Less they want to step outside.

I need someone who wants me to be there all the time,
Who won't have any friend who's not a friend of mine.
Just like springtime waters flow down the mountainside
I need someone to help me against the raging tide.

Someone who cares about me
Who'll always take my side
Won't let nobody curse me
'Less they want to step outside.

I need someone to hold me when the winter wind is cold
Someone who'll never leave me or let our love grow old,
Just like a little puppy who's left out all alone
I need someone to find me and take me to their home.

Someone who cares about me
Who'll always take my side
Won't let nobody curse me
'Less they want to step outside.

I need someone to love me most every time of day,
Someone who truly loves me, no matter what folks say,
Just like a tiny baby when nighttime shadows fall,
I need someone to love me more than anyone at all.

by Mickey Osgood and performed by
Steel Vulture, Canton, Georgia, 1973

Contents

viii

Preface

This is a work of fiction. All characters and situations are invented, and any resemblance to any person, living or dead, is completely coincidental and unintentional.

In Appalachian Georgia in the early 1970s, before the expansion of Medicaid benefits, prenatal care was unavailable to those who could not pay for it or who did not receive private insurance benefits. Pregnant teenagers, a population highly susceptible to complications during pregnancy and most at risk of giving birth to premature or low-birth-weight babies or those with birth defects, often had no access to prenatal care and nutrition and only saw a doctor for the first time when they appeared at a hospital emergency room ready to deliver.

DIANE MICHAEL CANTOR
Savannah, Georgia
2016

First Days

Atlanta, Georgia, 1973

My father was always very kind unless you crossed him. When it was time to return to college my junior year, I crossed him. I didn't mean to, but I was nineteen and knew what I wanted didn't include attending classes. At an early age I had figured out the reason my father's old army buddies called him "Bull" and why, when I acted particularly stubborn about wearing my cowgirl outfit out to a family dinner instead of the nice dress my mother had selected, or when I insisted I could pop open a can of spinach with my bare hand just like Popeye instead of using a can opener, I was just like him.

He never yelled at the people who worked at his downtown jewelry store. He considered raising his voice an admission of his inability to maintain authority, as well as ungentlemanly conduct. But when I told him I planned to leave college so I could be in the *real* world, he puffed out his chest like an aggressive Scottish terrier and yelled at me, veins showing in his neck, the muscles rippling in his arms as he clenched his fists.

"Laura, that's the dumbest thing I've heard of," he shouted, pounding the kitchen counter between us. "You're gonna throw away a scholarship to a New York college people practically have to die to get into so you can work in this health project doing something you're unqualified to do. It's out of the question." He turned away from me, focusing his attention on the special everything-but-the-kitchen-sink scrambled eggs he was fixing for us that Saturday morning, indicating that the matter was settled.

"It's not up to you, Dad!" I nervously dug my fingernails into the palms of my hands, but I still managed to speak up. "I'm not a kid anymore. You can't make me go to college."

"Maybe not," he conceded, dishing us up generous plates of eggs and setting down two mugs of strong black coffee. "But I don't have to keep supporting you either. Ever think of that?" His startlingly blue eyes stared me down.

"I'll live on my salary. I'll be fine. I'm not asking you to support me."

"Well, Miss Independence, how 'bout when you get sick of playing social worker and you've used up all your money just getting by, and there's no more scholarship? How're you gonna finish your degree then?" He doused his eggs with Tabasco sauce. "Don't come crying to me."

"Dad, I've never come crying to you," I insisted, knowing I hadn't done that even when I was a little kid and scraped my knee. "Anyhow, what about how you always say that all work is honorable? Besides, it's a once-in-a-lifetime opportunity. If some lady hadn't turned it down at the last minute, they'd never have considered me without a degree."

"Maybe they shouldn't. What do you know about social work?" he asked more calmly, clearly hoping to reason with me. "This is a dead end. Even if nobody cares right now because they're in a pinch, it'll mess you up later not having a degree. Doors will shut in your face. I can't stand by and watch you throw away your opportunities. If you only knew what your mother or I would have given for the chance to go to college full time."

I was tempted to say I *did* know since he'd told me a hundred times how hard it was after my grandfather died, when he had to drop out of school to support his family any way he could while he went to night school. But something about his frustration and the suffering in my mother's eyes whenever she relived memories of what had happened in Europe silenced me.

"But *nobody* told you what to do, Daddy," I reminded him. "They wouldn't have dared."

Even with his head bent over his plate, I could see the crinkling around his eyes as he started to smile. I had scored big acknowledging that no one pushed *Bull* Bauer around.

"You're right about that," he agreed proudly. "But I never tried to do things I knew nothing about. Being smart isn't everything. You don't know a thing about poor North Georgia towns or finding pregnant teenagers. Before they show, they'll be hiding. And what about all the people you can't help?" He sighed deeply. "Laura, you're too young to deal with turning people away when you're their last resort."

I assured him it wouldn't be that way at all. I had read the New Families Project guidelines and knew it would be easy to attract clients since the services were free and the families had so much to gain. I pictured myself leading a dedicated team, dispensing hope to those who had been ignored by an unjust healthcare system and abandoned by their boyfriends. I would be trained, just as high school assignments had prepared me for college and going away to college had equipped me for the challenge of standing up to my father, who, though he loved me, didn't know everything.

Chadwick, Georgia (a few weeks later)

I arrived at the Project office, expecting to be oriented by the administrator, who was driving over to explain our admissions process. Since I was early, I let myself in with the key I'd picked up in the Atlanta office and began glancing through the several large manuals on my desk. I had hardly slept the night before in my excitement about leaving student life for the work world. My parents had lent me money to buy a used Plymouth Duster, which though dented by its previous owners, I had proudly driven forty miles to work wearing my new blue suit. I had filled out and brought with me all the necessary application and insurance forms. I was ready for anything.

When after an hour the office manager had still not come in, I checked the blinking answering machine and learned she had stayed home with a sick grandchild. Another message informed me that due to a collision between a chicken truck and a logging trailer near Ellijay, the highway was shut down and Mrs. Cremins, our regional administrator, was unable to get through. I should review materials on my own and drive around town to get acquainted with the community. I might as well enjoy it, her brisk voice informed me, since once we were up and running, I'd likely never again have such an easy day.

I was disappointed, like someone who has dressed with care and anticipation for a party where no one asks her for a single dance. I read through my manuals for a while and sharpened my pencils. I placed pens in the holder on my desk and arranged my folders and notebooks in my desk drawers. I fixed a pot of coffee even though I wasn't sure how much coffee to put in the machine. I placed extra toilet paper in the restroom and changed a light bulb that had burned out in the conference room. I picked up the mail that had been pushed through the mail slot and placed it on the desk in the reception area. Then I was out of ideas, so the most productive thing seemed to be driving around to determine where clients might live and where high schools were located. I was starting out, car keys in hand, when I collided with a woman who was opening the door just as I walked out.

"I'm sorry, ma'am. Guess I come at a bad time," she said nervously, backing away. She laughed a thin laugh that turned into a bottomless cough. She covered her mouth with a tissue as I invited her inside. Since she kept coughing, I asked her to sit down on the couch while I got her some water. She took a polite sip and asked if maybe I had some coffee since only something hot was any good at stopping her coughing spells when they came on that way.

I knew my mother wouldn't approve of my offering somebody coffee that had been sitting around for a while, but I didn't want to take time to brew more with her seated in front of me coughing so hard. I poured a mug of the strong-smelling liquid left in the coffeemaker and added three sugars and several spoons of creamer, hoping to tone it down. She took a long drink of coffee, but then she coughed again so sharply I worried what to do. This must have shown in my face since, before I could reach her, she put up her hand, waving me off. So I sat there waiting awkwardly, as if witnessing a private struggle I should not have seen. She took another sip of coffee and pushed back strands of greying hair that had fallen from behind her ears. Then she tightly arranged her raincoat around her as if she were cold.

I asked what I could do for her. I hadn't been trained, but it was clear she was not a pregnant teenager. I wondered if she'd come to the wrong office but was too sick to move on to wherever she was supposed to be. I wondered what *I* should do with her. She looked sick enough to collapse right in front of me.

"Don't you worry 'bout me, honey. I'll be all right after a while. Now that y'all are set up, I come to find out what you can do for Judy. I been watchin' every day to see when somebody'd be here takin' applications."

When I asked who Judy was and if she'd come with her, she stopped talking and took her time drinking her coffee. She seemed to relish it, though I guessed it must have tasted very burnt even after all I had poured into it. Finally, her coughing quieted and she was ready to talk.

"I been working the mills since before you was even thought of, honey," she explained. "And before that, I was down at Chadwick's."

"Is that a store? We don't have it in Atlanta."

"So *that's* where you're from," she said knowingly, as if I'd revealed my ignorance by wearing a T-shirt advertising it. "You *must* have seen it driving in. You know, down the road, the long building with the tin roof? Looks like a chicken house, only bigger? Well, it ain't a coop. Inside they make all kinds of farm machinery. Mostly stuff for poultry. The work's real hard. Got to be fast or they take you off the line. They laid me off when I started breathin' hard this way. Said I couldn't stand the pace. And they got no retirement plan. No nothin'. Not even chicken feed."

"I think I did pass it," I said, recalling the long, metal building with the rusting roof. "There weren't any windows so I thought it was for storage. People work in that place?"

"If they can get it," she answered bitterly, as if I should know better.

Then another fit of coughing cut through her so violently I actually worried something inside her might break loose. No one I knew had ever coughed that intensely or looked so vulnerable. I took a few ornamental cushions from the easy chair at my side and propped them behind her, hoping she might breathe more easily. She smiled at my effort, but pushed them away and leaned back.

"Thank you, honey. But that don't do no good. Gets so bad some nights I hardly sleep a wink. Since they took the TV, ain't nothin' to watch. Readin' wears me out, but I still can't sleep. So I lie there. Judy and me used t'go to the show, but she don't want to no more. Sits there worryin' about her baby comin'. Don't help it none."

So there it was. Judy must be her daughter, but this lady looked far too old to have a teenaged daughter.

"Is Judy with you?" I asked again, glancing out the back windows to the parking lot. The Project living room, with its overstuffed couches, love seat, and hooked rug had been designed to look homey to encourage clients to feel they were in a friendly place, not a government waiting room. Through the curtains, I could make out an old grey station wagon but could not tell who was sitting inside it.

"She's out there all right." She cleared her throat and stared at me, sizing me up. I felt her eyes might bore through me. "She's already been through so much with folks down at the welfare office and the hospital askin' so many questions. I saw one of your flyers and figured I'd see whether y'all could help before puttin' her through more questions." She smiled proudly, sitting up a little straighter. "She's young, but she's not tough like her mama. All those pryin' questions shame her pretty bad."

So Judy was her daughter, and she was young. At least that was a start. I sat up in my chair, wanting to get on with the interview. It felt wrong for a pregnant girl to sit out in the car while her sick mother pled her case. I felt nervous to be taking an application without first observing someone else do it, and there seemed no point in talking at all without Judy.

"Honey, I know y'all are real busy startin' up this place and all," she said appreciatively, though the office was empty and our silence disturbed only by the hum of the refrigerator and the copier cycling on and off. "I reckon I'm takin' too long gettin' to the point, but it hurts to come in here beggin' for help after I worked so hard all my life. Can you bear with me a just little longer?"

I felt ashamed to have so poorly concealed my impatience. Her expression told me she saw through me. I might listen sympathetically to her, but I was actually interested only in Judy.

"I'm sorry, ma'am. I didn't mean to rush you," I told her, hoping to convey my regret. "You take all the time you need." I settled back in my chair, thinking of how my mother never interrupted anybody telling her a story. My father had also explained when I was small and sometimes accompanied him to his store when there was no one to watch after me that you should never push a customer when you're doing business. If they want to take their time talking things over with you before they purchase a ring or a necklace or even a pickle fork, then you just listen and wait until they're ready.

"Well, all right then. This is how it happened," she said gratefully, her thin body visibly relaxing once she knew I wasn't going to rush her. "Back after my operation, don't know what I would've done without Judy. She practically carried me like I was a child. They took out over half of one of my lungs. Used t'feel it aching when I breathed. Like a load of brick was falling. Now I don't feel nothin' there. But the other side, they say they got to open up again. I tell you . . . if it wadn't for Judy out there, I'd tell them, 'No.' I'd tell them go cut on somebody else. 'Cause I don't want no more scars. Down my front it looks like railroad tracks."

She coughed again. It ripped through her like scissors. She fumbled in her purse and pulled out a pack of Salems. Trembling, she stuck one between thin lips, greasy with pink lipstick, and finally lit it. A brief light of pleasure showed in her face as she inhaled until she looked cautiously over at me to see if I were judging her. I *was* wondering how anyone who coughed like that could stand to inhale cigarette smoke, but remembered my father explaining that people who don't smoke can't understand how good it feels and how hard it is to quit. He had begun as a young soldier during World War II, when smoking was encouraged to relieve stress and calm the nerves, and free cigarettes were distributed by tobacco companies. Although my mother and his cardiologist had forced him to quit, he confided that he still dreamed about smoking. The smell, which repelled me whenever I was in a closed room with someone who was smoking, filled him with longing, even after twenty years of abstinence. I tried hard to suppress my own desire to cough, either out of sympathy or because of the heavy cloud of mentholated smoke above our heads.

"What's it matter if I do or I don't?" she asked defiantly, mistaking my discomfort for veiled criticism. "They say don't smoke 'cause it makes it worse. But it don't feel no different. Sometimes it's like somebody lights a match inside me. But it goes away. It ain't always on my mind.

"'Less I start worryin' 'bout what Judy's gonna do on her own when I'm gone. I don't let on to her. She's worried enough 'bout the baby. But I know I'm not long for it. If they keep takin' lung, what you s'posed to breathe with?"

She took a long drag on her cigarette. Her body trembled as she let the smoke out.

"Judy wouldn't never have got in trouble if I hadn't taken sick," she said protectively. "See when I was laid up in the hospital after the surgery, she was all by herself. I kept tellin' her, 'Judy, you better call some of those girls you went to school with 'fore they forget you.' But she wouldn't. I don't really know why. Maybe she was ashamed to see 'em when she got left so far behind."

"Did they hold her back?" I asked as matter-of-factly as I could, trying to understand what had happened to the girl hiding in the car. Unless a person moved to a new community so nobody really knew about their past school failures, being held back was a defeat impossible for anyone to recover from, no matter how pretty they were.

"Yes, after she got the hepatitis she missed a lot of days. Then when she came down with the diabetes for a spell, she had to drop out of the vo tech. She was studying keypunch, but she had to quit. She's always been sickly. When she was a little girl somethin' made the skin peel off her fingers like when you're sunburned. And that same summer her toenails turned brown and shriveled up just like blossoms when they're spent. She couldn't hardly wear shoes come time for school. Always had to miss a lot. I reckon that's how come she's so shy." She laughed a wheezing laugh. "She sure didn't get that from me. I *say* what's on my mind. Least I did 'til Everett left me when the bills was sky high and I was flat on my back.

"I done the best I could to hold things together, but all my children left home early. Guess none of 'em saw no reason to stay. 'Cept Judy. Me and her was just natural close." Her gaunt face studied my own until I felt ashamed to be so tanned, well-fed, and healthy sitting beside her. Her pale blue, imploring eyes commanded me even as the tears ran down her face.

"Don't you go thinkin' Judy did it all the time. I know there ain't been others. That little girl never even thought about fellas. But being by herself, and him promising her things the way a soldier'll do a girl when he's home on leave. He told her he loved her and she was the kind of girl he'd like to settle down with. Then he got her to drinkin'. And well, you know the rest. It ain't nothin' new.

"It happened last time they put me back in the hospital when I started breathin' so bad. After I come back home and she told me who it was, I knew right off it was no use. 'Cause . . . now I can't tell you his name, but let's just say if they'd lock a fella up for what he done t'my Judy, there'd be a mighty fancy name down at the jail house."

I wanted to shout that it didn't matter who he was. He had no right to rape a teenage girl. That was exactly what it was since she was still a teenager. Right was right and wrong was wrong. "We don't have lawyers on staff here," I told her, choosing my words carefully since it was my very first day. I was also thinking that if Judy wouldn't even come inside to talk to me, she might never agree to answer a lawyer's questions. "Do you think Judy would talk to a lawyer?" I asked. "I could give you the number for Legal Aid. Or I could call down there, if you'd like to get her an appointment."

"Thank you, but there's no need, honey. The fella down there told us all about Judy's rights and paternity suits and stuff like that. But you know what our life'd be like if we tried one of those?"

She stubbed out her cigarette and then immediately lit another while she watched me, sizing up what I could know, with my Atlanta accent and my neatly manicured hands, soft with lotion, which had never suffered more than a paper cut.

"I reckon maybe you don't know." She studied my face and said wearily, "This ain't Atlan'a, honey. Up here's a lot different from down there. There's them and there's us. The ones who live in the big white houses and the ones that don't. They'd make our life so's a dog wouldn't take it. You know what they'd do if my Judy was to name names in court? They already threatened her."

She cleared her throat and took a long drink of coffee.

"See, she'd been callin', trying to make him do the right thing. And he always hung up on her. Or they'd say he wadn't home. But one night real late, after we was already in bed, this car come screeching up to the house and then somebody was layin' on the horn like to never stop. So Judy put on her robe to go see what it was. And it was *him*. Only he wadn't alone. She could see him coming up towards the house. His friends was still in the car blowin' the horn.

"So she went on out there. She was afraid if she didn't the neighbors'd call the police." She paused dramatically, waiting to see if I shared her indignation.

"He was filthy drunk. He started cussing her out like she wadn't even dirt. The whole bunch of 'em was fallin' down drunk. He had a bottle in his hand, and he smashed it out in the road against a tree. He called her every dirty name you can think of. Asked her how she come to think he'd want to hitch up with *trash*. Told her only trash gets knocked up. Nice girls didn't get themselves in trouble. Said he could tell he wadn't the first one anyhow." Her frail shoulders shuddered at the vileness. "Then he grabbed her and started shaking her like he wanted to knock the breath out of her. Told her if she ever told *anybody* her lies, if she ever tried blaming it on him, if she even *called* him again, he'd fix her so no man would ever want her. Then he pulled some money out of his pocket and threw it down on the ground. Said he figured he should have paid her in the first place.

"He said that to my *child*. Then they pulled the car up in the yard so he could get in. And they went tearin' out right through the flower bed, laughin' and throwin' bottles out the windows. You might even pass him on the street sometime. He's home from the army now, working for his daddy."

She sighed and lit another cigarette. "Honey, that's how it is up here." She began to cough so harshly she stubbed it out and struggled to catch her breath.

I felt helpless and ran to get her some ice water. It was all I could think to do.

"No thank you, honey," she finally said. "Water don't help. Just give me a second. I'll be all right." She cleared her throat and sadly shook her head. "It sure is a shame about those guidelines y'all got here." She was looking over the application laid out on the table between us. "The welfare lady sent us over since she can't do nothin' 'til after the baby comes. Guess she didn't know girls can't be more than three months gone t'get in your project." She calculated nervously on her fingers. "Reckon Judy's on to seven by now. But she's been took real good care of. Been seeing old Doc Wilcox right here in town. But he won't see her no more since we can't pay up. You got t'pay up by your seventh month or he won't deliver you. Said he was sorry but he wadn't no charity institution." Her eyes blazed at me. "You bleeve he said that to a little seventeen-year-old girl?"

So I was correct. Judy *was* a teenager, but she was out of luck. She was past our deadline. I had wanted to offer her new hope but saw now I had none to offer. And as hard as it was to face Judy's mother, I began to feel relieved Judy had stayed in their car.

"So you know what I done?" Her expression was proud and defiant as she called me back. "I tell you, honey, I did somethin' I never done before. I begged that man. I done without a lot before, but I ain't never begged none of those people. But I told that doctor 'bout me bein' laid off. And then how I had to leave the mill. Told him how Judy had to leave there, too."

I hadn't seen a mill driving into town. I knew about the textile plants further north in Dalton. I hadn't realized any mill would hire a teenage girl who was *pregnant* and with all the illnesses Judy had besides.

"I swore no child of mine would ever go to the mill," she continued. "But with the baby comin' and me sick, I let Judy try it. And she worked harder than anybody. But you know how it gets in a weavin' room?"

She looked at my hands and smiled as if she'd told a joke. "No, I reckon you don't know nothin' 'bout it. But, honey, you take my word. You get in there and the lint gets t'flyin' so you can't hardly breathe. And Judy's always had asthma. When she was a little girl sometimes she'd get attacks so bad we had t'thump her on the back to get her little lungs goin' again. One time she went in the hospital for a whole week when she was just a little bitty thing. So she couldn't take that mill. Even when they come out with the masks."

She started coughing so badly she sloshed coffee over the side of her mug as she tried to set it down. "I'm sorry, honey," she said. "I don't know why I'm so shaky today." She cupped both hands around the mug before she took another sip.

"Like I was tellin' you, they come out with these masks to keep out the fiber. Most of it anyhow. Made a big deal about giving them out for free. Same time as that energy bizness everybody was fussin' about on the TV. Then they told us they couldn't afford to keep the work rooms heated. Said if folks didn't want to take a cut in pay, they'd have to work with their coats on. You bleeve that! I told *my* child to come home.

"And I told that doctor. Looked him square in the eye. Told him I knew I wouldn't be around much longer, but if he'd take care of my child I'd pay his whole fee before my time comes. I'd get the money together no matter what I had to do. And as soon as Judy got back on her feet, she'd be back to work, too. We'd pay him right up before we paid anybody else a single penny.

"I was thinking, rich or poor, they're still mothers and fathers. They still got feelings. But he stared down at me like I was some ole rag to wipe up the floor with. And he says, 'Ma'am if I did it for you, there'd be ten more like you tomorrow morning. I'm sorry, but you go to the health department.'

"But the lady there said there was nothing she could do." She rolled her eyes. "'Cept to tell us when Judy's time comes to take her to the emergency room and one of the interns'd have to help her." She sank back into the cushions completely spent.

I drank the cup of water I had poured for her, not from thirst, but to give me time to think. I needed to conclude the conversation, but I could not bear to disturb her and walk her to the door.

II

"It ain't right I can't do nothin' but sit here and watch. At *my* age. Honey, how old you think I am? I bet you guess wrong. I bet you think I'm an old lady." She looked at me slyly, daring me to guess.

I was afraid to insult her by answering truthfully that she easily looked fifty-five. So I waited.

"OK, then I'll tell you. Next month, Lord willin', I'll be thirty-seven." She smiled ruefully, observing my surprise. "It's OK. You don't have to try to hide it. I know I look like somebody's ole grandma," she said indignantly, the idea incensing her, making her voice grow stronger.

"Honey, you might not believe it, but I used t'be pretty. Had a little meat on me. Men ran circles around me, and I won a beauty contest when I was barely sixteen. Had wavy blonde hair like on the TV. I was goin' t'be a beautician." Her voice fell. "Then I met Everett. And one thing led to another. I got married up." She sighed heavily. "But Everett's been gone since Judy was just a baby. He took t'drinkin'. Not just on Saturday nights either. He was drinkin' all the time. They fired him up at the mill. Fired him down at the dump. When he run out on us, it was no big loss." She sank back further into the brown and orange plaid sofa, which swallowed her.

"He never even sent us a postcard 'til 'bout a year ago. I got this letter from a hospital in Birmingham that said he had TB. Don't know how they found us 'less he told 'em we was his kin. But I had nothin' to send him. Seen him go through too much money in my time. Drinkin' his paycheck when there wadn't money for milk in the house. Judy'll get nothin' from him. She don't even remember what he looks like."

Thin and light as she was, it took all her strength to pull herself up from the couch, but she summoned her dignity and got up to go. She had had enough of my feeble sympathy and bad coffee.

"I won't take any more of your time, honey. Judy's probably sittin' out there getting' her hopes up. No need for that."

She took a scrap of paper out of her purse and handed it to me.

"Here's our number, honey. But I don't 'spect you t'call. Prob'ly won't have a phone much longer anyhow." She started toward the door. "Just don't seem right they make rules to leave Judy out 'cause she shows up a little late." She spoke directly, without pleading, simply calling for the world to be fair. "Honey, couldn't y'all make a special case just this once? Judy don't have nobody to help her. You're our last chance."

Then she closed her battered pocketbook and put it over her arm. She turned to me, patting my arm. "Don't you go blamin' yourself, honey. I know you want to help us. And you talk real nice." She smiled at me. "Don't you worry. We'll get by somehow. Looks like we always do."

My father and mother were working companionably in the kitchen preparing dinner when I arrived. She was cutting vegetables for a large salad while he basted a brisket roast that was simmering on the stove. I had smelled the aroma of garlic, onions, and mushrooms as soon as I opened the door, but was surprised to see my father so early since he usually did not make it home until seven o'clock. I had contemplated relaxing in a hot bath before facing him and acknowledging that he was correct. I hadn't been able to help anyone.

"Isn't it nice your father came home early to surprise you?" my mother asked brightly, enjoying the simple domestic duties she was sharing with him since he worked such long hours. She wore a yellow apron emblazoned with tiny red flowers and the words "World's Best Cook," which he had given her, and her eyes and smile seemed more joyful than when she was absorbed in tasks on her own. Her dark hair curled with particular enthusiasm, perhaps assisted by the steam released from a large pot next to the roast.

"First days are always rough." My father smiled warmly at me. "But you don't look so bad. You made it."

"Just barely," I confessed, telling them about my postponed orientation, and without naming Judy, sharing the story of my first applicant. "You were right, Dad." I tried but could not conceal my discouragement. "It was the saddest situation in the whole world. And I didn't do a thing to help her."

"Sounds like you did all you could do, Laura," he said sympathetically. "I know it felt awful to turn them away, but there'll be lots of others you will help. You know that, don't you?"

"That's not what you said before, Dad," I reminded him. "I think you were right. Tomorrow I'll just have to turn away more girls. I don't know why I ever thought I—"

"Wait just a minute." He closed the pot and set down his spoon to come put his arm protectively around me. "It had to feel terrible. Nothing anybody should have to deal with on their first day. But I was wrong to be so negative. I didn't want you to leave school. I still don't. So maybe I laid it on a little thick," he confessed. "I don't really believe you won't help anybody. *Of course* you will." He looked helplessly to my mother for support.

"Your father's right, darling," she said encouragingly. "And you would have felt differently if your day had been the one you expected." She shook her head. "You'll feel better after your training. Besides, you *did* help that lady. Maybe not the way you wanted. But she needed someone to pour her heart out to and you were there."

"But words aren't enough, Mom. I couldn't do a thing to help her daughter. They would have been better off saving the gas it cost them to drive over."

"Sometimes words are all there is, my dear," she answered softly, stroking my hair back from my forehead with her cool, smooth fingers, and looking off into some distant place where my father and I could not follow her. "I would have given a great deal in those dreadful days before I came to this country for a few kind words." Her radiance seemed to fade before our eyes, as it had done before, when a phrase or a smell or a strain of music recalled the horrors of her youth. "Kindness is very powerful," she said, her voice savoring the word. "Without it, some of us would never have made it."

. . . .

CHAPTER 2

In This Locale

"Now let's get a few things straight," Mrs. Cremins said a few days later, when she made it to the Project office. The regional administrator was a short woman, not even five feet tall, though she easily weighed two hundred pounds. She wore a dark blue suit that squared off her figure, and I discovered, since she had originally interviewed me in her Atlanta office, that her Southern accent thickened perceptively the further north she traveled from the city.

"I am very familiar with the people up here," Mrs. Cremins informed me. "Because I *was* one not so many years ago. My husband's people still live up in Tiger, and Mama was born near the marble quarries around Tate. So I know what you're gonna be up against, and I can't have you fallin' for their tricks."

I felt relieved that Nadine, our office manager, who had spent her entire life in the area, was at lunch so she could not hear our conversation. I had learned the first time I met Mrs. Cremins that her whisper was louder than most people's normal speaking voices. That afternoon she had stared at me so skeptically that I worried there was a stain on my skirt or that she had found something about me as flawed as she deemed our clients.

"I don't think anyone is trying to trick us, Mrs. Cremins," I suggested mildly as I could. "They don't even have to try. I've seen the most terrible poverty right in plain sight—"

"Just lissen a minute." She silenced my objection while she put another Carleton Extra Light in her cigarette holder and lit it. "I know you think I'm an old lady who gets lost where Roswell Road leaves Atlanta, but I got news for *you,* honey," she said in an exaggerated country accent. "This ole gal knows her way down a country holler a lot better than you do. With that olive complexion of yours and all that dark hair you look pretty foreign yourself. Where'd you say your people are from?"

"My father's family's from Atlanta, and my mother came from Poland after World War II."

"Then you got some things to learn about life up *here,*" she snapped. "I'm telling you how we're gonna run this project so we don't get taken advantage of. You can lissen *now*." She smiled with mock cordiality. "Or you can lissen later. But then it'll just be harder on you. If you're still around.

"Because I wouldn't have hired you if poor Melinda Ritchie wasn't struck down by cancer. Or if everybody else I interviewed wasn't desperate or foolish or lying through their teeth. At least all you've really got against you is being practically a teenager yourself.

"Besides, folks at Childcare Licensing think you're the best thing since sliced bread." She took another long drink of coffee and kept studying me suspiciously. "But taking a summer job there is one thing and leaving a private New York college to do *this* is quite another. Makes no more sense than all that new math they're pushing so hard."

She reached into a box beside her chair to hand me a thick binder. "So here we are. This is your new Bible, young lady," she said, laughing at her own joke. "I don't know if *you're* accustomed to studying your Bible or not."

I recalled my grandmother's saying, "Scratch a Christian and find an anti-Semite." I wondered if Mrs. Cremins was pushing me to acknowledge I was Jewish and too "foreign" for my job.

"It's none of my business whether you do or you don't," she said quickly as if she realized her unrelenting scrutiny had gone too far. "But you sure better study this one."

Then she pulled up the reading glasses, which hung from a gold chain around her neck. She settled them on the end of her nose while she examined a folder filled with forms completed in my handwriting. "On your application you said you understood the importance of following rules and adhering to procedures and maintaining proper records." She shut the folder and stared ahead coldly without blinking or meeting my eyes. "I certainly hope that was an honest answer. 'Cause I've just handed you the Project Manual, and out of that 563 pages about 375 deal with rules and regs.

"By the looks of your college transcript, you're a good student. But I'll hold you accountable for enforcing every one of these regs, so you better study this binder cover to cover. And don't you *dare* go changing anything without my say so. Do we have a meeting of the minds, as they say?" She laughed and lit another cigarette.

"Yes, ma'am," I assured her, hoping she could not read my mind. I was thinking how glad I was that her schedule would prevent her from spending much time in our area.

"Good. Now just remember you must find these girls in their first trimester and there'll be *no* exceptions. They have to attend every single class, and they absolutely cannot be over eighteen when they enter the Project, and I mean not a day over. Or out they go." She clapped her hands for emphasis.

"I know it sounds hard-hearted, Laura, and you're so green you'll have trouble turnin' them down," she observed critically. "Even with all the years I spent in public health nursing, it never got any easier. So you just focus on the ones you *can* help. We can't let the Feds close us down because we don't follow our guidelines."

Then she sniffed the air like a hound trying to identify an unpleasant smell. She looked around, wrinkling her nose.

"Don't you smell it? Can't say what it is, but it sure doesn't smell right in here. Talk to that landlord of yours. Must be something wrong with the HVAC system. Don't reckon you know much about things like that, do you?" she asked knowingly.

She glanced back at my employment application. "You're a real sweet girl, and it's fine to believe 'people are the same wherever they live and they all want the same things for themselves and their families,'" she said, mimicking me in a tone slightly tinged with ridicule. "Only you're wrong when it comes to people in *this locale*." She hesitated over her last words, particularly savoring them. "They're different from you and me.

"Read at least three books from this," she went on, handing me a long, single-spaced list. "I suggest *Looking Back to Appalachia, Down A Lonely Road,* and *Dirt Poor.* The authors confirm how proud these people are and that they don't want handouts or soup kitchens. And *I* promise you we would not be doing them any favors anyway by making things too easy for them. Because they have to be able to make it on their own when this project is over."

She looked around the room again in search of the offensive odor and stood up to examine the vent over our heads. "You better have somebody look at that right away since this used to be an old filling station. No telling what they might have left up there in the attic when they put in the ducts for the air conditioning.

"And one last thing. I know your heart's in the right place or we wouldn't be sitting here. But you can't let these folks take advantage of you. Young as you are, they'll try to wrap you around their little fingers."

She closed my file and reached back to place it in her box, her weight making me wary when the swivel chair creaked. I looked away, hoping we were near the end of my orientation so that I could walk her out and escape the odor, which had finally reached me. It was impossible, but it seemed to be emanating from Mrs. Cremins.

"You must be firm," she continued, placing her cigarettes into her purse. "I don't want to hear about you running folks to town on errands and spending your time listening to every hard luck story in the county. That goes for your staff, too. Be careful who you hire and make sure you they don't have more problems than the ones we're trying to help."

She closed the huge binder and picked up her purse. "Follow the rules just like they're laid out and we won't have any problems." She smiled slyly as she passed the front window. "You want to be creative, then you do something about those old curtains."

She stopped abruptly to look down at her stylish blue pump. "Would you look at that," she exclaimed in disgust, taking in the tracks she'd left behind on the new carpet. "Guess the joke's on me this time. Must have tracked this in from the front. Don't reckon you need to call the landlord unless you want to ask Mr. Tate to keep his dogs out of our parking lot." She took tissues from her purse and tore a few sheets from her yellow legal pad. "No, I'm fine. I'll make do with these," she said as she cleaned her shoe and dabbed at the soiled carpet. "Goes to show you. Even an ole country gal like me has to watch her step around here."

. . . .

CHAPTER 3

One Part Peanut Butter

I couldn't tell if Mrs. Murphy was sleeping or just closing her eyes against the afternoon sun. But once I saw flies lighting on the arms of her rocker, I knew she was asleep, since awake she would have sent them into the dust with one slap of her work-hard hands. With her long white hair wound about her head and fastened in a neat bun, and wearing her very best go-to-town dress with its print of pink and white flowers, she looked like someone to be reckoned with, even with her eyes closed.

Seeing the darning in her lap and the basket of tomatoes beside her on the porch, I hated to wake her. She managed all her own chores with only an occasional hand from her nephew when he wasn't on the day shift at Chadwick's. This meant all the cooking and housework, tending her flower-and-vegetable garden, and splitting her own firewood. More than anyone I could think of, she deserved an afternoon nap, and I was certain that despite her advanced years, she rarely had one.

When I tapped my foot and she didn't respond, I called out, "Mrs. Murphy?" I sat down in the porch swing across from her and hoped the back-and-forth motion and metallic groaning of its chain would wake her.

She started and sat up straight. "Oh honey, I'm ashamed to let you catch me like this," she said cheerfully, rubbing her eyes, embarrassed to be found napping. "I cain't believe I didn't hear you. What brings you out this way?"

The heat from the swing came right through my white slacks. I wondered how she tolerated it so easily. "Don't you remember, Mrs. Murphy?" I reminded her. "I'm here to take you to pick up your food commodities."

"Of course I do! I just dozed off for a second, and I forgot." She stood up surprisingly fast for someone of her age and hurried inside to get her hat and pocketbook. "Now, I'm ready," she announced, starting down the steep steps. "I sure do 'preciate it, honey. I'd walk there myself, but it gets so heavy totin' all those things. Lady said last time I come in, 'You must not need 'em much if you wait so long to come after 'em.' But that ain't it. I declare I cain't carry a big ole thing of flour 'n lard 'n meal and those great big ole jars of peanut butter."

She apologized as we walked over to my car. She couldn't remember if she had locked her front door and needed to check it. Then she stooped to retie her high-topped shoe. "I tell you, honey," she said, "if they'd just give me the money I'd buy somethin' a whole lot better than peanut butter. I'd get me a bigger garden goin' and raise me a few chickens. And buy some Ivory soap. Did you know they don't give you soap or toothpaste or nothin' like that? How you s'posed to stay clean? I tell you I'm lucky I don't got teeth left 'cause I sure couldn't 'ford to keep them."

I had met Mrs. Murphy when I got lost looking for a family living on Apple Orchard Road. The directions had made sense when I wrote them down, but driving there I couldn't figure out where one apple orchard left off and the next one started in order to make the prescribed right turn after the second orchard on the right. I'd been driving up and down the same stretch of road doing nothing but raising dust when I spotted Mrs. Murphy sitting on her porch.

"Well, howdy there, young lady," she had said as I approached her house. "I've been wonderin' who you're lookin' for." She motioned for me to sit down in the porch swing behind her. "I know *who* you are and that you're lookin' for girls in the fam'ly way 'cause nothin' stays secret around here longer than it takes to blink your eye. But you didn't think I'm expectin' now, did you?" She laughed at her own joke and poured me a glass of ice water before she told me how to find my destination, Collard Valley Road.

As I walked away, she said, "I reckon you'll have your hands full lookin' for these girls and carryin' them to the doctor an' all. But you're always welcome to stop by if you'd like to rest a spell. You're welcome to as much ice water as you can drink, and I can tell you some good stories. I know everything there is to know about this county." Suddenly her eyes implored me, though her tone remained the same. "And if you ever have a few minutes to spare—and you're goin' into town *anyway*—maybe you could take me by to pick up my c'modities? 'Cause they sure get heavy when I have to try to get 'em home in this ole red wagon used to belong to my nephew. These days he's hardly ever off during the daytime to help me."

I no longer had a grandmother, so I looked forward to visiting Mrs. Murphy. She always invited me to have a glass of ice water or sweet tea if she had it, so her porch became a refuge for me. Everywhere else I went people were suspicious of me, as though I were the tax collector or a caseworker coming to see about a complaint. Even the ones who needed the services of the Project were still wary of what hidden price or obligation they might incur by dealing with an outsider.

"Even one as nice as you," Mrs. Murphy explained on my first visit, when she also asked me about my Jewish star. I had forgotten I was wearing it since I usually tried to draw as little attention to myself as possible. I wore almost no jewelry of any sort, much less religious necklaces, as I went about my duties. Day to day I did not encounter other Jews in this land of Primitive Baptist churches and revival camp meetings. Even our other staff members, who were more educated and worldly than our clients, confided in me, if religion came up in passing, that I was the first Jew they had ever met. This identification made me feel a great responsibility since any accidental slight or misjudgment on my part might affect their impression of an entire religion, not just their opinion of their supervisor.

"I put a lot of store in the Old Testament," Mrs. Murphy told me after she observed my star. "Jesus was a Jew, and it was good enough for him. I still don't understand why Jews don't hold with the New Testament. But that's all right, honey. You got a right to believe whatever your people do, and I don't hold with what some folks say about Jews being cheap and stingy." She laughed out loud. "We got some rich folks around here who don't pay fair wages and act so mean they'd throw something away 'fore they'd give it to anybody else, and they sure aren't Jewish."

When I told her that the star had belonged to my great-grandmother and that my grandmother, my father's mother, had given it to me, she was very touched. "Don't you ever part with that," she advised, wiping away a tear. "When times got so bad, I had to pawn the gold necklace my mama gave me when I got married, and I'll never get that back. Any star named for King David is a whole lot more special. You hold on to that, honey, and you wear it proud."

She told me stories about the people living up and down the country roads around her, though she always grew silent when I asked for the names of girls she thought might need our services.

"I know you wouldn't mean to let on, honey. But your face would give you away. They'd know who told you since folks have seen you stoppin' by here so often. You best just keep talkin' to people and passin' out your flyers. Maybe drive over to some of the high schools. But don't be countin' on me to be your eyes."

So despite Mrs. Cremins's warning not to accept refreshments to avoid diseases associated with well water and unsanitary conditions, I drank Mrs. Murphy's ice tea and enjoyed an occasional biscuit or piece of pie she saved for me.

When I told Nadine about meeting her, she smiled and complimented me on keeping such good company. "Ruth Murphy's one of the finest folks you'll ever find," she said. "She's alone since her husband passed and their only boy got killed overseas. You go by, you'll learn a lot and you might get yourself a slice of the best apple pie in the county. She's got the blue ribbons to prove it. And a chest full of the most beautiful quilts you've ever seen. She does that fine, old-time stitchin' nobody bothers to do anymore."

I tried to drop by Mrs. Murphy's at the beginning of the month, when the food commodities were distributed. The first time I drove her to town and saw the weight of what everyone was supposed to haul off, I was shocked. I thought she had exaggerated until I saw other older women and mothers carrying babies with toddlers clinging to their skirts, struggling with their heavy parcels.

Mrs. Murphy didn't want me to come inside with her. "No need for you to get out of your car, honey. You just set here a minit." She winked at me. "I reckon I can get curb service."

A few moments later she returned to the car holding a small booklet of pink, green, and yellow pages. It was called "Cooking with Commodities." A man followed behind her carrying two large cartons that would have required several trips for Mrs. Murphy relying on her red wagon. He was red-faced and sweating in the sun when I handed him the key to my trunk.

As she got back in the car beside me, Mrs. Murphy pushed the booklet into my hand and said, "Now if you want to see somethin' funny, you read that first page." I started to read silently, but she stopped me. "No, read it out loud. I don't want to miss a single word."

It was a recipe called "Ham Patties Surprise," written in rhyme with cartoon characters illustrating the steps. There were dancing hams and smiling jars of peanut butter in the margins, and two little robins tweeting along and pointing with their wings toward the recipes on the next page.

"Go on, read it," Mrs. Murphy said impatiently.

"Make your family a delicious treat that's fun to eat," I recited. "All you need is:

"One part peanut butter

"One part deviled ham

"One part pickle relish

"Mix the best you can. Stir it all around. And put it in a pa—"

"That's enough, honey," she said, laughing. "Can you 'magine what that would taste like? Ain't it funny what rich folks think up for poor folks t'eat?"

. . . .

CHAPTER 4

My Little Girl

"Hi, Vernon. Want to join me?" I invited him over to my table though I'd gone to lunch purposely to escape my concerns about our social services director. As he approached, I thought that he would be good looking if he lost thirty pounds, despite being fidgety and constantly cracking his knuckles. He had regular features and prematurely gray hair, which might have seemed distinguished if he hadn't been so soft. When he shook your hand, his own felt clammy, and he was always wiping his face with his handkerchief, even in the air-conditioned office.

"I could use some lunch." He wiped his shiny face and laughed nervously. "But the fact is, we've kind of got a problem back at the office."

I waited impatiently, wishing he would just spit it out.

"This girl Trina Kitchens locked herself in the bathroom, and she won't come out. I've tried everything. She wants to talk to a lady, and Susan's out on a home visit to Jasper." He sat down and wiped his sweaty brow. "I've been looking all over town for you."

I handed money to the waitress and started out the door with Vernon following me like a puppy. I couldn't believe he'd left her in the office all alone. What if she were suicidal?

"Her husband's with her, Laura," Vernon told me, as if he could read my thoughts. "I'll meet you back at the office," he added, nervously rattling his keys.

"No, I'm coming with you. So you can tell me what happened."

He reluctantly opened the passenger door for me. His car stank of air freshener. One of those plastic spruce trees hung from the rear view mirror, and a can of lemon scented deodorizer lay at my feet. Beneath these chemical smells was another odor that disturbed me, the sweet smell of bourbon. I quickly looked around for a bottle but didn't see one.

"It wasn't my fault," he said defensively. "I asked her a few questions and gave them the forms to look over. Next thing I know she's locked herself in the bathroom. And he's banging on the door like a maniac."

When we entered the office, they were seated close together on the sofa in the waiting room. The man was average height and wiry, not the hulk I'd imagined. His red hair was close cropped, and he wore a green jump suit. He smiled, sheepishly averting his very blue eyes. I could only see the girl's long brown hair, since her face was pressed tightly against his chest. Her arms were thrown around his neck like a desperate child's.

"Please tell me what's the matter," I said. "I'm Laura Bauer. I'm in charge of this program."

"Bill Matthews," the man said, sitting up straight to meet my eyes. "And this is Trina." He looked embarrassed. "Afraid I had to take your door off the hinges. Couldn't take a chance of something happening to my little girl in there. But ma'am, I didn't hurt it none. I'll put it back up for you just as soon as Trina settles down." He stroked her cheek with his large hand. She turned her head slightly to look at me.

I sat down beside her. "What's got you so upset?" I handed her a tissue. "Maybe we can help."

She turned away and pressed her face again into Matthews's neck. Vernon walked over to the window and began to pace.

"She's real shy, ma'am," Matthews explained. "Reckon she feels kind of silly about that door." He whispered tenderly, "But it's OK, honey. I'll fix it."

"Have some water, Trina." I filled a cup at the cooler and placed it in her hand. She took a few tiny sips and watched me shyly. "Take your time. You can tell me about it whenever you're ready."

"It was just the forms," he said. "When we got to the part about whether we was married, she felt real ashamed." He watched my face anxiously. "I kind of let on to Mr. Blakely here that we was married, but the fact is, I'm still married to somebody else. But we haven't been together for a long time, and I'm trying to get my wife to give me a divorce so I can do the right thing by Trina here."

He looked down at the floor. "See, I don't have much money. That's why we come in here. And we were doin' all right about the marrying part until she forgot and give out a different name than mine. We didn't set out to hide nothin'." He looked over at Vernon. "No offense, but she got flustered trying to talk to a man. So she run in there, and then I got kinda excited." He squeezed her shoulder. "Sorry about the door. But it won't take no time to put it back good as new."

It seemed odd Trina was so upset about talking to a male counselor when she'd had no problem having sex with a married man. She acted so timid I had trouble imagining her speaking to him, much less sleeping with him.

Matthews smiled and kissed her on the chin. "Didn't figure you'd mind if I read your pamphlets while we waited for you," he politely informed us. He pointed out a page to Trina, who managed finally to look at me. "Says right here that this Project don't care if you're married or not. But anyhow, soon as I'm free, we'll get married." He put his arm around Trina's shoulders. "'Cause this is my little girl. As far as I'm concerned, we're good as married already." He stood up and took out his pocket knife. "Now, I'll see to that door for you, ma'am."

Vernon followed him over to the bathroom. They were soon down on their knees hunting for a missing screw.

"While they do that, could we finish your application, Trina?" I asked tentatively, not wanting to scare her again.

"All right." Her voice was small but steady. "I *guess* I can do it now." She took another sip of water.

I examined what she'd written in a rounded, childish hand. "You didn't put down how old you are."

"I'll be fifteen next month."

It was hard to hold in my sadness, realizing we were only four years apart. I'd gone out with men two and even five years older, but Matthews looked easily twice her age. "What grade are you in?"

"I finished seventh. But I don't 'spect I'll be going back this year. With the baby coming and all."

"How old is Mr. Matthews?" I asked, filling in the blanks.

"He's thirty-six," she announced proudly, as if to convey, *He's a real grown up, and he loves me.*

"How far along are you?"

"I haven't seen nothin' in two months."

"Seen nothing?"

"You know," she whispered, "my monthlies."

I blushed, embarrassed by my clumsiness.

"Y'all got many girls signed up yet?" she asked hopefully, clearly not wanting to be the first.

"No, we just opened up."

"I know somebody else who might want to join." She hesitated, watching me anxiously. "Only you can't let on how you found out 'cause her husband's real proud. He'd pitch a fit if he thought I told somebody they need help."

"Don't worry. Anything you say stays between us."

"Her name's Mandy Barfield," she blurted out. "We grew up together, and she and James live right down the road from Mama and Daddy. Of course they don't have as nice a trailer with a swing and flowers like Daddy fixed up. They're on the back end of Mountain Breezes." She stopped for a moment to see if I was following her. "You *do* know where Mountain Breezes Trailer Park is, don't you?"

The trailer park I remembered was shadeless and so near the dump that I could not connect it to mountains or breezes.

"You know the one," she tried to convince me. "Where that boy got killed when some fellas were taking target practice early this summer? There was a big picture in the paper." She pushed her bangs behind her ears. "Anyhow, if you're coming out from town, you take the third gravel road after you pass the Mountain Breezes sign next to the wagon wheels. It'll be on your right. Mandy and James live about a mile up that road. Their trailer's got a bunch of old cars out front."

"That sounds easy enough to find. You feel better now?"

"Yes ma'am."

"You have any questions?"

She shook her head "no." "I'm sorry I got so upset," she said apologetically. "I shouldn't have carried on that way. Only sometimes I get scared Bill won't marry me. Mama don't think he really means to leave Candy."

Her voice grew very wistful. "I sure don't want my baby growing up without a daddy. But Mama was pregnant when Daddy married her. And James married Mandy." She folded her arms and looked at me thoughtfully. "It does make a man take you serious, don't it?"

She smiled as she watched Bill working on the bathroom door. "I know he really wants to marry me as soon as he can. 'Cause he loves babies. He's got four already."

We watched him set the door back on its hinges. Her gaze was loving and admiring. "He's cut it so short now you can't really tell," she confided. "But he's got the prettiest red hair. I sure hope the baby'll take after him."

. . . .

CHAPTER 5

Mountain Breezes

I took the road out of town past Millie's Beauty Shop and the burned-out remains of a barbecue joint, then poor farms and ranch-style houses with two or three cars in the yard or a pickup next to an old boat on a trailer. I saw the Mountain Breezes Trailer Park sign and turned near the main entrance, marked by wagon wheels, as Trina had directed. Just a few hundred yards off the highway the road changed to dirt. I rolled up my windows against the red clay dust that rose in clouds. I noticed clotheslines covered with work clothes, diapers, shirts, and dresses catching the dust.

The remote road was lined with scruffy pines. Wild flowers grew out of the ditches and ruts. Goldenrod. Aster. Touch-me-nots. But Mountain Breezes overlooked the dump. I could smell the garbage even with my windows up. Flies lit on my car as I slowed down to check my directions. Most of the trailers rested on concrete blocks unanchored against tornadoes. Several people in town had told me the same story about a trailer carried off in a storm that left behind it the complete, unmarred border of blooming yellow daffodils that had surrounded it.

The Kitchens trailer was easy to find. I recognized the yard by the rope swing hanging from the oak tree and the flower bed bordering the front porch, just as Trina had described it. The neatness of the yard, from the woodpile to the carefully tended flowers and rows of vegetables, showed a pride untouched by hardship. I sat in my car a few minutes, considering how to introduce myself if Trina were not home, and I had to talk to her parents, who might not even know she was pregnant.

"Have you lost your way, ma'am?" A woman in her mid-thirties walked toward me. She was plump and wore a blue, checked shirtwaist dress. Her dark hair curled around her face. As she came nearer, her face looked so weathered I decided she was much older than I'd initially guessed. "You need directions?" She was polite, but clearly concerned by the presence of a stranger.

"No, ma'am, I'm not lost." I smiled as I approached her. "My name is Laura

Bauer. Is Trina around?" It felt odd not explaining why I was there, but I thought I should say as little as possible.

"She's inside." She pointed to a straw-bottomed rocker on the porch. "Have a seat please, ma'am. I'll call her." She asked anxiously, "She's not in some kind of trouble, is she? I'm her mama."

That would depend on your definition of trouble, I thought, trying to keep my expression inscrutable. "No ma'am. I'd just like to talk to her for a minute."

She stood firm, waiting for me to offer more.

"It's private, Mrs. Kitchens. I'd rather you let Trina answer your questions."

She stuck her head in the door and called out sharply, "Trina, you get out here right now. There's a lady here to see you. Now wake up!"

Trina came out rubbing her eyes. Her hair was tousled. I kept my voice down and turned my back to Mrs. Kitchens. "I'm sorry, but I made a mistake yesterday," I whispered. "Since you're not eighteen or married, one of your parents has to sign the application so you can join the Project."

"But *Bill* signed. We're gettin' married soon as he gets his divorce. We're close as you can get to being married."

"Close ain't nearly good enough," Mrs. Kitchens insisted, determined to join our conversation. "He's no closer to marrying you than he is to marrying me."

"Mama, you don't understand about me and Bill," Trina protested. "He loves me."

"You got no business fooling around with a married man. He belongs with Candy and those kids."

"But he don't love her anymore. He wants to marry me as soon as he's free. You don't believe it, but it's true."

"He won't ever marry you." In her agitation, Mrs. Kitchens stepped between me and Trina. "What kind of father would he make anyway, if he's gonna leave the four kids he's already got? And one of them not even a year old."

"The kids don't have nothin' to do with it." Trina began to whine like a child, her bottom lip trembling. "He never loved her. He loves me."

"If he loves you so much why didn't he keep you from getting pregnant?"

"Mama!" Trina's face turned red and tears came to her eyes.

"If you're embarrassed, you've got cause to be. Now get back in the house so I can talk to this lady."

"She didn't come to talk to you. It's my baby. It's got nothin' to do with you."

"You're gonna bring a baby into this house and that has nothin' to do with me? You think you're all grown up, but me and your daddy'll have to figure a way to get you out of this mess."

"Me and Bill will take care of our baby. I won't need no help from you." Trina wiped away her tears, trying hard to sound defiant. "It's *not* a mess. Bill loves me. And how come you're so upset about it?" Her eyes turned accusatory. "You were pregnant when Daddy married you."

"You spiteful little slut." Mrs. Kitchens slapped Trina hard enough to leave a mark on the girl's face. "You wait 'til your daddy gets home. You're not too old for a lickin'."

Mrs. Kitchens had spoken harshly, though her face was sad rather than angry as Trina ran sobbing into the trailer. We stood outside in a tense silence I didn't know how to break. Mrs. Kitchens picked dead leaves off a large basket of purple hearts that hung from the porch railing.

"Let me take a look at those papers you need me to sign," she finally said.

I showed her the application Trina had filled out and the packet describing all the services. She studied it all carefully, tracing the words with her finger.

"She'd get to have the baby in one of those high-risk hospitals? With the incubators and monitors and all that stuff? And there's no charge?" She looked skeptical and apprehensive. "I'd do anything in the world for that girl, but we don't have the money for things like that. I sure never had it with none of mine."

She turned the papers over and over. "Well, I guess she better get in the Project and *stay* in it. 'Cause he's sure not gonna help her, and there's not much we can do." She turned toward the door. "That's still my little girl in there. I know she was talking ugly before, but she didn't really mean it." Her voice grew friendlier. "Come sit back down, Miz Bauer." She indicated the porch swing. "Make yourself to home." She picked up a bowl of green beans. "You don't mind if I finish snapping these, do you?"

"Please go right ahead. Don't mind me."

"They came right out of that garden," she said. "I can make anything grow—tomatoes, peppers, cucumbers, all kinds of greens. I have to, to feed this family." She looked out across the yard. "'Course most of it's gone by now. But it was beautiful earlier in the summer."

"The flowers are still lovely," I said, admiring the brilliant red geraniums and thinking how seldom my family managed to grow any vegetables to maturity. Worms destroyed our squash vines, and squirrels took a bite out of every tomato. Nothing ever ripened, almost as if it didn't have to since it was just our hobby, not food we depended on for our supper. "You sure must work hard at it."

She smiled with satisfaction. "I won't tell you I don't. But I get a lot of help. The whole family worked that garden. Fact is, that's how I first figured something was goin' on with Trina. She kept carrying on about how workin' in the sun made her feel woozy. When it never bothered her before."

"So you guessed she was pregnant?"

"'Specially since I felt the same way with each of mine. Only I couldn't figure out how it happened to Trina. Shy as she is, she never even dated. She wouldn't go to the school dances. It didn't seem natural for a girl her age not to go with boys." She set down the bowl of snapped beans.

"It must have flattered her to have a grown man interested in her."

"Trina thinks he *means* it when he says he loves her." She sighed deeply. "When he don't even take care of his own family. Only works regular half the time. Construction work when he can get it. And odd jobs." She shook her head regretfully. "He's closer to my age than hers. We grew up together, and he's always been no 'count. I should have known not to let her spend so much time around him."

"You *knew* she was seeing him?" I couldn't believe any mother would knowingly let her fourteen-year-old daughter spend time with a grown man. A married one at that.

"Of course I knew," she said crossly, her tone showing she didn't appreciate my question and doubted my ability to understand anything. "Trina started baby-sitting for them when she was twelve. You know how young girls want to make a little pocket money.

"And Candy needed somebody to mind the kids so she could take in sewing. They needed the money bad. So did we after Trina's daddy cut his hand at Barnwell Poultry gutting chickens. He was real good at it before his accident. Then they cut him down to two days a week 'cause they said he was too slow. So there wasn't money for lots of things we needed. I was real glad when Candy asked Trina."

"You think it started when Trina was twelve?" I tried to be straightforward without revealing my horror at what she might answer.

"No. It couldn't have happened 'til Candy took sick after her last baby. They were both so sickly she was always running back to the hospital." A look of remorse came over her. "Maybe I should have known better, but the Good Lord knows I didn't see anything wrong with Trina staying the night. She'd already been sitting for them so long. And the days Bill had to leave real early for his construction job, we had no way to carry Trina over there. So that's how it started." She looked in at Trina, who was stretched out on the couch watching television. "They might have did it like a man and a woman, but she's still a little girl."

She leaned forward confidentially. "I finally got it out of her. I sat her down and made her tell me what was going on." She shook her head. "Poor child. She didn't have a chance. He come after her when she was asleep."

Statutory rape, I was thinking. Maybe even worse if he forced a fourteen-year-old girl with his own little children in the same room.

"She was so sleepy she probably didn't know where she was. Bet she dreamed she was back home. Being the oldest, she's used to somebody getting scared and crawling into her bed at night. By the time she woke up and realized what was happening, he was holding and kissing her." She blushed slightly. "Miz Bauer, I know you got to tell these girls to say 'no,' and I'm not trying to make no excuses for Trina. But when a man good looking as Bill Matthews crawls into a girl's bed and looks at her with those pretty blue eyes and starts to stroking her, there's no way she's gonna say 'no.'"

"Does Candy know?"

"I hated to hurt her. 'Cause Candy's sweet as she can be. But I figured she should know he was doin' her that way. Besides Lonnie was wantin' to shoot Bill. He did rough him up some. Told him *never* to come anywhere near our daughter again."

"But Mr. Matthews brought her to our office."

"I can't watch her every second," she said defensively. "Do you know *anything* about teenagers?"

I didn't answer, not wanting to admit most of my knowledge was recent and firsthand and hoping my blue suit made me appear older.

"I didn't think so," she said critically. "You don't look much older than one yourself. But I'm not trying to give you a hard time. Let me finish looking at those papers." She picked up the pen but then set it down again. "There's one thing I still don't get." She pointed to the small print. "This part about y'all followin' the baby the first year of his life. We'll be giving this one up for adoption." She looked out at the children playing on the woodpile. "We got enough kids around here already, and Trina's not ready to be a mother." Her face was determined. "It'll be hard at first, but she'll get over it."

"No, I won't!" Trina came bursting out of the trailer. She had heard us over the television and had come outside to defend her rights. "It's my baby.

You can't take it, Mama. I'll run away when it's time to have my baby. You'll never see me again."

"Baby, you don't know what you're saying." Mrs. Kitchens pulled the sobbing girl into her arms and cradled her head against her chest. "You're not running anywhere. I'm on *your* side. I'm trying to help you. 'Cause you don't know a thing about men and how they'll do you."

"I know Bill. He's *going* to marry me." She turned to me. "You heard him."

Mrs. Kitchens wiped Trina's eyes with her apron. "Calm down, baby. Don't make such a fuss in front of company. Besides," she said authoritatively, "all that crying takes air away from the baby." She stroked Trina's hair back from her forehead and made a place for her in the swing. Trina leaned against her and closed her eyes.

"Mama, I *am* going to get married. Bill's going to leave her."

"I'm sorry, baby." She kissed Trina's cheek. "I know it's hard to believe he could give you a baby and then forget all about you. But men do it all the time." Her face was resolute. "So me and your daddy have to do what's best for you."

Trina jumped up and ran to me for protection. "Miz Bauer, you can't let her take my baby away. You'll help me, won't you?"

"She can't go against your own mother." Mrs. Kitchens stepped between us. "You're not even fifteen. I'll decide what's best for you. *Not* Miz Bauer." She looked apologetic. "I'm sorry, ma'am. Nothing personal. But I know what's best for my child." She turned to Trina. "Now you just go back inside and cool off. I got to talk to Miz Bauer. There'll be plenty of time for talking later." She pushed her firmly toward the door.

"I don't care if you beat me 'til I can't sit down," Trina screamed from the safety of inside. "I'll never give up my baby."

"I've never beaten her." Mrs. Kitchens began to cry. "Lord knows, maybe I should have and none of this would've happened. But I never harmed that child. You got to believe me, Miz Bauer."

"She just wants my baby so she can sell it to one of those ladies that can't have a baby," Trina accused her, standing just inside the doorway. "She wants the money. That's all she cares about."

"That's plain foolishness. You don't know what you're talking about," Mrs. Kitchens said angrily, clearly insulted by her daughter's accusations. But her irritation quickly subsided, and her voice turned fierce with love. "Your life was gonna be different. You were going to finish high school and have the church wedding I never did and live in a real house. Not some old trailer.

You're still gonna have that. Do you hear me?" She stepped quickly toward Trina, hugged her tightly, and began to cry, still clinging to her daughter.

"Mama, it don't matter about the trailer. That's what you and daddy got. I wouldn't want to marry anybody better than Daddy. Aren't you two happy?"

"Don't talk to me about happiness," Mrs. Kitchens said wearily. "You get what you get. No point fussing about it. Rich people are the only ones that can change their luck."

"That's not true," Trina insisted, looking for my validation. "Tell her it's not true, Miz Bauer. I *am* gonna be happy with Bill. Just me and him and our baby. 'Cause he can't talk to Candy anymore. Ever since her last baby come along, it's been over between them. That's how come he turned to me." Her eyes smiled. "He said I'm his happiness." She sighed. "And least 'til our baby's born, I guess he'll be all of mine."

CHAPTER 6

....

In Its Proper Place

"Good morning, ma'am," Mr. Johnson, the principal of Clayborn High, said reluctantly, rising stiffly, not offering me a seat in his office. "I got those flyers you brought by." He lowered his voice and nervously moved the papers around his desk. "I'd already seen them at the superette. I'm afraid we won't be able to help you."

He came out from behind his desk to make it clear our interview was over. In his grey suit, he stood lean and tall, an impressive array of football trophies in the display case behind him. "If I let you put those flyers up and one of them found its way home to a parent, I'd have a war on my hands.

"Folks don't want their kids bringing something home from school about babies and 'single' mothers." He laughed nervously, then whispered, "Don't get me wrong. I believe girls in the family way need medical care and such. But it was hard enough getting parents to let their kids take Health and Family Life."

He cracked his knuckles as he ushered me out of his office. "But talk to Miz Lynch, our guidance counselor," he said, gladly passing me off to someone else. "Maybe she can help you."

I passed through two sets of double doors to reach the counseling office. Grey metal chairs were arranged around an old library table. The bulletin boards were covered with announcements for school events, sports calendars, and SAT testing dates. The bookshelf was filled with yearbooks and college catalogs wedged in so tightly and with such an even margin, it seemed certain no one ever removed them.

Miss Lynch came forward immediately to receive me. Mr. Johnson had obviously called ahead to warn her. "I understand you're from that project in town," she said coolly. She was small and trim with a "no nonsense" expression and stiffly sprayed grey hair. I could easily imagine her lecturing girls about chastity.

"Come this way," she said. "We'll talk in my office." She looked pointedly at her secretary. "Margaret, don't let anyone disturb us. I don't want students coming in here for *any* reason."

Everything in her office was carefully arranged. Even the philodendron knew exactly how many leaves to display. The framed needlepoint behind her desk read, "Everything In Its Proper Place."

"I understand having a program like yours for a few unfortunate girls, but school is hardly the place to advertise it," Miss Lynch insisted once we were seated, ready to dismiss me.

"We wouldn't intrude in any way, Miss Lynch." I tried to sound accommodating and nonthreatening. "If I could just talk to your teachers. Or leave flyers with them in case they know a student who needs help."

"I won't have your literature around here." She looked with undisguised repugnance at the flyer on her desk. "Perhaps at some time in the future you could speak to a faculty committee."

"Could we start with the coaches? They know everything that's going on—"

"I meant the *lady* teachers. It would be totally unsuitable to involve the male faculty." She folded one flyer and stuck it in her desk, handing the rest back to me. "You may find *someone* willing to distribute these at other schools, but I certainly can't post them in *our* restrooms. Besides we've hardly ever had a girl get herself in trouble," she said proudly.

"I'm glad to hear it. It's surprising, considering the large number of teenage pregnancies in this county." I sat back, wondering how she would meet the challenge of statistics.

"I imagine there *is* a lot of need among the colored." She lowered her voice genteelly as if speaking of venereal disease or some equally disgusting matter.

"Why would that be?" I could predict her prejudiced beliefs but was determined to make her express them out loud.

"When you consider their habits." She paused, watching my unsympathetic face. "Well, you know . . . their disadvantages. The only case I am familiar with this year concerned a girl from the colored community. Do you know where Coo—" She quickly corrected herself. "Raccoon Hollow is?"

I told her that I knew it. But I didn't say what I thought of this tiny community of shacks on the most eroded, worthless land in the county downwind from the dump. Many of the families lived without toilets or running water, either because those *luxuries* did not exist in their neighborhood or because their landlords did not maintain them. Even on still days when the air hardly moved, the smell of putrefaction was staggering. This was the "community" where the black mill workers and ditch diggers and their families sought their evening rest.

"Now you listen to *this*," Miss Lynch said, her reticence temporarily displaced by incredulity. "I know this is the gospel truth because my nephew drives the county ambulance. And Annie Stokes was a student here, but of course she *never* confided in anyone. Even though some folks tried to help her.

"She was the *only* case of that sort that we've ever had. She'd always been real heavyset, but then her P.E. teacher started noticing Annie was getting mighty big through the middle. So she asked her if she was pregnant. And the girl flat out denied it.

"Only she kept getting heavier. So they sent her to my office—we don't have a school nurse—thinking I could talk to her about not stuffing herself that way.

"She had the perfect opportunity to tell me. But she just sat there dumb as a doorknob. So there was nothing I could do for her.

"Then about two months later, Terry—that's my nephew—gets a call to go see about a teenage girl in trouble, and when he gets there in the ambulance, what do you think he found?"

I could tell no response was required or expected of me so I waited until Miss Lynch felt ready to reveal the climax of her story.

"I'll tell you *exactly* what he found." Miss Lynch's eyes opened wider. "That Annie was lying on a filthy kitchen floor and right beside her in a dishpan was this tiny baby about the size of a monkey.

"Terry asked her why she hadn't called sooner. And she told him she didn't know she was having a baby.

"She was home alone with her sister. So when the pains came on so strong, she just lay down on the floor and had that baby." She shook her head in disgusted amazement. "It was premature of course. Hardly weighed three pounds, I hear. But now Bessie Mae, this girl who does laundry for me, said she saw the baby at church a few weeks ago, and she's looks just fine.

"*Those* are the people who need your project. You best go talk to the colored ministers."

In Atwell, the principal hardly let me through the door. He was an old man wearing black army-issue glasses and the thinnest tie I'd seen in years. Holding the Project guidelines and a flyer in one hand, he glared at me. "I don't mince words," he said sternly. "Miz Lynch called me yesterday and told me you'd been up to see her. I can't stop programs like yours, but I don't have to let you in *my* school. You put ideas into young folks' heads they'd never come to on their own. You throw so much birth control at them, it's no wonder they get in trouble."

He spoke so vehemently he grew red in the face. "Far as I'm concerned, you people are as bad as the abortion people. They murder babies and you make it so easy, every girl may as well have one since you pay for it all. It's a total misuse of public funds. Why do you people get all this money when we can't afford decent band uniforms or get a grant to renovate our gym?"

He looked me straight in the eye. "You say you want to help this community, right?"

"Yes sir," I agreed heartily, wondering if I had unfairly judged him, since he seemed about to make a suggestion.

"Then do us all a favor and stay out of it."

I was back in Atlanta, where no one would accuse me of encouraging teenagers to have sex. I could drink beer with friends in the warmly lit, comfortable wooden booths of Manuel's Tavern and forget about the terrible hardships I witnessed each day at the office. Rob, my boyfriend, a graduate student at Emory University, gathered a bunch of his friends, who crowded around one of the big wooden tables, sharing cheap pitchers of beer and descriptions of the novels they were writing, though these existed mostly in their heads. They argued politics with Manuel himself, a garrulous older man, who loved to walk the room playing the friendly devil's advocate. It was comforting to listen and laugh with well-nourished, relaxed people with nothing worse to worry about than defending dissertations or finding teaching positions— serious concerns, of course, but minor challenges compared to the problems of my clients. I ignored the cigarette smoke and blaring TV sports, which both normally irritated me, in the joy of being surrounded by happy people. If they were loud or slightly drunk or talked too much, they weren't ruining someone else's life, and they weren't pregnant teenagers.

When Rob and I arrived at his apartment, Chadwick, Carrollton, Blue Ridge, Clayton, and Blairsville seemed far away, along with all my responsibilities. He put on a recording of Bach's Second Brandenburg Concerto, and while we listened to Maurice André's miraculous high notes, Rob put his arm around me and pulled me close in the soft lamp light. I sneezed, disturbing our reverie, since despite neatly arranging his many books, magazines, and newspapers, Rob rarely dusted. But then we relaxed again on his old leather couch with his posters of Breughel's happy feast scenes and the framed silk prints of Parisian streets his mother had brought back from Europe, indulging our fantasies of traveling together. Rob listened intently, perhaps more to the trumpet playing than to me, but then his soft, black hair touched my cheek and his dark eyes appeared to see only me.

"We can still hear the music from the bedroom," he whispered, caressing my neck with gentle kisses and taking my small hand in his much larger one.

Since I was accustomed to college dorm rooms with mattresses on the floor and gently undulating water beds, Rob's bedroom, with its cherry bedstead and dresser dating back to his parents' home, made me glad to have left behind the milk-crate bookshelves and lava lamps of my peers. He was eight years older and resided in that independent land beyond parents and undergraduate life.

In the semi-dark, as he embraced me, looking down so that his thick mustache and wavy hair seemed as romantic as a pirate's against the white sheets where we lay together, I was where I most wanted to be. We both loved staying up late, lingering after lovemaking, talking of silly matters and serious things. Rob was sometimes too reticent when we went out together, but the dark seemed always to enliven him, and I felt our strong connection, even as we lay back silently.

"What are you thinking about?" he asked, tracing my breast with his finger, delicately yet persistently.

"I can't think of anything when you do that." I giggled, suddenly conscious of my own arousal.

"Then I'll stop for a moment," he said, seriously contemplating me, his long- lashed eyes watching me. "You've got that faraway look you have when you're worrying about something. Like the state of the world or how you're going to find clients when nobody will even say the word 'pregnant' out loud." He gently combed my hair with his long fingers.

"Well . . . you mentioned it," I answered, leaning back against the pillows and pulling the sheets over us, glad to talk about what was troubling me. "I can't get the word out if nobody'll let me into a high school." I told him about my miserable showing and how Miss Lynch had called ahead to warn her colleagues about me.

"You can't give up, Laura," he encouraged me. "You're the one who always reminds me there are good people everywhere. So that applies to high school principals, too, right?" He smiled, pleased with his logic. "You *just* opened up. Have faith in yourself. If you believe in what you're do—"

"If you start reciting 'The Little Engine That Could,' I'm going to scream, Rob," I warned him.

"OK, forget it," he said, turning away so that I thought I had truly offended him. The record ended and the room was suddenly completely, painfully silent. Just as I started to apologize for cutting him off when he was trying to help me, he spun around and kissed me tenderly.

"Let me help you forget about it. *All* of it," he whispered in my ear. "At least until Monday morning."

Two weeks later, the principal at Mobley High, a tall, smiling man in a bright red sweater that bore his school emblem, thanked me for coming to see him and offered me a cup of coffee.

"It's about time somebody owned up to the problem we've got around here," he said, rubbing his bald head. "I don't know what they say at other schools, but too many girls are getting pregnant around here. They try to hide it, and they don't know the first thing about taking care of themselves.

"How about if we put up your flyers in the boys' and girls' restrooms? And I'll give some to the guidance counselor soon as we're done." He was making notes on his desk pad. "This afternoon we'll put 'em in the faculty mailboxes. And maybe next month you'd like to speak to our Family Life classes?"

He laughed at my obvious surprise as he refilled my coffee cup. "So this isn't the reception you've received most places?" he asked confidentially, nodding toward the secretary outside his office door who was busily typing. "Her sister-in-law is Mary Lynch," he whispered. "Miz Lynch called over here to warn her about you."

He turned his back to the door and continued softly, "I'll wager she called every high school this corner of the state. But don't you worry." He sat down and generously added sugar to his coffee mug. "Folks have heard plenty from Mary Lynch the past thirty years. But some of us have learned to ignore most of it."

CHAPTER 7

Mondays

It was 5:30 on a Monday afternoon. Mandy Barfield was cooking pork chops in her tiny kitchen, knowing James would be home soon wanting his dinner. The first day of the week was always hard on him, so she was hurrying to get everything ready. It was so hot in the trailer she could barely stand it. She propped the back door open with a broom, yet with the heat from the stove and the heavy grease smell rising from the frying pan, she felt like she was cooking along with the chops.

She hated the trailer. It wasn't how she'd expected to start off her married life, but she couldn't let on to James she was disappointed. He already felt ashamed he could give her so little. She cringed remembering the pitying expression on Laura Bauer's face that first morning she'd stopped by to explain about the Project. No matter how much air freshener Mandy used, the trailer always smelled like last night's dinner, and their few pieces of furniture were dated and shabby. Laura was very friendly, yet Mandy had been embarrassed by the sympathy in her eyes.

She'd wanted to convince Laura that their place only looked bad because the porch railing had come loose the week before, and James had been too tired to mend it. If she could just come back another day, she would see how nice they kept the trailer and the porch that James had added on as a surprise for Mandy before they moved in. But then she realized she couldn't even fool herself with her excuses. Anyone could see the rusted-out tool shed and the old cars and spare parts James was tinkering with. He worked such long hours she couldn't fault him for not always getting to the yard on the weekends. Weeds and ragged grass stuck up everywhere, and Mandy knew if she tried to clean up herself, James would feel like he'd been criticized. They'd never talked about it, but they both understood that the yard was his place just like the kitchen was her own.

She'd felt terrible when Laura told her about getting stuck on a dirt road full of ruts that was the turnoff just before Mandy's road. She had actually driven up the old logging road, which was so rough you needed a jeep to get through. It shamed Mandy that Laura thought she was poor enough to live up there. *Nobody* had ever lived on the old logging road. Not even the poorest colored people.

Then Laura told her she hadn't been looking for Mandy. She was just driving around the county letting people know about the New Families Project. Laura had looked Mandy right in the eye, but Mandy couldn't help wondering if somebody had told her she was expecting. She didn't mind so much for herself, but she knew it would kill James. He'd die before he'd let anybody know they needed help.

Like when the ladies from the church came by. They'd heard she and James had hardly any furniture or kitchen stuff. So one afternoon a few of them brought by this huge box just filled with things she wanted real bad. Dish towels. Bed sheets. A crock pot still in the box from the store. Kitchen curtains. A clock radio and a TV that worked on all but one channel. She'd gotten excited thinking how nice everything would look in their trailer. They'd be able to watch TV together in the evenings. She would make a big bowl of popcorn with butter and get James a cold beer.

But he'd pitched a fit. He got so angry he turned red in the face and started cursing and slamming things around. He told her nobody in his family would have anything they couldn't pay for themselves. He wouldn't have her shaming him in front of the whole church. No Barfield had ever taken charity, and no Barfield ever would.

He talked so mean and stood there looming over her until she couldn't believe he loved her at all. Then he picked up that whole big box of things she was dying to have and carried it outside and threw it in the road. Just like it was a bunch of garbage. When he got to the TV, he looked at it real hard, but then he picked it up and chucked it out with the rest of it. When she heard it smash in the yard, she felt like her own heart was breaking.

She turned down the light under the chops and went into the bathroom to splash cold water on her face. But it didn't refresh her. Instead, she felt dizzy like she might really faint. So she sat down on the edge of the tub with her head down between her knees. She'd heard this would keep you from fainting.

Ever since she got pregnant, she hadn't felt right. The pamphlets Laura left her said the morning sickness would stop after the first few months. Only she was starting her third month, and she still got it nearly every morning. Her mama told her to keep crackers by the bed and eat a few before she got up in the morning, but they didn't help. The smell of the coffee set her off every time, and James needed his coffee. When she tried to drink milk, that did it, too. Laura said she should drink a quart a day, but every time she even *thought* about milk—

Suddenly, she realized she wasn't going to faint; she was going to throw up. She moved over to the toilet, gagging on the sour taste, yet relieved it would all be over in a moment.

When she returned to the kitchen, the chops had scorched. She quickly scraped them up with her spatula and added some Crisco. It spattered and smoked in the hot pan. The burnt smell made her gag again. She'd wanted so badly to make the chops nice and brown. She held her breath and forced herself to stir the green beans. *I will not throw up,* she told herself. *I will not get sick again.*

She tried to think of other things. Leaves changing colors. Cool weather. It had to be coming with fall just around the corner. She couldn't remember any year when summer had held on so long. She went out to the living room and sat down in the gold recliner. Laura had said it was important to rest even for a few minutes when you were woozy. The gold velvet felt so soft under her hand. Everything else might be old and beaten up, but their recliner was as nice a chair as you'd find in anybody's living room.

She jumped up just in time to save the beans. They were perfect, cooked with onion and ham hocks, just the way James liked them. She'd been careful not to boil them dry as she'd done the greens the night before. She checked the biscuits. They were browning fine on top and would be ready right on time. If only the chops didn't look so dry.

She heard the truck pull into the yard grinding over the gravel. Then James's heavy footsteps coming onto the porch. He was a big man who made lots of noise even when he tried to be quiet.

He dropped his work shoes by the door, and seconds later, he was there in the kitchen beside her. "Hi," he said. He kissed her quick on the cheek, different from when they were first married. She smelled beer on his breath. She figured he'd stopped for a few quick ones with the fellas after they left work, but she didn't mind. Her mama had always told her, "Don't worry so long as it's just beer. A man won't get into trouble with beer. He can't drink enough to do himself no harm."

"What's burning?" he asked, walking over to the stove.

"Nothin'. Just a little grease in the pork chop pan."

"Looks like they're burning to me." He lit a cigarette and leaned back against the counter. "What'd you do today?"

"That real nice lady came by again to tell me about this new project they got in town to help girls have healthy babies. You get to see doctors and have your baby in a hospital. And they got all kinds of classes and meetings. They teach you all about eating right and taking care of the baby. It sounds real nice, Jimmy, and it don't cost a cent. I want to join."

"There's a catch in it some place," he said suspiciously. "It don't figure, them giving you doctors and the hospital or the rest of it for free."

"It's 'cause it comes from the state, Jimmy. Here're the papers she left for us to look over."

He leaned back against the counter. "Tell them you don't sign nothin' 'less your husband sees it first. You hear me?"

She reached over to hug him. She didn't want to fight. She just wanted him to hold her.

"It's too hot for that." He pulled away and went into the living room. She could hear him pacing.

When she brought the food to the table he was leaning back in his chair, staring at the ceiling. She had let down her hair. She pinned it up to cook, but she thought a woman ought to look nice when she sat down at the table. She might be losing her figure, but she knew she had pretty blonde hair. James always told her so before they were married. Now she could hardly get him to look at her.

She set the biscuits in front of him and dished him up the two biggest chops. Then she started eating. She hadn't realized she was so hungry, what with feeling so queasy, but suddenly she was starving. She guessed it kind of made sense you'd get hungrier eating for two.

"Aren't you ever going to learn?" he said irritably. "Look at these." He stabbed a chop with his fork and held it up. "Burnt on both sides."

They were a little black, she had to admit, but they weren't really burnt. It was only that the scorching grease had colored them. She was sure they'd taste fine.

"Just cut around the edge, Jimmy. They're all right. Really, they are."

"Aw, shit." He threw down his fork and slammed out of the house.

She couldn't move. Looking at all that food made her want to cry. He said she looked so ugly when she cried. One time he told her he knew she was having a baby, but he hadn't known he was *marrying* one. She didn't know why he got so mad because she was sure he loved her. He'd bought her a red heart filled with candy on Valentine's Day. He told her the curtains she made for the living room were as pretty as anything in the stores. And she could always depend on him. That was one reason her mama hadn't been against him.

"Seventeen's awful young to be marryin'," her mama had said. "I'd hoped you'd finish high school first. But if you're dead set on it, I'd rather you marry an older fella like James Barfield than one of those good-for-nothings that's always wrecking cars and runnin' around drunk."

James was thirty-two and steady. She knew he didn't run around like some men did when their wives were pregnant. And he always paid the bills on time. He'd never once gotten behind on their trailer payments. But he felt bad about not having enough money to take her to a doctor for the baby. She knew that's why he was so angry about the Project.

She wished he wasn't so proud. Getting hurt and storming out. She was sure it wasn't really the pork chops that made him so mad. They weren't that bad. She wanted to cry when she looked at that table full of food she'd spent all afternoon fixing for him. She turned off the light and rested her head on the table.

Hours passed. It was pitch dark, but she didn't feel like moving to turn on the lights. *I'll just sit right here and wait for him,* she thought. *He'll be back soon.* Then she felt a cold shiver of fear. *What if he never comes back, and it's just me and the baby with nobody to look out for us? And we lose the trailer and don't have nowhere to live? Everybody will know he walked out on me?*

She heard his footsteps. She could have called to him, but she didn't make a sound. She wanted him to find her. To see how he'd left her. He flicked on the light and jumped back as he saw her out of the corner of his eye.

"Why are you sittin' in the dark like that?" he asked gently. She could tell he felt bad about hurting her.

"Waiting for you."

He went to her quickly. "Please forgive me, Mandy." He sat down and reached out to pull her onto his lap. "I'm sorry, honey. Guess Mondays make me pretty mean. Come here." He held out his hand. "Come on. You're still my baby, aren't you?"

He settled her in his lap and hugged her real close like before they were married. He whispered in her ear until he made her smile.

"Did you get yourself some supper, Jimmy?" She remembered he hadn't eaten a bite. She worried when he didn't eat. Doing that heavy work laying pipe.

"Naw. I just had a few—" He stopped suddenly. She knew he didn't want to let on that he'd had more beers, but she'd already smelled it on his breath.

He was acting like a little kid pretending he didn't know who ate the cookies out the cookie jar when there was chocolate smeared across his face.

She wanted to do for him. She told him she could heat everything up in two seconds. But he wouldn't let her get up. He said he'd eat it just the way it was.

"These are good chops, Mandy," he said enthusiastically, holding one in his hand and taking hungry bites of it. "I don't know what got in to me. I'm sorry I snapped at you, baby. And I'll look at all that Project stuff tomorrow." She could see in his eyes that it cost him a whole lot to say it.

Mandy sat across from him, proudly watching the way he was enjoying the food she had prepared, even if it was cold. She passed him her chops since she felt too tired to eat. She smoked a cigarette and drank iced tea until he was ready for bed.

CHAPTER 8

Girl!

"Girl, you a mess! You walk up that hill on your face?" Mavis laughed and laughed. So did the little children playing underneath the porch. Three large yellow dogs ambled over, not aggressively, since they knew me, but they sniffed curiously around me and where I had disturbed the mud.

"You look like somebody threw a mud pie in your face."

Only Mavis would think it funny that I fell in the mud walking up her hill. I dabbed futilely at my face with the few tissues in my pocket. "It's slippery, so I fell," I told her defensively.

"You sure did! You wait here. I'll get you some rags to clean up with. I'll be just a minute," she said more sympathetically. Then, unable to resist a last jab, she added, "Think you can stand here a minute without falling?"

The children made a circle around me, still laughing. They were all Mavis's brothers and sisters, but hers was such a large family I couldn't remember their names.

One little girl said, "Nobody never fell down out here before."

A small boy said, "Uncle Ray did one time he was drunk."

Another girl asked politely, "Miss, are you a drunk lady?"

Mavis returned with the rags, some wet, some dry. "Here you go. This'll take care of you, but you sure messed up those pants."

I managed to clean my arms and face, but my white slacks were hopeless. "We need to go now, Mavis," I said, giving up on further reclamation. "It's a twenty-mile drive and we're alrea—"

"You're goin' to the doctor lookin' like that?"

"I don't have extra clothes with me. Besides, he'll be looking at you, not me."

Mavis reached in the passenger window and touched the car seat. "I can't sit on that," she said. "It's too hot."

I grabbed a newspaper from the back seat and placed it on the hot vinyl. She reluctantly got in. I blew my horn to scare the dogs out of the road.

"You sure do drive slow," she said as we took a bad curve on the way out to the main road. "My brother'd take it twice this fast." I had seen Mavis's cool-dressing brother in his souped-up black Camaro. "Laura, how come you don't have a nice car when you got a good job?"

"I don't care to discuss how I spend my money, Mavis." I jerked the wheel more than I needed to avoid a pothole. I hated to admit how much she got to me and how prissy my words sounded even to my own ears.

"You don't have to get so touchy. I just asked a question."

"I'm sorry. I have a headache."

"You want a cigarette? Always makes me feel better." She lit one for herself and held out her pack of Kools.

"Mavis, you know shouldn't smoke. And you're sure not going to do it around me."

"I don't believe you," she protested, but nevertheless tossed her cigarette out the window. "You don't smoke. You always fuss after me to eat right and never drink anything but milk. Don't you ever have no fun?"

I laughed, imagining the poor opinion Mavis would have of my kind of fun. Foreign films with subtitles, opera in the park with Rob, and a fancy picnic. Hiking in the North Georgia mountains. An afternoon at an art museum.

"You ever go to a bar with a fella?"

I hesitated, thinking what Mrs. Cremins would have to say about discussing personal drinking habits with our clients.

"Come on, Laura," Mavis persisted. "Since you know so much about *everything*, What do you do when you're with a fella and he gets in a fight and pulls a knife on somebody?"

I gripped the wheel tighter. She obviously spoke from experience, which she imagined corresponded to my own, yet it was preposterous to think of quiet, laid-back Rob threatening someone with a knife. Even my father, who had marched into Buchenwald to liberate the survivors of that horrible place, opposed weapons in the hands of civilians. He did not keep handguns at his store or in our home and had never even owned a knife larger than the small sterling penknives next to the pocket watches in his display case. "During the war, I did what I had to do," he had admitted. "I was a soldier defending our country and the Jewish people. But in peacetime, Jews and guns don't go together. We're the People of the Book."

"Come on. You know what I mean," Mavis said, pulling me from my thoughts. "You're with one fella and somebody makes eyes at you. You smile back and then the one you're with wants to get up and cut him."

"Did that really happen, Mavis?" I couldn't conceal my shock.

"A bunch of times. Willie's the jealous type. He won't even let me say 'hello' to another fella."

"But Willie doesn't carry a knife, does he?"

"Girl, you never believe nothin' I say." She shook her head at my ignorance. "I asked him not to carry a gun so he carries a knife."

"He better stop carrying anything or he'll end up in jail."

"They won't never catch Willie. He can spot the police a mile off. He don't really need a knife anyway, he's so big. And he don't go lookin' for fights."

"I'm glad to hear that."

"But don't think Willie won't fix 'em if they push him. Hell, I'd fix anybody messes with me. Sometimes I take my own knives. I got real little ones. I put one behind me and one right here." She pointed to her cleavage. "Some of those cafés got some real rough people waiting to start something. Even the girls got scars. You gotta be ready to cut them before they get a chance to cut you."

I pictured Mavis and Willie together in a roadhouse with neon signs and murky darkness. Men swigging beer, leering at any woman accompanied or alone. Mavis tall and powerful, her hair in a short Afro. Her sleeveless dress cut low, deep red against her truly black skin. Her smoldering eyes. And Willie still taller. A high school tackle. His T-shirt bulging over his biceps and his blue jeans so tight they seem painted on. I pictured them standing in a haze of smoke, Mavis smoking a Kool and grooving to the blaring rock and funk and falsetto soul. Jacked-up cars with mag wheels ripping through the parking lot.

"So for fun you just read all the time?" Mavis asked, taking in the back seat of my car covered with library books.

"No. But I do read a lot," I admitted, glad we were getting away from drinking and knives and bar fights.

"That makes *no* sense. If you're out of school and you got a job, why you want to waste your time reading?" she asked, her tone more curious than accusing. She reached back to retrieve a large volume. "What you reading anyway? '*The Death of My Family*,'" she read aloud. "'A loving memoir by the sole Jewish survivor of a small Polish village after the Nazi occupation destroyed every member of his family. His struggle, his search for what happened to his family, his neighbors . . . his entire world.'" She studied me suspiciously. "Are you *Jewish*?"

"Because I'm reading that book?" I challenged her. "There's another book back there about slavery in America. If I'm reading that, does it mean I'm black?"

"I just asked, that's all. Not only because of this book," she insisted. "I thought about it before. 'Cause you don't really look like people around here.

You're not black, but you're a lot darker than the white folks around here." She laughed out loud at her own awkwardness. "I didn't mean you don't look *nice*. But now it makes sense." She smiled at me, satisfied with her analysis. "I knew you were *something*. You got such dark, curly hair and your eyes are almost black."

"Mavis, it's a religion not a race. I have cousins with blonde hair, and my father has the bluest eyes you've ever seen." I tried to keep driving carefully, but I felt the conversation going somewhere I didn't want to go.

"My daddy says the Jews killed Christ. And he should know. He's a preacher," Mavis said. "But he's not the only one. A lot of folks say it's true."

So there it was. What I had feared.

"He's entitled to his opinion, Mavis." I chose each word carefully, not wanting a confrontation with her father, who might make her leave the Project, yet unwilling to take responsibility for killing Christ. "But he wasn't around then. I believe it was a mob, Mavis. A bunch of hateful people who turned violent—"

"Like lynch mobs."

"Exactly like that." I didn't want to talk about Pontius Pilate or the Roman soldiers. I wished we could get out of the car and end the conversation.

We drove on in silence. I avoided further discussion by looking straight ahead, pretending that the traffic required my complete attention. Yet I kept imagining Mavis's father fomenting hatred against the Jews, when I doubted he'd ever met one. I wondered what stereotypes they would be sharing around their dinner table that evening once Mavis told them I *was* one.

I turned off the busy road lined with fast food restaurants onto the access road leading to the doctor's office. I pulled into a parking space. Mavis got out and stood by the car, waiting for me to join her.

"You go ahead, Mavis," I called to her. "I'll wait out here." I still felt hurt, and I needed a few minutes away from her. It wasn't her fault what her father believed, but her explanations didn't satisfy me at that moment.

"You're not coming in with me? You *always* do." Her voice sounded plaintive, genuinely disappointed. "What if there's something wrong with me? You know they'll want to take my blood and make me pee in a cup so they can tell you every last thing about me."

She sounded again like her usual fearless self, but Mavis's panic showed in her face, so I couldn't maintain my resolve to put a little distance between us. I got out of the car and walked around to her side.

"I'm glad you're coming with me." She didn't swagger, and she looked right at me. "Laura, I'm sorry about before. What my daddy said about *Jews*—

your people." She hesitated, almost afraid to say the word. "Well . . . a lot he says is pretty hard on *all* kinds of people. Besides, way back in those old Bible days, nobody was too nice to anybody with them sacrificing people to God and wanting to stone that lady taken in adultery. Or stealing their birthrights—whatever that is—for a bowl of some kind of soup."

When the receptionist called her name, Mavis changed her mind, telling me I didn't need to come inside. Unless I got some kind of special kick out of seeing her in one of those little paper gowns.

I didn't. And it actually felt restful to sit quietly for a little while, going through the stacks of old magazines in the waiting room and reading recipes I would never have to prepare for lavish Christmas desserts and congealed summer salads. I didn't see Mavis come over to get me, but out of nowhere I heard her impatiently address me.

"Can we *please* get out of this place!"

"Sure. But what'd the doctor say, Mavis?"

"Everything's fine. They're sending you a report," she said sharply. "Can't we just go now?"

I was glad to get going, but almost as soon as we were back in the car, I knew something *was* wrong since Mavis was quiet. She didn't complain about my driving or try to change the radio station or smoke in my car or complain the air conditioning wasn't working.

"Is everything OK, Mavis? Did he say something you want to talk about?"

"Just the same old stuff about the iron pills," she answered wearily. "I told him they melt. He said to put them in the refrigerator. I told him the kids take 'em out to play with 'em. He said put the bottle on a high shelf."

"Was that it?" I didn't see why that should bother her so much.

"He says it's gonna be a big baby and there ain't nothin' wrong with me he can tell." She seemed annoyed at having to tell me about it. "Say how 'bout instead of lunch you take me somewhere to get a beer. That would make me feel a whole lot better."

"I'd like to keep my job, Mavis," I said as calmly as I could. "I can't buy you beer. And I got to thinking while you were in there. What are you doing going to a bar with Willie anyway? You're not eighteen."

"Girl, nobody waits 'til they're eighteen to go out drinkin'!" She laughed at my astounding foolishness. "Besides, I'm eighteen anyhow," she acknowledged sheepishly, tensely watching my face.

"That's not what you said when you applied." I tried to sound stern, though more than being lied to I worried that Mrs. Cremins would make Mavis leave the Project when she caught the error in her next audit. I hadn't remembered any hesitation when Mavis had given her age as seventeen when she applied, but she hadn't had a driver's license to show proof of age. She had claimed she couldn't find her birth certificate the day Willie brought her to our office, and though she promised to bring it later, she never produced it. It was my own fault I'd forgotten to follow up. But deep down I knew I hadn't wanted to face the truth; I could see how badly she needed our services.

"I'd just turned eighteen the month before. So I didn't fudge *much*, Laura," Mavis implored me, speaking in a tone she'd never used before. "I was *so* scared you wouldn't let me in." The tears ran down her face as if to attest to how truly frightened she was.

"Now . . . don't cry, Mavis. We'll figure this out," I said in my gentlest voice, hoping Mrs. Cremins wouldn't turn Mavis out if she discovered her age. "But tell the truth about *everything* from now on, OK?"

"I don't lie, Laura," she said with quiet dignity. "That was the only time." She wiped her eyes. "But there is one other little thing I ought to tell you."

I was afraid what would seem "little" to Mavis after what she had already disclosed. I waited anxiously for the rest of her confession.

"I just got my dates wrong, that's all," she said, more quietly than I'd ever heard her speak. "Maybe I was just a little bit past three months when I joined the Project."

"How much past?" I could not make myself look at her, and I worried what the doctor had said about her baby's size and what his report might reveal.

"I don't know. I never kept track of the curse that close. Maybe I was two or three more weeks gone than I told you. But I promise I been doing everything else right."

I heard the panic rising in her voice as she nervously twisted her seatbelt strap. "Please don't make me have this baby at home. I know this girl almost *died* having her baby on the kitchen table. She started bleeding and the midwife couldn't do nothin' to stop it, and the baby wouldn't come out no mat—"

"Hey . . . nobody said you're having your baby at home," I comforted her, not wanting her to return home so upset she would make herself ill. Yet Mrs. Cremins's lecture about enforcing the Project regulations went through my head as clearly as if she'd been sitting between us in my car.

"I'm sorry, Laura. I know you're mad."

"Well . . . no more drinking until after that baby comes," I said, using my advantage. "And no more excuses about not taking your vitamins and drinking a quart of mi—"

"Okay, I'll take those old horse pills. And I'll wash 'em down with milk. But I'm still goin' to the café with Willie. I can't give everything up. I won't *really* drink. I'll just take a swallow to get the bad taste out of my mouth. Or maybe a sip of sweet wine. My Aunt 'Rene says if you drink that while you're expectin', the labor will go easy on you."

A construction detour made us creep along the rest of the way to Mavis's house. Despite the annoying stops and starts in the heavy traffic, Mavis seemed to grow more companionable.

"Laura, what you think I should do?" she asked deferentially.

"About what?"

She looked away. "With the baby coming, you think I ought to marry Willie?"

I was flattered that she would ask my opinion about something so important.

"Mama and Daddy say I got to. 'Specially with Daddy being a preacher. He says the preacher's daughter can't go having babies if she don't have a husband. Mama just keeps crying and saying how I ruined myself so nothin' good will ever come of me. Daddy was gonna whip me but I told him, 'You lay a hand on me, you'll never see me again.'"

"What does Willie say?"

"Willie's *real* quiet 'less you rile him. When I told him about the baby, he said he'd marry me. Said if he had to marry somebody, he'd like to marry me as much as anybody else he could think of."

I thought how crushed I would feel if that was all someone felt for me. Rob and I were enjoying the present and hadn't yet discussed our future. But I knew how fast I would walk away if he acted like marrying me was the best choice he could make in some second-rate cafeteria line. I tried to keep my expression noncommittal and didn't trust myself to speak.

"Girl, I wasn't lookin' to get married neither. So I can't blame Willie." She sighed deeply. "Didn't know what I'd do after high school." She winked. "Thought maybe I'd go to Atlan'a. Get me a job and try out that big city life. Or maybe see the world in the army." She shook her head in disbelief, smacking her chewing gum. "I sure didn't plan on getting trapped like this. Or ending up at no welfare office neither. I went last week to see could I get me some money 'cause I can't get no mill job five months gone." Mavis pointed to her distended belly. "That welfare lady just shamed me. Asked why I didn't think about that before I got pregnant. I told her the damned rubber broke. Did she want to check it out? That shut her up good."

Her voice sounded bitter, but I could also hear her fear of being stuck at home where she was miserable, or marrying Willie and giving up her hope of a life away from that isolated road. They would live on what he made from odd jobs, and soon she would have more babies to care for in their own broken-down trailer.

"You know how hot it is at Daddy's place?" she asked, seeming to read my thoughts. "He's so cheap. Nothin' but concrete block walls just like the jail house and that rusty tin roof with the sun beating down on it all day. He takes money from the collection plate to buy clothes for everybody but his own kids." Mavis tried to sound hardboiled. "I swear I'll leave the baby with Mama. She likes them so much, they can give it to her straight from the hospital. I didn't ask for it no more than measles."

"Mavis, if you feel that way, maybe you should put the baby up for adoption. So it can have parents who really want a baby. I'll go with you to talk to—"

"Girl, don't you go trying to give my baby away. I told you before. This is my flesh and blood. You want to help me, you find me a job. That's what I need. Not all this counseling crap."

We edged up the hill to her house, my wheels spinning in the soft mud. The dogs came running. The children were burying a dead cat wrapped in a cellophane bag. They lowered it into a hole. One little girl threw dandelions into the grave. Then, looking as solemn as church deacons, they prayed over it.

"Can't you find me a decent job?" Mavis asked longingly. "Something pays enough not to get married?"

"If you can't take it at home anymore, you could stay in a church home until the baby comes. We could put you up in one of our field offices for a few days until we find one with space."

"Girl, you think I wanna go to one of those places with people praying over me all the time or with you watching everything I do? I sure ain't gonna have a baby and give it to those welfare bitches neither."

The children finished the burial and marked the grave with a Coke bottle. Then they came running to Mavis's side of the car, laughing and jumping up to greet her.

Mavis scooped up a tiny little girl in a diaper and muddy T-shirt. "I guess one more won't make much difference," she said. "Mama'll help me, and Willie won't be so bad. He *is* good looking. And he don't preach all the time."

"Do you think he'll be a good father?"

"It don't take much to be a father, Laura. Or a mother neither. It just comes natural. Didn't you know that?"

CHAPTER 9

A Beautiful Build

"Ma'am?" the little girl asked shyly to get my attention. She wore white shorts and a green halter top and looked so summery I forgot about fall in the air.

"Hi," I said. "I didn't see you come in." I was surrounded by stacks of hamburger patties and a big mound of meat still to be attacked. She waited as patiently as if I'd walked into *her* office. Finally, I said, "What can I do for you? I'm Laura Bauer."

"That sure is a lot of hamburgers."

"We have a big group coming for supper. Are you here for that?" I guessed she was a new client who had been dropped off early.

"No ma'am. I'm not in the Project yet. But Susan came out to see us first of the week. She said if I was interested I needed to talk to you."

"You must be Lisa Landrum." It came back to me.

"Yes, ma'am. I guess Susan told you all about me." She looked at me as hopefully as an eager puppy.

"She said you might be by this week. But she didn't tell me *all* about you." I didn't want her to think we passed her complete life story around like a magazine.

"My mama was gonna come down, too, but she's workin' today. So I got a ride down with Miz Ledberry. She has the toothache and was comin' in to see Dr. Weems. Susan said y'all could carry me home later."

"You *have* to see Lisa soon," Susan had told me, looking poised as ever, even sitting on a stool with a cracked, vinyl top. We were eating lunch together at the drugstore soda fountain, probably the same one where Susan had come for French fries and cherry Cokes after high school cheerleading practices. "She'll break your heart," she said of Lisa. "Thirteen and dead set on having that baby. I found out about her 'cause Miz Malden, the lady at the retardation center, goes to my church. She told me there's another daughter, sixteen, who got pregnant, too. Miz Landrum got so mad at her, the girl ran off, and they haven't heard a word from her in two months.

"So when Miz Landrum found out that Lisa was pregnant, she went down to the center to talk to Miz Malden. And Miz Mal—"

"Why'd she go to the retardation center instead of the health department?"

"She knows Miz Malden from way back. On account of Bert, Lisa's older brother, has been going there since he was a little boy." In a softer voice, she continued, "He's not *real* retarded. But when they put him over at the regular school, the children made fun of him. And of course he does talk kind of funny. He's twenty-two now. To look at him you wouldn't know anything's wrong, but once you talk to him, you can tell."

"Anyhow," she said, crunching on the ice left from her tea, "Miz Malden arranged for me to visit them. I went around suppertime to make sure Lisa's mother would be home. She waits breakfast and lunch at a little café. And you know where they live?" She laughed out loud, not cruelly, but loud enough that people at the end of the counter looked up. She whispered, "In an old *superette*. You wouldn't believe it. The name's down, but there's still Coca Cola signs up and the parking lot's marked off with yellow lines. Miz Malden *told* me, but I didn't believe it 'til I saw it. Inside there're still most of the counters and partitions. There's a tiny kitchen and some furniture and things, but it really looks like a cleaned-out grocery."

She lit a cigarette, took a deep drag, and in deference to me, exhaled over my head. "We sat down where they had a few kitchen chairs and a couch made up like a bed. Her two little brothers, I guess around three and four, were playing on the floor, and Bert was making a dog collar. They taught him that at the center."

She flipped her long, blonde bangs out of her eyes and nervously twirled the end of her hair around her fingers. "It felt so odd, Laura. I asked Lisa all the usual questions, and she answered me. But every time I tried to lead up to who the baby's father was, Miz Landrum led me away real quick. I couldn't put my finger on it, but something was strange. It was like when you know without even turning around somebody's coming up behind you." She shivered as if she still couldn't shake the feeling. "I don't know. Maybe it was just being in an old superette like that."

"I'm glad to meet you, Lisa," I told her and started making hamburgers again. I didn't like leaving them out in the heat. "Can you stay for supper? Afterwards, we'll be glad to run you home."

"Yes, ma'am, I'd like that. 'Cause I want to join up reg'lar. You need help with those hamburgers?"

"Sure." I was relieved she talked so easily. "And I'd enjoy the company."

She worked neatly and quickly. I forgot she was only thirteen as she told me all about her family.

"It's been hard since Daddy died. The doctor'd just told us how sick he was. Then he was gone like somebody blowing out a candle. Mama had to start waitressing, but she don't make nearly enough to take care of all of us the way Daddy done. See, he was a real good carpenter. Everybody was after him to work for them.

"But most everything he'd saved went for the hospital and the doctor. Mama couldn't keep up the house payments so we moved into the superette. It's all right 'cept in the summer. 'Cause they took out the air conditioning, and the windows don't open."

I noticed that all her hamburger patties were perfectly shaped. She'd finished her portion of the meat and was reshaping some of mine.

"You're doing a great job, Lisa."

"This is easy," she said, making light of my compliment. "Anybody can make hamburgers. I get a lot of practice helping Mama with the cooking at home. Since Cindy run off, there's more to do. But Bert stays with Matt and Dan during the day, and he'll keep the baby for me when the time comes. He's good with children. Real gentle and all. So I can go back to school, and the baby won't hold me back hardly at all."

I wanted to convince her she didn't have to become a thirteen-year-old mother. She could grow up and get out of the grocery store before she had a child.

"Lisa, it's early in your pregnancy. There's still time to . . . to talk about options. Are you sure you want to have the baby?" I felt shy speaking this way to a child. "Maybe it'd be better if your mother's here when we talk about it."

Her face and voice grew fierce. "You're talking about abortion," she accused me. "My fam'ly's always gone to church. We don't believe in murdering babies. And Susan already told me 'bout adoption. But I can't give my baby to somebody else. I want this baby." Her voice broke and she began to cry.

"Lisa, I'm sorry." I stood there helplessly with my greasy hands. "I didn't mean to upset you. I just wanted you to know you had choices."

"It's OK," she said smiling, pushing back her brown hair. "You don't have to 'pologize. You got to ask. You want to know anything else?"

"Is there something you'd like to tell me?"

"No. But could I show you my pictures?" Her face brightened. "Lemme wash my hands first so I don't get 'em all greasy."

We washed up at the kitchen sink and put the hamburgers in the refrigerator. Then we sat down at the table, and she carefully took a small red photo album from her pocketbook.

"This is Cindy. My big sister."

A shot to the waist of a pretty girl in a maroon V-neck sweater. A slim blonde, hair perfectly curled in a flip. Smiling wide like a cheerleader.

"Ain't she pretty? She always did take a good picture." Her voice was sad. "We were real close 'til she run off. But I know she'll write once she settles down someplace.

"And this is Dan and Matt. Dan's the taller one in the brown pants. We made these in the machine at Woolworth's. Made them feel real grown up to have a picture like everybody else."

Two little boys. China white skin. Pale as the lowest-fat milk. Sandy hair clipped at the brows. Striped T-shirts. Four frames. Four variations of *Look at me now! Look at me smile.*

"And this is Bert. My big brother. He *is* big, ain't he?"

He was tall and his powerful shoulders were revealed by the thin straps of a red tank top. Shoulder-length black hair, washed and brushed until it lay thick and straight. Brown eyes. The slowness showed no trace in those eyes. He was grinning like any boy in a school picture, hiding nothing.

"Ain't he cute? Don't he have a beautiful build? I think he looks just like David Cassidy."

Then we drove to the store for a few items I still needed for the dinner. She laughed and reclined her seat.

"I like your car," she said, when we pulled into the parking lot. She admired the mag wheels, whose flashiness had embarrassed me when I drove it off the used car lot. "This is fun," she told me, as we entered the store. "I know I'll like the Project if we get to do stuff like this." She ran ahead of me. "Oh look!" She pointed to the candy counter. "Don't you just love choclit? I could eat it all day long." She looked puzzled. "Why are you buying so much milk? Wouldn't everybody rather have Cokes or tea?"

"We're trying to get all the girls to drink a quart of milk a day."

"Ooh. I don't drink a quart a week."

We went through the check-out line and carried our brown bags out to the parking lot where the sun baked the rows of cars. We were standing by my green Plymouth Duster while I fumbled for the keys. I don't know why then, but I turned around to face her, and it suddenly occurred to me. I was squinting into the sun. I asked awkwardly, afraid of her answer, "Lisa, is . . . are you saying . . . Bert's the father?"

"Yes," she said, smiling unselfconsciously. "Don't he have a beautiful build?"

CHAPTER 10

A Red Velvet Sofa

"You get a little foolish sometimes," Mrs. Walton told me, cracking the knuckles of her large rough hands. "You can't afford it, but one day you go out and buy the nicest thing you can find, and *hang* the bill collector. That's how come I bought that red velvet sofa you're sittin' on. If I didn't get one pretty thing once in a while, I couldn't stand it no longer."

A red velvet sofa that would look cheap in a good store and pretentious in a second-hand shop. When the velvet was worn after a few years, it would look worse than vinyl.

"Usually we don't set in here. I save it for special occasions," she said proudly. "Oh no! I wanted *you* to set there," she hurriedly assured me. "I'd druther look at it from here. If I sat next to you I couldn't see it."

She lowered her voice. "I'll call Nell for you. But don't feel put out if she don't say much. She won't hardly talk to strangers. Guess she can't help acting that way, not being real bright." She shook her head in dismay. "She takes after my first husband. Couldn't carry on a conversation to save his life. But he was a handsome devil." She laughed a harsh laugh. "Poor Nell. She got his brains, but not his looks. Guess she missed out all around."

When Nell walked in, she made me think of a child with a bloated stomach. She looked ill, not pregnant. Her black, straight hair was cut as if someone had put a bowl on her head and hacked it off at the ears. She wore a white smock over blue jeans. She seemed an old-woman child, awkward with her extra weight. Then there were her dark eyes, following but revealing nothing. Not anger, sadness, shyness, or fear. She just watched.

"Nell, now you answer Miz Bauer's questions," Mrs. Walton said sternly. "She's from that project I told you about. She came all the way out here to see you. So you talk now. You hear?"

Nell nodded and lowered her head. She sat down in the chair next to her mother's, her eyes on the floor.

"Don't you mind Nell, ma'am. She never did mix real well, and since we moved up here, she's gotten extra shy. But she don't mean nothin' by it, do you, honey?"

Nell smiled halfheartedly, the way a dog tentatively wags his tail when he is uncertain of what may come next.

"We moved up here in June when my husband got a new job in Cartersville. He's a mechanic, and he's doing real well now." She pointed to pictures on the coffee table. "Jeannie Lee, my oldest, lives in Roopville. She's married. That's her baby right there, and she's got another due next month. And Jimmy—you prob'ly saw him out in the yard with his daddy's shovel—is six. And Nan's four. And Louise is eight. She's the only one got the pretty red hair from my side of the fam'ly." She passed a hard look at Nell as she picked up a small framed photograph from the coffee table. "This here's Nell's school picture from last year. She looks a whole lot older now being . . . well, you know. Anyhow, she's fifteen like I told you on the phone."

"How have you been feeling, Nell?" I asked directly, fighting to make her look at me and trust me with even a few words.

Mrs. Walton answered me, as if Nell were incapable of speech. "In the beginning she was belching all the time. Guess it made her full of gas. But I got a big bottle of Maalox and that stopped it, one, two, three." She snapped her fingers for emphasis. Her hair was frosted three variations of champagne and set in a frozen pompadour. I looked from one face to the other seeking a resemblance. I tried to imagine Nell's hair frosted, teased up, and stiff with hairspray, but the image wouldn't take.

"Are you still in school, Nell?"

"Nell ain't going to school no more. She never liked it, and now she don't have to with the baby coming. She'll be sixteen by then anyhow. She finished six months of eighth grade before we moved here. I hold a lot more with vocational school anyhow."

"What would you like to study in vocational school, Nell?"

"The best thing for Nell would be the nurse's aide course. Only takes a few months before you go to work making $2.25 an hour. She'll live here and go to Jasper to school. There's always jobs for nurse's aides."

Mrs. Walton sent Nell out to the kitchen for coffee. In a moment she returned with a plastic tray heavy with coffee mugs and a plate of homemade chocolate chip cookies. Nell pushed a mug towards me.

"Where's your manners?" Mrs. Walton snapped. "Give her a napkin and the cream and sugar."

"There's no need to bother, Mrs. Walton. I like it black. This smells delicious, Nell." I wanted so badly to make up for her mother's harshness that I enthusiastically took too big a swallow.

"Nell, you shouldn't fill the mugs so full," Mrs. Walton said, handing me a napkin. "It's gonna be your fault if you burn somebody."

"It was my fault. I shouldn't have taken such a big sip."

Nell relaxed, realizing she wouldn't be blamed. She took two cookies and dunked one in her coffee.

"That's about all she eats these days. I told her she's gonna get fat. But she don't listen. Just keeps eating cookies and drinking coffee and Cokes. I cook up fresh vegetables every day, but she won't touch them. She likes choclit chip best."

Nell bent over her cup eating quickly, never looking up, as if she feared her mother might snatch the cookies.

Mrs. Walton picked up one of the brochures I'd placed on the coffee table and looked it over. "I'd be glad for Nell to come to some of your programs down there," she said. "It's kind of far though." Her voice became long suffering. "I guess me and Bill could bring her down some evening."

"How about Wednesday? We're having a family supper. Nell could meet our staff and some of the girls and their families. You and your husband would be welc—"

"I'm sorry, but she couldn't come Wednesday night. That's when I do my Tupperware parties. Do you use Tupperware? I couldn't *manage* without it. Besides, I need the extra money. I'm hopin' to get a chair to match that sofa by Christmastime."

"I'll come for you, Nell." I was determined to get her away from her mother. "I'm picking up somebody who lives nearby anyway."

Nell looked up, finally summoning the courage to speak. She had a soft, husky voice. "If it wouldn't be too much trou—"

"But you always help me with the parties, Nell," Mrs. Walton complained. "It's an awful lot for me to do on my own. You know it is."

"I can see why Nell is such a help to you." I tried my most conciliatory tone. "But couldn't you manage without her just this once? This is important for Nell."

"I'm sorry as I can be. If it was any other night I'd come myself. There's just too much to do. Besides, I hate for you to come all this way just for Nell."

"It's no trouble, Mrs. Walton." I was determined to win. "I'll already be in the area."

"Well, what d'you think, Nell? You gonna leave me to run it all by myself? You want to go down there without me where you won't know a soul?"

Nell stared at the floor.

"Now I'm not tellin' you what t'do, Nell," her mother insisted. "It's your life, honey. You sure you don't want to go?"

Nell shook her head "no."

So I lost. Bitter thoughts overcame me as I agreed to take Nell to the Project doctor the following week. I wondered how she'd ever gotten far enough away from her mother to get pregnant.

Mrs. Walton walked me to the door. Nell stood in her shadow like a small child. "Well then, we'll expect you next Thursday, Miz Bauer. Nell and me sure do 'preciate you comin' to get us. We'll get all those papers filled out in the meantime." She smiled triumphantly. She knew she'd won.

She handed me a Tupperware catalog. "You look this over before you come back." She smiled at me. "It's a big help for working girls." She held the screen door for me. It was starting to rain. Small drops left their marks in the dusty red clay of the yard.

"Thank you for coming, Miz Bauer. Say good-bye, Nell."

Nell smiled as timidly as a child told to say "thank you" to a stranger for a lollipop. I sat in my car for a few minutes watching the rain. I felt foolish and defeated. I stared at the little white house with the green tarpaper roof. And the red velvet sofa.

CHAPTER 11

Afternoon Tea

"You shouldn't go up there." Nadine spoke with the authority of a mother warning a child.

"Why not? It's only afternoon tea."

"You listen here." She kept filing as she enlightened me, not wanting to waste one moment assigned to her official duties, being as conscientious as an Eagle Scout. "You may know Ray Lee Tate as a landlord, but I know him as a neighbor . . . and a *man*." She blushed. "Folks talk a lot. I guess you realize he's not inviting you up to drink *tea*."

"Nadine, he's sixty years old! He's just being friendly. He'd be insulted if I didn't go."

"D'you *know* what he calls you?" she asked sternly, and then blushed and looked away, buttoning her blue cardigan sweater, as if even the thought of Ray Lee Tate made her wish to cover up.

"What?" I asked directly, unconcerned by her hints about Mr. Tate.

She wouldn't answer or look at me. I could only see the back of her head, her brown pageboy hairdo neatly turned under.

"Nadine, you brought it up. So you have to tell me."

"It's not nice. That's all I'll say." She moved across the room to the supply cabinets and began straightening up. "Listen to me for once. Don't go."

I went to stand in front of the cabinets she was working on so she had to address me. "Either you tell me, or we'll stand here all day."

"Well . . . you know how he comes in here all the time." She looked away. "And if you're not here, he'll mosey over towards your office, and he'll peek in and then he'll come up to me . . . *brazen* as the devil and he'll . . . he'll—"

"Go on!"

"He'll say right out, 'Where's *Jugs* today?'"

"Meaning . . . oh my God!"

"You made me tell you," she complained, embarrassed to repeat his vulgarity. "I didn't want to, but now you know why you shouldn't go up there."

"But look at his note, Nadine."

She put on her pink glasses to examine it. Nadine had a grown daughter and was in no danger from the town flirts, but she was much too vain to wear her glasses all the time. She read out loud, "Hi. We've missed you around here. When you close up shop, come up for a little afternoon tea. Bring Nadine with you."

"He wouldn't dare pull anything with you along. The man's not a fool."

"Did I say anything about going with you? I won't be your chaperone."

"Maybe he *is* offering us a drink, but that's all there is to it. What's the harm in that?"

"You're making me gossip and I don't like it." Her eyes scolded me. "When Ray Lee's first wife Myra took sick so fast with the cancer, he hired a housekeeper. She was there to help nurse poor Myra, who looked like death even when she was still alive. But anyhow, not two months after she died . . ." Her voice grew hushed. "He married Paula."

"Paula?"

"The housekeeper!"

"Maybe he always liked her, and when he was free, he found he loved her."

"She's at least thirty years younger than him!"

"Well . . . look at . . . Strom Thurmond."

"Go ahead. Come up with all the examples you want, but it's not right for a man's wife to die and he up and marries a woman half his age who was his *housekeeper*." Her tone was scorching.

"I'm sure Paula will be there this afternoon. He wouldn't try anything in front of his wife."

"I'll bet his brother Ollie'll be there, too. And he moonshines and gambles and Lord knows what else."

"The more you say, the more exciting it gets." I couldn't resist riding her. "Come on. Go with me."

"No, ma'am. You go on and laugh," she said. "I just hope the last laugh's not on you."

When the time came for me to leave, Nadine changed her mind and agreed to accompany me. "If you're bound and determined to do this," she said as we got into her car, "then I'm going with you. But when *I* say it's time to go, we're leaving."

Nadine drove quickly up Mr. Tate's steep driveway. I knew she could back down a mountain road if she felt like it, but I worried there'd be no place to turn around. So at the top of his hill, she turned around and pulled in behind a blue pickup. We walked up on the porch and rang the bell. Wooden signs made to look rustic announced we were on "Paula's Porch" at "Ray Lee's Ranch."

"Welcome ladies!" Ray Lee Tate greeted us, squeezing my hand. I tried not to show it, though he made me uneasy. I could smell his heavy cologne as soon as he opened the door and was unsure whether he actually leered at me as we walked in or if I'd been unduly influenced by Nadine's opinions. He was missing two fingers from a farm accident when he was a boy, which I noticed again as he smoothed back his thick, black hair, just starting to grey at the temples. He was a powerfully built man gone thick in the middle and wore a maroon and navy velour top.

"We were just startin' to wonder if y'all was even comin'," he said, smiling to Nadine as he ushered us in.

"Mr. Tate, we don't often get asked to tea," I said, trying to capture the right degree of flippancy. "We wouldn't miss it."

He smiled back, long and heavy. I wished he'd release my hand. He led us into a plywood-paneled den with a plaid overstuffed love seat with matching chairs and a worn corduroy recliner. It didn't seem the setting for the richest man in the county. I wondered if people exaggerated his wealth. The only visible signs of it were his two late-model Buicks and a huge horseshoe diamond ring, made more striking by its juxtaposition to his missing fingers.

I couldn't forget the stories I'd been told about the wad of bills—big ones—always present when he paid for anything from a candy bar to a piece of property. This ready cash supposedly explained his ability to deliver elections. There was also a rumor he had a fortune in old gold coins buried in his cow pasture.

"He's a millionaire through no good sense of his own," Nadine had told me. "Years ago he bought up this whole passel of worthless land. Everybody told him it was a dumb thing to do 'cause it wadn't good for anything. And for a while it just sat there. Then *purely* by chance, they decided to dam a creek and make Lake Chigawasee and build a whole resort of lake homes. And the closest land to that creek was Ray Lee Tate's so the deal fell right in his lap. He tries to take credit for being a good businessman. But he don't have half the brains of a good dog. He's just lucky and mean."

"He's shrewd all right," Susan had warned me. "Acts like he's just this simple country boy to fool everybody so they won't watch him. But he's clever as they come." Then she'd looked perplexed. "The only thing that doesn't figure is why he can't spend his money. The man's *loaded*. And his house is all right, but it's no kind of place for a man with that kind of money.

"And you won't believe this! Two years ago he built a big ole swimming pool. Then one day—just like it was nothing—he filled it in so he'd have more space to park his milk trucks." She shook her head. "It's a waste for folks like that to have money."

Ray Lee called me back to reality. "I wantcha t'meet my brother Ollie from Ellijay and Whit Barlow, my fishing buddy."

Both men stood up and smiled.

Ray Lee said, "Y'all, this is Laura. She's from the new Project. And of course y'all already know Miss Nadine." He put his arm around Paula while he made introductions. She was a honey blonde. His three fingers stroked her pink cheek.

Ollie had all his fingers. And green plaid pants. He stood a head taller than Ray Lee. His blue eyes were glued on my chest.

"Hello there, J— Laura." He blushed furiously. "Pleased t'meet you. Ray Lee thinks a lot of you."

Barlow was a turnip with legs. He sat down quickly as if his legs would give out. There was an empty highball glass beside him.

"Ladies, now I *could* offer you tea," Ray Lee said. "But I was thinkin' . . . maybe after workin' all day . . . well, you know . . . I thought you might like somethin' a little more relaxing."

"I'll have what you're having, Mr. Tate," I said, ignoring Nadine's dirty look.

"Call me Ray Lee, please." He grinned. "Nadine, what can I get you?"

"I'll have a Coke please. And you can just leave it in the bottle."

Ollie sat down next to me. Just a little too close. Barlow grinned like a Cheshire turnip. "What's a matter, Nadine? You afraid he'll slip somethin' in it if he pours it in a glass?"

"I'm not afraid of Ray Lee or anybody else," Nadine said in a withering tone that made me wish I'd come by myself.

Ray Lee brought out a half-gallon Haig and Haig Scotch bottle. Only the liquor inside it was clear. Paula carried highball glasses full of ice. Ray Lee poured the liquor generously and handed glasses round to everyone but Nadine.

Maybe it's vodka, I thought. *Maybe Haig and Haig makes vodka.*

"Ladies, to your health!" Ray Lee raised his glass, which I noticed contained hardly any ice, and downed his drink quickly.

"What is this, Ray Lee?" I asked, inching away from Ollie.

"That," said Ollie, patting me on the back, "is the finest moonshine you can find from Mississippi to Tennessee. I can guarantee it 'cause I make it myself. One hundred eighty proof and clean as a whistle."

Blindness. Horrible deaths. I'd heard all about it on public television. How you're supposed to light it to see if it burns with a clear blue flame. I didn't dare look at Nadine.

"Drink up, honey. Don't be afraid of drinking the barrel dry." Barlow topped off my glass. "It's a deep well."

The second round was easier, sort of like riding a bicycle. Once you know how, you never forget and you don't fall off.

"Maybe you'd like to go fishin' with me and Ray Lee sometime?" Ollie asked, smiling down at me. "We got two Cessnas and we fly down to Florida. Take a little beer, have a lot of good times."

Barlow had moved onto the arm of the love seat and was easing himself closer to Nadine under the pretext of lighting her cigarette. I watched her face for signs of concern, but she simply got up and moved to a chair close to Paula, who was doing needlepoint and drinking a Coke.

"Do you make this up in Ellijay?" I asked Ollie.

He winked at me. "I ain't one for givin' out professional secrets, but considerin' we're friends . . ." He put his arm over the back of the couch behind me. His weight knocked me into him. "Les just say me and Ray Lee got us a little place where we make just enough for us. But back in the old days . . . we made quite a bit."

"Quite a bit—hell!" Ray Lee was excited. "'Scuse me, ladies. But we used t'make so much, there wasn't hardly a truck from here t'Ellijay carryin' milk cans with milk in 'em!"

"That's the truth!" Barlow slapped his thigh. "Tell her 'bout them night runs, Ray Lee."

"I don't want y'all t'think we was bad fellers or nothin' but durin' Prohibition a man was gonna drink, and he was gonna get it somewhere. We figured it might as well be from us." He smiled contentedly as Paula's eyes followed him. "We'd make it up near Ellijay. Then we'd carry it all over the state at night."

"Thas right," Barlow said. "Folks musta thought we had the biggest dairy in the state."

"Now, don't confuse our friends," Ray Lee said. "Nobody ever seen us 'cause we always drove late at night."

"And honey, don't fret over the stories they tell in Atlan'a." Ollie patted my arm. "That stuff about blindness—well, maybe it does happen—but not from our whiskey. I never sold a man nothin' I didn't try myself. And just look at me." He thumped his barrel chest. "It ain't hurt me none." He poured a little of the liquor into a saucer and ignited it with a match. "See that clear blue flame," he said proudly. "That's good, clean whiskey."

"Anyhow," Ray Lee said impatiently, "I knew ev'ry back road in this county. 'Cause you couldn't go cruisin' down Highway 41 with the revenuers out there thick as flies. We used t'go seventy miles an hour in the pitch dark down roads I wouldn't go forty on today in broad daylight." He sat up straight with excitement at the retelling. "There was this one night me and Whit had the biggest load we'd ever hauled. It was a clear night with a big ole full moon shinin' overhead, and we was nearly home free. When all of a sudden Whit says to me, 'Ray Lee, look in that mirror. There's somebody followin' us.' Sure enough I could see the headlights in my mirror." Ray Lee was on the edge of his chair. "I knew we was in trouble. In the pitch black all we could see was those lights followin' us straight as if we was givin' out directions."

Barlow's little eyes opened wide at the memory of their adventure. He looked over at Ray Lee, as proud as a fellow veteran during the retelling of their war stories.

"So," Ray Lee said, "I looked at Whit and I told him, 'I don't know about you, but I'm for makin' a run for it. Ain't nobody gonna pinch me like a sittin' duck.' 'Cause I knew it had to be a revenuer. There wasn't nobody else had business bein' on that road. Anyhow, I gunned that pickup for all she was worth. I used t'call her the Blue Streak. She didn't look like much, but she could move like a rabbit.

"We were flyin'. I could hear gravel and rocks poppin' all around us. But I knew that road—ev'ry single pothole. And I tried ev'ry last trick I could think of. I'd ditched them city fellas left and right many times before, but this one stuck. So I flew up this little dirt road that wadn't hardly more than a hikin' trail. And I slammed off my lights and turned her real sharp off the road so we just vanished into the night. But then the other fella vanished, too. We didn't see him go by." He frowned, furrowing his thick brows, remembering his consternation. "And then I figured it out. I turned on my lights and pulled back into the road, and do you know who was following us?"

He paused, like any good storyteller, making us wait for his punch line. He laughed nervously and his eyes sparkled, as he savored the suspense he had created.

"Come on, Mr. Tate. Tell us what happened," I urged him, my curiosity fueled more by what I'd had to drink than the power of his delivery.

"All right then. I'll tell you," he agreed, still taking his time to do so. "It was that big ole moon shinin' on the tops of my milk cans!"

Everyone laughed hilariously except Nadine, who would never have granted Mr. Tate the approval of her laughter, and Paula, who smiled politely, probably having heard this same story fifty times before. Besides, all she was drinking was Coke. And, maybe like me, she believed it was just another fish story.

"What d'you say? You wanna go fishin' down t'Florida some weekend?" Ollie kept moving closer. I was running out of space. "If you want, we'll fly down an' get you in Atlan'a. We'll touch down right in your backyard."

"Paula, I'd love to see your needlepoint." It sounded foolish, but it was the best escape I could invent. I got up quickly to examine her work, which was displayed on the wall behind the recliner. But as soon as I was standing, it hit me. I was *drunk*. I was determined not to show it since I could feel they were all watching me. I turned to Paula as if she were about to show me priceless etchings.

"I'm makin this for the baby's room," she said, holding out to me the quilt she'd been working on. "It's the Sermon on the Mount. I like religious things, don't you?" She smiled with pleasure at my apparent interest.

I had my glasses on, but the room felt fuzzy. They've done it, I thought. They've gotten me drunk while they don't feel it more than if they'd had one weak mixed drink. Pretty soon it will be me and the Turnip and Ollie on a Cessna to Florida.

"Would you like to see the baby's room?" Paula asked.

"Yeah, you wouldn't want to miss that," Ollie said, making a joke of it.

"Sure she's dyin' to see it," Barlow said, catching the mood as he drained his glass again. "I bet she's never seen one before."

"I like a joke as well as the next man," Ray Lee said angrily, "but don't you sit here makin' fun of Paula's work." He stroked her cheek protectively. "I don't care if I am the one blowing her horn. Paula's a *genuine* artist. She's won awards at craft fairs from Alabama to North Carolina. When it comes to needlepoint with a religious message, nobody can—"

"Now, Ray Lee, stop it. You're embarrassing me," Paula said. "I don't do anything that special."

"She's just being modest," Ollie said, trying to make it up to Ray Lee. "Ole Ray Lee here—he's just a good ole boy—but I 'preciate real art. And Paula here ought to have her work in a museum. Wait'll you see for yourself."

As I followed Paula across the room, I stumbled. I passed it off as the crepe sole of my shoe sticking to the thick carpet, but Nadine sensed the truth. "I want to see how Paula's decorated, too," she said brightly. Then she whispered, "I'm right behind you. See if you can remember how to walk. I *told* you not to come here."

The baby's room was snowy white from the shag carpeting to the ceiling outlined by a border of pink and blue bunnies. The crib and dresser were fairly dancing in hand-painted butterflies and flowers. The curtains were patterned with storks and baby dolls in pink and blue. We had entered the insides of a sugary confection. The embroidered wall hanging read, "Hush Little Baby, don't say a word. Mama's going to buy you a mockingbird." The design showed a sleeping baby with a blanket pulled up to its chin, covered with mockingbirds. A small embroidery on the opposite wall displayed the face of Christ defined in several shades of lavender, pink, and blue. And centered above it was a banner embroidered in pink and blue, which declared, "Let the little children come to me. Mark 10:14."

But where was the baby? Had they recently adopted or was she pregnant? She certainly didn't show it. And the room looked finished as if a baby were ready to arrive any day. There were toys in the playpen and supplies arranged in readiness on the changing table.

"It's a beautiful room, Paula." I hesitated, afraid I was about to say something tactless. "I didn't know you were expecting. Is it a boy or a girl? I'm surprised Ray Lee hasn't said anything."

"There's not a baby *yet*." She looked at me sheepishly. "Sometimes God takes a while to grant your wishes. Ray Lee says it's his fault 'cause he's too old. But I keep prayin' and doin' what the doctor says. 'Cause I want a baby so bad."

She'd built a shrine for an unborn child. It made me feel lonely to think of her sitting at home sewing curtains and stenciling "Jack and Jill" on a new dresser while Ray Lee was out playing poker or having "afternoon tea" with his friends. Her need was as frightening as an addict's.

"This room is pretty as a picture," Nadine said, breaking our awkward silence. "But could I take another peek at what you've done with the Sermon on the Mount?"

"Before we go back out there, could I ask you something?" Paula asked tentatively. "It's a little embarrassing."

"Sure. What is it?" I felt obligated to let her confide in us, though what I most wanted was to get away.

"I don't feel like Ray Lee and me are ever gonna be blessed." She spoke shyly as she looked around the room. "We've been trying awhile . . . and I don't mean to get real personal or anything, but Ray Lee's not as young as he used to be.

"So . . . I was wonderin' if I could get in touch with one of those girls who can't get into your project. Or maybe one of the young ones who's not ready to be a mama."

"I don't understand," I answered uneasily, uncertain if this was still the effect of alcohol or if Paula was somehow pressing me for information I should not give out. "What did you want to do for them?"

"I want a *baby,* Laura. Ray Lee and I could adopt one. It would never want for anything. And Ray Lee would be a great daddy. After all, he already is one. His kids are grown, and they all turned out just fine."

I was amazed at how wrong Nadine's conjecture had been. Ray Lee didn't have designs on *me.* He wanted a baby for Paula.

"We'd be able to give a baby a much better life than these poor little girls who've got themselves in trouble," Paula said. "How could it possibly hurt for me just to talk to one of them?"

"Paula, our records are confidential. I couldn't give you our clients' information." I found myself backing out of the room toward the others to escape her.

"I know some of your girls. I could call 'em so you wouldn't even have to get involved. Please help me, Laura," she implored me.

I was relieved to feel the firm pressure of Nadine's hand on my shoulder, easing me out of the room. "Come on," she said firmly. "We really need to be getting back, Paula. Thank you so much for having us."

"We have plenty of money," Paula said, tears in her eyes. "How much do you think they'd want?"

"We know how bad you feel, Paula. But we can't sell babies, honey," Nadine said, more gently than I'd have expected.

"Of course not. That's not what I meant," she hurriedly assured us, though it certainly appeared that she had. "Only Ray Lee's counting on me to ask you. What'll I tell him now?"

"I'm sorry, but you just need to tell him the truth," I said, wishing so much I had listened to Nadine and never come. "We're not an adoption agency. And I'm not aware of any girl we've enrolled who wants to give up her baby."

"Fact is, Laura," Ray Lee said, suddenly appearing and joining our conversation. "Some of those girls' mamas want 'em to give up the babies 'cause they know they can't take care of 'em. Paula and me talked it over, and I know the mama of one of 'em you could talk to. I'm pretty sure if you told Trina Kitchens's mama about what we're offering, she'd be fine with it."

"I can't do that, Ray Lee."

I had speculated that Trina would be better off surrendering her baby, but I'd imagined an anonymous adoption, not Trina handing her baby over to the richest man in town, whom she'd have to see each week at church and the grocery store.

"Then, I can do it myself. Trina's folks rent their place from me."

"Ray Lee Tate, I'll go to the police if you try to swap rent for that baby," Nadine said. "Or try to force that family out of their house if Trina won't give you her baby. I won't stand by and watch that."

"Who said any such thing?" Ray Lee said with amazement. "You're comin' up with some mighty strange ideas, Nadine. On nothin' but Coca-Cola."

"I'm sorry," Paula said, drying her eyes on handkerchief. "I shouldn't have asked you."

"That's absolutely right," Ray Lee said. "You don't need their permission. You can call Trina right now. People arrange adoptions all the time."

I felt suddenly sober and angry, but also helpless to stop them from calling Trina or her mother.

"Ray Lee, I shouldn't do that." Paula's eyes opened wide. "Not when Laura says Trina wants to keep her baby. I wouldn't want to shame her."

"She's a minor, Paula. She's got to do what her mama tells her."

"I don't want to *make* her give up her baby."

"A baby's no different than anything else," Ray Lee said cynically. "You want it, you pay for it. Long as there ain't no law against it."

"I've heard about enough," Nadine said. "Thank you for your hospitality, Paula. I'm leaving now, Laura. You coming with me?"

Before I could answer, Ray Lee laughed a hard, ugly laugh and said, "Hey, don't hurry off. No hard feelings. We won't call Miz Kitchens about Trina's baby. We'll stay out of it. Besides, she's bound to have another one in a year or so. We can wait."

. . . .

CHAPTER 12

For Three Lousy Bucks

"The trouble with you hicks," the superintendent said, spitting into the dirt, "is that you're lazy." He stared down at the men in the hole. It was noon, the broiling point. Resting on their shovels, squinting into the sun, they stared up at him. Vibrations from the borers and bulldozers moved across the cleared land where the red clay was piled up like giant ant hills.

"Barfield, I'm warning you," he said to the big man who returned his look sullenly. "You smoke on company time once more and you'll be back on the farm where you belong."

Barfield jammed his hands in his pockets, his powerful body tensing, his anger threatening to explode.

"You got something to say, Barfield?" The superintendent cupped his hand to his ear, pretending to be hard of hearing. "You'll have to speak up so I can hear you." He swaggered, his eyes full of contempt for Barfield and the rest of them. When Barfield made no answer, he said deliberately, "I didn't think you had anything to say. In case you change your mind, remember what I said. And that goes for the rest of you." He turned away in disgust.

Barfield savagely sank his pick into the clay. *For three lousy bucks an hour,* he thought, *I gotta take this shit. I kill myself all morning digging through rock and laying these pipes like some kind of mule, and then I stop to smoke one lousy cigarette and he gives me hell about it.* He kicked the dirt piled up in front of him, but couldn't contain himself any longer. "Damn son of a bitch," he said, louder than he'd intended.

"Shut up, Jimmy, or he'll hear you," his buddy Eddie Davis said protectively.

"I don't care what that bastard does. Let him hear ev'ry word I got to say." He spoke angrily but nevertheless lowered his voice.

"Come on, Jimmy, don't take it so hard." Davis thumped him on the back. "It's time for lunch anyhow."

They drove to a little superette down the road, and then they sat under a tree to eat their sandwiches. Davis talked nervously and told lots of jokes, trying to make up for Barfield's silence. He was worried Barfield would get fired if he stayed angry. His temper was legendary. He wasn't mean, but he wasn't a fellow you wanted to aggravate.

"What d'you say tonight me and you go have a few beers?" he asked Barfield. "Listen to a little music. Relax awhile. Forget about work."

"I don't feel like goin' nowhere. But I'd sure like to bust that guy. All it'd take is one punch."

"Well, you know you cain't. You even *look* wrong at that guy, he'll can you and have somebody working in your place tomorrow. And you and Mandy got a baby comin'. You better quit talkin' that way."

"Shit. I'm sick of takin' it off some guy who never worked a day in his life. I'd like to beat the crap out of him."

"So would everybody else, but nobody's gonna do it. And you're not either." Davis's voice was caught between annoyance and regret. "It don't matter how big you are, Jimmy. You cain't beat guys like that. You gotta take it like everybody else."

"OK, Eddie." The big man smiled. "Reckon I ain't cornered the market on hating him, but I sure as hell would like to knock the living—" He stopped himself and tried to relax. "Where you wanna go when we knock off?"

"I was thinkin' maybe we'd try something a little different." He spoke carefully, watching Barfield's face. "The new place that just opened up. I heard they got real nice girls. *Dancers*—that is." He couldn't keep the secret to himself. "Guy told me they got a topless show!"

"Come on, Eddie. My wife's gonna have a *baby*!"

"That don't mean you cain't look!"

At 5:30 they drove Barfield's pickup north towards Cartersville. The place was nearly halfway to Rome, Davis had been told. Barfield thought of calling Mandy to tell her he'd be late but knew she'd be disappointed he wasn't coming straight home, so he put the dime back in his pocket.

The bar was what Barfield had expected, dark and sleazy. Neon lights advertising "Girls, Girls, Girls" flashed on and off. The windows were covered and the doors shut quickly as if to say, "Wait'll you see what we've got inside."

Barfield couldn't help feeling excited, as he walked by a long bar with black leather stools and a long, mirrored wall. A lot of men were crowding the bar or sitting at tiny tables hardly big enough to hold two drinks. Two girls were dancing on platforms. They were both down to black G-strings on the bottom and nothing on top. They stared out over the heads of the men, their heavily made-up eyes looking dazed. One had platinum blonde hair piled up on top except where it had fallen loose. The other dancer had curly black hair ringing her face in tight coils. Barfield and Davis felt lucky when two men vacated a table up front. But as they sat down, Barfield couldn't deny his guilt as he thought of Mandy. Davis seemed to read his mind. "Remember, Jimmy," he said, squeezing his friend's shoulder, "it don't hurt just to look."

"Two drafts," Barfield said when the barmaid appeared. She smiled and emptied their ashtray. He took in her trim figure in her skimpy outfit. He remembered that Mandy used to look a whole lot prettier than her and was glad it wouldn't be long 'til she had the baby. He was tired of seeing her all blown up.

"Now that blonde one's got what it takes," Davis said, jarring Barfield from his own thoughts. "She's got much better tits than the other girl. What I wouldn't give to get inside her pants." He looked her up and down. "What even holds that G-string on? Hell, I wish she'd wiggle wrong one time and give us get a peek." He sat on the edge of his chair. "You can see the crack in the back. But it's what's up *front* I'm after."

"Shut up, Eddie. Somebody's gonna hear you."

"I don't care. There's not a man in here wouldn't like to put it to her if he had the chance. Unless you're sayin' *you* wouldn't."

Barfield didn't really think he would. He liked it as much as the next guy but not with some kind of dancing whore who'd probably do it with anybody. But he couldn't explain how he felt to Davis. So he said, "I ain't sayin' that. But you don't have to sit there with your damn tongue hangin' out."

"OK, ole buddy," Davis said, looking away from the stage. "I'm just feelin' good." Then he called to the barmaid, "Hey, honey! Bring us a couple more."

"Eddie, why're those guys over there starin' at us?" Barfield was beginning to feel uneasy and struggled to pull his friend's attention away from the dancers.

"You sure do pick a funny place to watch men," Eddie teased him, his eyes still on the stage.

"I'm not kiddin' around. See the big guy over there in a yellow shirt? The one who just picked up his beer. Sittin' next to a man in a grey suit? They both keep lookin' over at us."

"You figure they're queers or somethin'?"

The barmaid brought the beers. When Barfield tried to hand her money, she pushed his hand away. "You don't have to pay for this round, sugar." She looked at him curiously as if she were surprised. "Your friends over there," she said, indicating the men Barfield had just pointed out, "are standing you a round."

Barfield was about to insist she take the money when the two men walked up to their table.

"Mind if we join you fellas?" The man in the plain grey suit spoke in a voice which made even that simple question sound intimidating. He was tall and lean and wore wire-rimmed glasses. The big man standing beside him had on a bright yellow shirt rolled up to show a Marine Corps tattoo.

Barfield stood up. He didn't understand the invitation and felt uncomfortable. "Do we know you, mister?" he asked the man in the grey suit, determined to let the fella know he wasn't about to play games.

"I don't guess you do. But we'd *like* to be your friends." His smile looked slimy to Barfield, like he was hiding something unsavory behind it.

"How's that?" Barfield stood his ground, and didn't ask them to sit down.

"Invite us to join you, and we'll tell you all about it."

But the man didn't wait for an invitation. He motioned to the big man, who pulled two chairs up to the small table. Davis looked nervously back and forth between Barfield and the others, not saying a word.

"I know you work for the county, and I know your boss gave you a pretty hard time this morning," the man in the grey suit told Barfield. "Don't ask me how I know. I just do." There was an authority in his voice that made questions impossible.

Davis took a long drink of beer. Barfield sat tight, unsure what to say, but not liking it one bit.

"I hear you have a hard time getting along with bosses," the man said to Barfield. "But I don't hold that against a fella." He took out a cigar, which his goonish sidekick lit quickly for him. "Fact is, I've had a lot of trouble with bosses myself. They try to put a young man down because they're scared of what he can do." Barfield felt the man's eyes appraising him. "I know what you're going through 'cause I was a young man a lot like you." He smiled appreciatively. "I bet they don't recognize half your talents." He took a drink of beer while his words sank in. "That's why I wondered if maybe you boys might like to work for me."

"What kind of work you in, mister?" Barfield asked. He wanted to show this guy he wasn't scared to ask questions of his own.

"I'm in the moving business, son," he said, leaning back in his chair. "I truck things all over the country. And I happen to need a few drivers I can count on."

"What *kind* of things do you move?" Barfield asked cautiously, suspecting a trap.

"You name it, I've moved it," the man answered ambiguously. "Lots of times I don't even know what I'm moving. Some folks are cautious, you know. Don't like anybody to know their business. They just tell me how many trucks they need and where the load's going, and I move it. No questions asked."

Barfield didn't say anything, but he didn't like the sound of it. He tried to answer firmly, ignoring the goon's threatening expression. "Well, we're not truck drivers, mister, and we already got jobs." He added hurriedly, "But thanks anyhow."

"I know you have jobs, son." The man's voice was still cordial. "But I figured maybe you'd work for me evenings. 'Cause most of my shipments are at night. You could make yourself a nice little nest egg."

"How much you talkin' about, mister?" Davis asked, his face lighting up with interest.

"I'd figure on you and your big friend here working together. I promise my customers security, you know. You'd each get ten dollars an hour. You work a few nights, you'd turn yourself a nice little profit. You want to put in more hours, you can do a weekend move. Sometimes on special jobs there's even bonuses. I'll do right by you boys."

"Where would we have to go?" Barfield asked guardedly, trying to make up by his own reticence for Eddie's eagerness. He could feel his friend's boot tapping the floor, and his nervous fingers drummed the table.

"Nowhere too far away. Atlan'a. Chattanooga. Mostly short hauls."

Barfield didn't like it. Something didn't feel right, and it didn't help the way Davis was acting like a little kid on Christmas morning.

"You boys could always try one run." Grey Suit smiled again. "If you don't like it, we'll call it quits. Nothin' lost, you know. I'm not askin' you to quit the county. Just givin' you the chance to pick up a little extra cash."

"That's the way to look at it, Jimmy," Davis said. "We got nothin' to lose. It's not like we'd be tied into—"

He stopped short, obviously confused when Barfield's work boot pressed down on his own beneath the table. He wondered why his friend was so tense.

"Do you mind if Eddie and me talk this over a minute?" Barfield looked Grey Suit in the eye. "We need to do that before this goes any further."

"Sure, you take your time. Link and I'll just mosey over to the bar and watch the girls for a minute." He stood up and the big man followed at his heels like a well-trained dog.

"Why'd you do that?" Davis pointed at his foot.

"So you'd shut up," he answered angrily. "Don't you know better than to show your hand in front of a guy like that?"

"You don't have to get so sore! What's botherin' you? You afraid we'd make too much money?"

"It's not on the level, Eddie. Makin' deliv'ries at night, not knowin' what we're drivin'. Him knowin' about me gettin' chewed out by the foreman. Who's he been talkin' to and what's he want with us? We never been truck drivers." He shook his head. "I don't know what it is, but something's wrong with it."

"Jimmy, this is our chance to get ahead," Davis insisted. "We can make a lot of money just for drivin' a truck. We'll never get another chance to—"

"That's right, because it *ain't* for just drivin' a truck. There's somethin' crooked goin' on, and he figures we're too dumb to know or too poor to care. But not me, buddy."

"You mean you're gonna turn him down flat?" Davis asked incredulously.

"That's right. And you better do the same thing. Or your next question'll be how many phone calls you get to make after they pick you up!" He downed the rest of his beer and motioned to the men at the bar.

They walked confidently across the room and sat down. Barfield bet they didn't get turned down very often. He wondered if Link carried a gun.

"Well, boys?" The man in the grey suit smiled genially. "All set to give it a try?"

Link contentedly picked his teeth, waiting for his next order.

"Don't think I can help you, sir." Barfield smiled, trying to act friendlier than he felt. "My wife's gonna have a baby soon, and it'd worry her real bad to have me away at night. You know how a woman gets at a time like that."

"I don't have no baby comin' but my old lady'd have a fit if I started stayin' out late," Davis said halfheartedly, trying to convince himself. "She'd figure I was up to somethin'."

"Sure am sorry to hear that, boys. I was just tellin' Link here, you boys looked like you'd take me up on my offer. But I guess my eyes are just foolin' me these days."

"Maybe some other time, mister." Davis spoke as if they'd turned down a game of pool. "But thanks anyway."

"You say your wife worries 'bout bein' alone?" The man turned to Barfield as if Davis hadn't even addressed him. "Don't blame her one bit with all the trash runnin' around at night. And her with a baby on the way.

"Yes sir, even Link here gets kind of anxious. Ever since he come home from Nam he's been restless. Sometimes he prowls around all hours of the night. Guess he misses the action. Ain't that right, boy?"

The huge man looked up with his watery blue eyes. At the mention of his name, he grinned wide, revealing snaggled yellow teeth.

"You're wise to be concerned, son," the man went on. "You can't be too careful with her in the family way. You sure wouldn't want nothin' to frighten her."

Barfield didn't respond. He could tell a threat when he heard one, but he wasn't sure what to say. He didn't want trouble.

"I hope you boys'll change your minds. They say it's only women who do that, but plenty of men do as well. But I'd 'preciate you boys not mentionin' my proposition to anyone else. Man don't like folks to know he's been turned down." He started to turn away, but then, as an afterthought, he said, "Case you do change your mind, just leave a message here for Mr. Jones. Or Link." He smiled at the big man the way you look at a favorite dog. "I'll be watchin' out for you. I always keep a lookout for fellas I take an interest in."

All night Barfield couldn't sleep. Every time the wind stirred, he jerked awake, afraid Link might be hiding in the bushes.

"What is it, Jimmy?" Mandy touched his cheek in the dark.

He felt bad disturbing her rest, but when he spoke, his voice was belligerent. "Stop worryin'. I told you, nothin's wrong," he said dismissively. He tried hard not to show how concerned he was since that would make her worry, which was just what Mr. Jones and Link were counting on.

"I wish you'd tell me, Jimmy." She sat up and turned on the light. She wore a long white nightgown, and her blonde hair fell loose and soft around her face. In the soft light she looked so young to him, so delicate, even with her pregnant belly. He wanted to protect her from Link and Mr. Jones and everyone in the world.

She broke into his thoughts again. Her tone was pleading. "Jimmy, talk to me. At least if you'd tell me what it is, I wouldn't have to worry about what it idn't."

"Honey, it's nothin'." His voice was kinder and he placed his hand gently in the small of her back and pulled her to him. "I'm just restless. Workin' like I do—sometimes it gets to you. It's hard having to stand all day in the sun with those foremen yelling at you, telling you how to do things when they don't even know—"

"Jimmy, you're not in trouble at work, are you?" She stared deeply into his eyes. "Promise me you didn't cuss the foreman ou—"

"Mandy, would you quit worryin'! D'you think you married a fool? I don't want trouble at work." He plumped up the pillows around her and turned off the light. "It's nothin' but the weather. Lord, I wish it would rain."

"Not before this weekend, they say." She turned her back and nestled against him so he could tuck her head beneath his chin. "Feel him move, honey," she whispered, placing his hand on her stomach. "I feel him more and more all the time."

"He's gonna be a real football player, that boy." He smiled at the back of her head and kissed her neck. "Now get some rest," he said. Then he leaned down to press his lips against her stomach and whispered gently, "And *you* go to sleep, too. Let your mama get some rest." They both laughed when the baby moved. "Hey, this is your daddy talkin'."

The baby stopped moving immediately. They laughed again, and even though he knew it was probably a coincidence, Barfield said proudly, "See, he already listens to his daddy. And he ain't even born yet."

A week later Barfield thought he spied Link at the superette half a mile from their trailer. He had stopped for a few things Mandy needed on his way home from work. While he was standing at the register, he was positive he saw Link in a red pickup in the parking lot. He didn't wait for his change. He raced home, hardly able to breathe until he saw Mandy at the kitchen counter fixing biscuits.

"Jimmy, you're gettin' to be an old worrywart," Mandy said the next morning after she'd heard him on the phone asking her sister to stay with her during the daytime. "I'm fine here by myself. It's a long time before this baby comes, and you're going to make me a wreck if you have people hovering over me for three months. What's got into you?"

He tried to think of an excuse to explain his concern. "I heard on the radio," he told her, "that a woman gets real lonesome and depressed towards the end of—"

"That's *afterwards*, Jimmy." She laughed, touched by his concern and kissed his cheek, not minding the roughness of his beard and the sour smell of a long, hard day. She felt tender toward this big man who was so worried about her, but she couldn't resist teasing him. "I've a good mind to stay pregnant all the time," she said. "'Cause you never carried on like this before if I felt a little blue."

James had always kept a pistol in the nightstand by their bed, but he never took it out to even look at it. But suddenly, Mandy noticed he was checking it all the time. When he thought she was asleep, she'd see him reach for it as if he expected trouble. She worried, despite his assurances that he'd not had any trouble at work. Even when she tried not to touch him, she could feel his tense body beneath the sheets. One night she got up to go to the bathroom. As her pregnancy advanced, she'd found it harder and harder to make it through the night. Sometimes she had to get up two times. This particular night, when she noticed how deeply James was breathing, she tried to be extra careful not to wake him. She was almost to the bathroom when the floor creaked. James jumped up like an alarm had sounded. He grabbed the gun from the drawer and yelled, "Who is it? Tell me who you are right now or I'll blow you to king—"

"Jimmy," she screamed in terror. "It's me. Don't shoot!" She ran to the bed crying, gasping for breath. "I cain't live scared you're gonna shoot me if I go to the bathroom in the middle of the night. What's going on?"

He knew she had a right to know, only he couldn't figure how to start. He hated to tell her about the topless bar and Mr. Jones and Link, realizing how terrible it would sound to her. She was so young and didn't have any idea of the things that happened to a man out in the world.

"James Barfield," she said, taking his head in her hands, "you tell me the truth."

"One night a few weeks ago, me and Eddie stopped to get a beer and we met some guys who tried to get us to—" He was interrupted by the telephone. He felt relieved to have an excuse to stop explaining his nightmare, until he remembered it was 3:30 in the morning. The phone ringing had to mean somebody had died or was taken sick. Or Link was calling to shake him up.

He bit his lip as he answered the phone. He waited for whoever was on the other end to say something.

"Hey, Jimmy, is that you?"

"Are you crazy callin' in the middle of the night, Eddie? Or did something happen?" He was scared waiting for his friend's answer.

"I'm in bad trouble, man. So listen good 'cause this is the only call they'll let me make."

"You're in *jail*, Eddie?" It was worse than he'd imagined.

"Yeah. They picked me up about an hour ago near the Tennessee line."

"What in God's name were you doin'?" He stopped short, not wanting to believe Eddie had gotten mixed up with Mr. Jones and Link. "You didn't start drivin' for that man?" He heard the panic in his own voice. "Eddie? Answer me."

"I know it was a fool thing to do. But it didn't seem like it when I done it. See I ran into that Mr. Jones again. I started thinkin' 'bout what I could do with that extra money. For Helen, you know. Hell, three bucks an hour don't even leave you somethin' to eat on after you make your car payment and your trailer payment. So I went and did it. First two times it worked like clockwork. I made my deliv'ries on time. Nothin' to it. Both times I went to Atlan'a. Somebody paid me off like they was supposed to. I never knew what I was haulin'—just like he said. He always sent another fella with me before. But this time, I had to go by myself.

"I was on 75 North right before the turnoff for Rome when I seen this blue light flashin'. I wasn't speedin' or nothin' but of course I pulled over. These two state troopers got out and one of them said, 'Buddy, you step out of there real easy with your hands up. Don't try nothin' smart or you won't try nothin' ever again.' I still couldn't figure out what they was stopping *me* for, but I did everything real easy just like they said.

"Then one of them said, 'You can look at this if you want to.' And he stuck a paper in my face. It was a search warrant. And he says, 'So just hand over the keys to the back of the truck and we'll get this over with.' But the funny thing was I didn't have the keys. Mr. Jones said there wadn't no need for me to have 'em. Said his customers felt safer knowing the driver couldn't mess with their cargo."

"Just tell me what happened, Eddie," Barfield said impatiently. "They ain't gonna let you talk all night."

"Well, they searched me and of course they saw I was tellin' the truth 'cause there wadn't no key. They laughed like it was some big joke, and then one of them jimmied the lock. They pulled out some of the cartons and tore off the tops. They was full of pillows. Regular ole feather pillows. I was getting nervous thinkin' about what Mr. Jones would say when he saw what they done to the cargo. Until all a sudden they pulled out all these little bags full of white powder.

"'Look here, Harry,' the fella who found the bags called out to the other one. 'There must be a quarter of a million dollars worth in here at the very least!'

"'Of what?' I asked them. I figured at that point I had a right t'know.

"'You really don't know?' He shined his flashlight in my face, studyin' me hard, waiting for me to give something away. But of course I didn't know nothin'. Then he said, 'You know, Harry, I think he don't know what this is.' He held the bag up in front of my face.

"'No sir, I never seen that before.'

"'Boy,' the other one said, pointing his rifle at me. 'You got enough heroin in here to shoot up a whole herd of elephants!'

"You believe that? So they brought me down to the station, and I didn't even know that man's real name." He sounded sheepish. "He *said* it was Jones and remember he called the other fella Link, but I don't reckon that was the truth. Guess I'll never see 'em again." His voice quickly grew frightened as he hurried to explain, "They said I could make only one call, Jimmy. So I called you. I didn't know what else to do. You said we shouldn't work for that man. But I did it. And now I don't know what to do. I figured Helen'd be so upset she'd just break down. Would you talk to her? And you gotta help me get a lawyer. I never had one before."

"There ain't no point in waking her and the kids," Barfield said. "There's nothin' she can do in the middle of the night. Or anybody else either." Barfield couldn't help feeling sorry for his friend even though he'd warned him not to do it. "You listen to me. You sit tight and don't answer none of their questions until you talk to a lawyer. I'll see you get one tomorrow."

"I don't want to put you out. I may as well just tell 'em what I know, Jimmy. I had to answer some of their questions. I figured they alrea—"

"Don't say another word. Tell 'em you're waitin' on your lawyer. 'Cause anything you say, they can throw back at you in court."

"But I didn't know what I was haulin', Jimmy. I *swear* I didn't. If I'd known what was in that truck, you couldn't a-caught me within a mile of it."

"*I* believe you, Eddie, but you're in big trouble."

"I gotta hang up now. But you'll talk to Helen for me?" His voice was plaintive and urgent.

"First thing in the morning. Try to sleep now, OK? You'll need to be on your toes in the mornin'. And remember what I said. Not another word to anybody."

"OK, I'll sit tight." He sighed audibly. "Jimmy, you figure you can talk to somebody over t'Legal Aid? 'Cause you know I can't afford a lawyer."

"I'll be there tomorrow soon as they open up. They ain't hurtin' you or nothin', Eddie?"

"No, they're all right. One of the deputies dated my sister in high school."

"Yeah, well, don't get too friendly."

"You can count on me, ole buddy. I won't say another word. And thanks, man. Sorry I had to bother you and Mandy."

"What's happened, James?" Mandy asked as he hung up the phone. "What's Eddie done?"

"Something real dumb, Mandy." He led her back to bed, sighing as he lay back against the pillows and closed his eyes. "Let's not talk about it now. I'll tell you in the morning."

"But why's he in jail? You're not in trouble, too, are you?" She grabbed his arm.

"Of course not. Stop worrying. I didn't do nothin'." He made her lie down beside him. "Eddie fell for a stupid line even a kid could see through. But I'm gonna get him a lawyer in the mornin'." He kissed her and held her tightly in his arms. "Now, you try and rest, baby. Ain't nothin' we can do for Eddie right this minute."

"I'm so scared, Jimmy," she said. "Please don't let go of me."

He kissed her on the nose and tucked her head beneath his chin the way he knew she liked.

"Don't worry, baby," he said. "Just close your eyes. I'll be watching over you."

When she drifted off to sleep, he listened to the peaceful rise and fall of her breathing until he fell asleep himself. In the early morning, he slipped out of bed to call Helen. He was careful not to wake Mandy and tenderly covered her.

For just a moment longer, he stood by their bed watching her sleep, listening to her calm breathing and imagining their baby growing inside her. Thinking of Eddie lying there in jail, Barfield figured how lucky he was. Even if he did have to shovel dirt for three lousy bucks an hour, he wasn't in jail. And no man could tell him what to do when he came home at the end of the day. When he came home to her.

CHAPTER 13

Just an Accident

There was no way to ignore an office fire, particularly one started by a non-smoker. I had to find out what Vernon had been doing in his office. As soon as I arrived, he opened his office door barely wide enough to admit me. We sat down on opposite sides of the ruined desktop, next to the trashcan where the burned blotter had been stuffed. Even with a fan running, the smoky smell hung heavily in the windowless room.

"It was just an accident," he said defensively. "Could have happened to anyone. I don't know why Nadine made such a big deal out of it. There was no need to involve you." He sounded like a child who feels someone has tattled unfairly to the teacher.

I knew Vernon's assessment was incorrect. Nadine was unflappable and had resolved completely by herself nuisances like an aggressive sow and her piglets that had made their home under our front porch and the drunken young men she'd caught painting graffiti across our parking lot on a Saturday night. So when she called to tell me Vernon had started a fire in his office, and I'd better come quick and talk to him since she could tell there was more going on than he wanted to admit, I jumped in my car.

"So what happened, Vernon?" I asked as matter-of-factly as I could, though the problem lay menacingly between us.

He wiped his forehead and paced the small room. "It was dumb," he acknowledged sheepishly. "See, the air smelled so stale in here I lit this bayberry candle I'd picked up at a crafts fair."

"And you're telling me the fire went through the blotter and burned the desktop while you were sitting here?" The damage we were looking at was too extensive to have occurred in the seconds it would have taken to extinguish it if Vernon had been present when it started.

"Of course not!" he said, recovering quickly. "I guess I'm kind of absent-minded so I didn't notice I'd left papers so close to the candle. And then I went up to the front to make copies. I took longer getting back to my office than I'd intended." He sounded like he'd been practicing his story. "Because a family came to the door to find out about enrolling. You *know* how long that can take. So I was away from my office maybe ten minutes."

I couldn't accept his explanation. Nobody else's office smelled bad. I had a very bad suspicion about the odor he had been attempting to cover up. "That's really all you want to say?" I asked critically, any pity I had for him destroyed by the insult of his imagining I could believe this story.

He scowled, speaking mechanically, avoiding my eyes. "You don't have to worry, Laura. No matter how bad the smell gets, I'll *never* light a candle in the office again." He was focusing on the odor rather than the severity of his own actions. "It might be mold or varnish from the new paneling. Or some cleaning product they used when they shampooed the carpet. I'm sorry it got to me and this happened."

"I wish we *could* chalk it up as an accident," I said regretfully, watching him squirm. "But I've had concerns ever since you left Trina Kitchens locked in the bathroom."

"I admit that was poor judgment, but it has nothing to do with this situation," he answered defensively, his remorseful stance vanishing quickly, unlike the smoky odor around us.

"But I should be able to rely on the judgment of the social services director of this project, right?"

"There's nothing wrong with my judgment," he protested. "I was working with families years before you ever thought about it." His voice turned self-pitying and resigned. "But if you want me out of here, go ahead and say so. Just stop lecturing me."

"I don't *want* you to leave," I confided, wondering where I'd find another male counselor to work for our salary. "But I'm worried what could happen next, Vernon."

"Meaning what?" He looked cornered and grim.

"Meaning if you don't stop drinking."

"You have no right to accuse me with no proof whatsoever. Where do you get off—"

"If you'll get help, I think we can work this out," I said, without any real idea how I was supposed to handle him. There was no section about alcoholic employees in the manual Mrs. Cremins had given me.

"I don't *need* help." His voice rose sharply in anger. "You have no grounds to say I'm an alcoholic. Somebody must be pressuring you to force me out."

"You're doing it yourself. I've smelled alcohol on you before. I didn't say anything, but it was overpowering the day Trina locked herself in the bathroom."

"OK," he admitted. "I shouldn't have, but maybe that day I *did* have one drink at lunch."

"You told me you hadn't been to lunch," I reminded him.

"I was worried about what happened with Trina so I forgot I'd already eaten." He smiled nervously as his lies piled up, almost tangibly, in the space between us.

"This is a dry county, Vernon. There's nowhere you could have gotten a drink with lunch." I raised my voice to stop his protests. "What about the air freshener in the car and the breath mints?" I looked across the burned desk. "We both know what you were covering up."

There were tears in his eyes. "You did smell whiskey in my car," he confessed. "I had a flask that leaked. But I only brought it that one time. You have to believe me. I've been sober a long time. I swear I have. I just felt so nervous starting out here." His face was resolute. "But it won't happen again. I promise you."

"How did the fire really start? I'm responsible for this project. I need to know."

"I kept a bottle in my desk. I'd never touched it before today. I just needed to know it was there." He looked down. "But everything started piling up on me." His eyes were tense, his voice strained. "So I took a drink. Just *one*. That's all I was going to have. I was putting the bottle away when I heard Nadine coming down the hall. I was so scared she might walk in, I knocked the bottle over, and the smell was so strong I lit that scented candle. Then I went out to wash my hands, but I got involved in something she needed and with that family I told you about. I guess some papers were too near the flame and well . . . you know the rest."

I wondered how much of the "rest" I *didn't* know. I couldn't have an alcoholic making decisions when I wasn't around or burning down our office on Nadine's day off. I knew what Mrs. Cremins would say even though Vernon had been very successful in getting the boyfriends and husbands to agree to join the Project. She had always questioned my decision to hire him, and I feared for once I should have listened to her.

"It's your funeral. But why you want to hire an Episcopal priest to work with these families is beyond me," she'd said dismissively when she reviewed his application. "There are plenty of social workers out there trained to do this job."

If there were any, I couldn't find a single one interested in the low wages we offered and the obligation to travel all over North Georgia. Vernon was absolutely the best of all the applicants. As a priest he had done marriage counseling, and unlike other candidates, he wasn't embarrassed to talk about birth control and knew social services didn't involve party planning.

"Laura?" Vernon said tentatively, pleading with me, tears in his eyes. *"Please* give me another chance. I can't lose this job. I hadn't mentioned it yet, but Cathy's having a baby. We just found out last week. I can't let anything upset her. She'd die if she thought . . . I was . . . you know . . . drinking again. *Please,* Laura. You said yourself I'm doing a good job. And nobody else could have gotten the father's group to even *talk* about using birth control."

"If you get caught drinking, we'll be shut down," I said sternly, thinking of Mrs. Cremins. "I want a call tomorrow from wherever you're going for treatment." I tried to sound tough, but heard the sadness in my own voice when I told him, "I'm putting you on probation. I don't know what we'll do without you, but don't come anywhere near this office until we've agreed it's all right for you to return to work."

"Laura, you won't be sorry." He squeezed my hand tightly and didn't let go. I wished I could run out of the room before he hugged me in relief. "Can we keep this between you and me?" he asked urgently.

I couldn't imagine he thought I would tell our clients or Mrs. Cremins. Did he actually believe Nadine had not figured it out after the fire?

"I'm writing this up and putting it in a sealed envelope in your file. If you get help and nothing else happens, it stays sealed. If I find out you're drinking—even *one* drink—then you're out. That's it." This time *I* couldn't meet his eyes. "I won't be able to think about Cathy's pregnancy. I'll be thinking about the girls in the Project and what will happen to them if we have a scandal and get shut down."

I realized I had just committed myself to watching him all the time when he returned, going over his work as if it were my own and dropping in on him at unexpected times to be sure there were no relapses. I hoped I had sounded threatening enough, since I could feel myself shaking as I pictured the trouble there would be if he didn't stop drinking. I felt very young and alone.

When Vernon left, Nadine rushed into my office. She patted me on the back. "I know that was hard," she said sympathetically. "You got way too much on your plate. So don't you worry about that desk. I'll get somebody to haul it to the dump tonight and we'll fumigate that office. By tomorrow you won't smell a thing. I'll send Vernon a bill just as soon as I figure out how much we paid for it."

"I'm not concerned about the *desk,* Nadine," I confided, feeling my stomach tighten with worry. "What if Mrs. Cremins finds out and she uses it as an excuse to shut—"

"Well, *you're* not gonna tell her. And I wouldn't tell that woman the time of day. And Vernon's sure not gonna say a word. So you got nothin' to worry about on that score."

I was about to thank her and sit down at my desk to drink a cup of coffee, staring at nothing more complicated than the wall. But I could see from her expression that she was waiting to tell me about something else.

She nodded towards the waiting room. "I'm afraid it ain't over yet, honey," she said. "Trina Kitchens's mama just came in real upset. I told her you were tied up and asked if she could come back another time. But she says she'll wait as long as it takes to see you."

I figured it was better to get it over with—whatever was upsetting Mrs. Kitchens—so I went out to the waiting room. As soon as I saw her, I was alarmed since her eyes were red and puffy as if she'd been crying for hours. When I escorted her back to my office, she was too agitated to even sit down.

"You got to help me, Miz Bauer," she implored me. "I got nobody else to turn to. Lonnie's on a run to Omaha. I can't call him to come home. He'd lose his job, and it was too hard to come by. We got to have that money."

"What's wrong? Please sit down, Mrs. Kitchens."

"Trina ran off with Bill Matthews," she blurted out.

"When did they leave?" I thought guiltily of an earlier phone message from Mrs. Kitchens I had not returned.

"Yesterday morning. Right before lunch," she said wearily, sinking into the chair beside my desk. "Candy called me when Bill didn't pick her up at the hospital. He dropped her off for her iron treatment, but he didn't come back for her. Her sister had to come all the way from Jasper to carry her home, and when they went inside, there was a note on the table saying he'd gone to Atlan'a. He'd be back by the weekend. The children—even the baby—were there all by themselves. Candy called 'cause she figured Trina should have been lookin' after them. Nothing had happened, but she was pretty hot Trina'd just go off and leave them."

"Why would she expect Trina to be there? You said she couldn't baby-sit for them anymore."

"I guess Candy was so upset she plain forgot." She looked mournful. "Anyhow, look what I found in Trina's room." She handed me a note penciled in a childish hand:

Dear Mama,
You don't understand and you never will. But I'm grown up and Bill loves me and not Candy and I'm going away with him. I'll write you when

I can. You give Corrine any of my stuff she wants. I don't need it no more. Bill's going to get me new things. I love you, Mama. Please don't worry. I'll be all right.

Trina

"Where do you think they went?" I asked.

"I'm guessin' his sister's in Atlan'a. He prob'ly don't have the money to go nowhere else." The tears ran in streaks down her tired face. "She busted her piggy bank. It wouldn't surprise me if that's all the money they got." She shredded the tissue in her hands. "I don't know what to do."

"You should call the police. She's a minor. He's kidnapped her. They'll start looking for her."

"That'll scare her to death. Besides, no telling what could happen if he's been drinking."

"Call his sister. See if you can talk to Trina."

"I have to go there. Talking on the phone won't do no good. I got to get her away from that man. Please go with me, Miz Bauer," she begged me. "She'll listen to you. I'm afraid she'll run if it's only me."

"I can't leave here now, Mrs. Kitchens. I'm sorry. You really should call your husband. See what he thinks you ought to—"

"I can't reach him 'til tonight. Who knows where they might be by then?" She stood up and looked at me resolutely from the doorway. "Don't know how I'll get there, but I reckon somebody'll have to carry me. I'm sorry to have bothered you—"

I started to let her go. But when I looked outside, the parking lot was empty. She had either walked to our office or someone had brought her and hadn't waited. I was surely her last hope, and if I didn't drive her, she would try to get to Atlanta without a car. She looked so despondent I feared she might collapse by the roadside.

"Come on," I said. "I'll take you."

"I told Candy I *knew* you'd help us," she acknowledged gratefully. "Poor thing, she's beside herself, and some days she's so weak she can hardly stand up. And now it turns out she's pregnant again. Guess that was his farewell present to her before he ran off with my baby."

CHAPTER 14

No Special Trouble

Bill Matthews's sister lived just south of Atlanta in a garden apartment complex, which had been built cheaply and allowed to run down a little more every day to avoid maintenance costs. The mature trees had been bulldozed during construction, leaving behind stretches of patchy grass and a few stick-like saplings planted by the developer. The original landscaping had dwindled to a few stunted, yellowing bushes, so that the whole place was functional but charmless, only one step above a housing project.

We rang the doorbell and waited anxiously several moments until Matthews's sister opened the door and let us in. "Annie, I'm so glad you're here," she said to Trina's mother. She welcomed us into the living room. "I knew I should have called you earlier," she said regretfully, as if she expected to be criticized. "But I was waiting for Billy and Trina to go out so they wouldn't hear. Then when I finally got my chance, nobody answered at your house."

"I guess we'd already started out. This is Miz Bauer," Trina's mother said. "She drove me down here."

We sat down on the overstuffed floral print sofa. "I know it idn't your fault, Mary," Mrs. Kitchens said understandingly. "But where are they?"

"I don't really know." She called the two small blond boys who had been playing in the middle of the floor. "Y'all go play in your room. Mama's got to have a grown-up conversation right now."

They got up reluctantly, pulling a wagon full of blocks and army men behind them. The smallest one sucked his thumb and glanced back suspiciously at the ladies who were occupying his mother's attention.

"Are Bill and Trina coming back?" Mrs. Kitchen's face was tight with fear that we were too late to find her daughter.

"Of course," Mary said enthusiastically. "Billy said they'd be back by suppertime. Their suitcases are still here. And a six-pack." She laughed heartily. "Billy would never walk out of any place and leave beer in the fridge."

"Did they say anything about their plans?" I asked, wondering if

Matthews's sister understood my role or thought I was a simply a friendly neighbor.

"To tell you the truth, the whole thing's a puzzle to me. Lord knows Billy and Candy have had their problems. He's messed around before. That don't shock me." She rolled her eyes. "Nothin' men do could surprise me. But running off with a *child*?" She lit a cigarette and dragged deeply on it. She blushed slightly as she asked, "You do know she's pregnant, don't you?"

"I don't reckon you know more about my child than I do," Mrs. Kitchens said testily as she began to pace. Then more sorrowfully, "I'm sorry for talkin' like that, Mary. I'm just so worried. We got to wait around 'til they come back. You want us to stay in the car?"

"Don't be silly." She put her arm around Mrs. Kitchens and led her back to the couch. "I tried to get her to call you, but she said she couldn't do that until they're married."

"You know he can't *marry* her. She's not even fifteen. Besides, he's still married to Candy." Mrs. Kitchens was indignant. "She knows that. I don't know what's got into her."

"I tried to warn her. 'Cause I know my brother. He's good lookin' and charming. But he's an S.O.B.—pardon my French—and a liar and a cheat. If he weren't my brother he wouldn't set foot in this house. I told her he wouldn't get a divorce, and she ought to just call her mama and go home. I even offered to drive her, but she wouldn't hear of it. And I was scared to call you for fear of setting Billy off."

"I understand, Mary. Really, I do." Mrs. Kitchens looked nervously at her watch. "How long they been gone?"

"I don't know exactly. Maybe three or four hours."

The little boys began making Indian war whoops down the hall. "I killed you," one of them yelled. "I killed you first," the other insisted. Then the phone rang. Mary picked up the pink princess phone quickly.

"Honey, what's wrong?" she asked after a few seconds. "Why are you crying? Your mama and Miz Bauer are here. When will y'all be back to the apartment?"

Mrs. Kitchens grabbed the phone. "Trina, where are you?" Before there was even time for Trina to answer, she went on, "I'm not going to *make* you do anything. I just want to talk to you." Her eyes filled with tears. "Oh my Lord!" She covered the receiver with her hand. "He's left her." She spoke very gently. "Honey, just tell me where you are, and we'll come get you." She listened, looking confused. "I better let you talk to Miz Bauer. She'll prob'ly understand better where you're at. Baby, you just hold on 'til we get there. Everything's gonna be all right. Mama's comin'. Don't you worry. Mama's coming."

I couldn't think of any reason they had gone to a clinic except to get blood tests. But even that didn't make sense because he was already married, and she knew it. Blind as love can be, it couldn't have made Trina forget about Candy and four children.

We found her standing alone on a rundown street on the outskirts of downtown Atlanta. A blue and white sign advertised the Women's Clinic. As soon as I saw her ashen face, I knew what had happened.

Mrs. Kitchens understood, too. She jumped out of the car before we were completely parked and ran to embrace her crying daughter. "Baby, baby, what have you gone and done?" she asked soothingly, as if speaking to a small child.

I helped them back to the car. Mrs. Kitchens sat in the back seat cradling Trina in her arms. I began driving in circles through the neighborhood. I thought if we parked, they would be too aware of my presence. I didn't want to be an audience to their pain.

"Baby, are you all right?"

"I feel kinda strange, Mama. It don't hurt so much now. I just feel real tired. Like I could sleep forever."

"Why'd you do it?" I watched her stroking Trina's hair back from her forehead. "I knew all along he'd leave you, but I would have helped you. You didn't *have* to do this." I could hear the choked tears in her voice. "I know you were upset when I said you'd have to put the baby up for adoption. But I *never* meant you should do this!"

"He tricked me, Mama. He told me to dress grown up as I could since we were going somewhere real important. I figured it had to do with getting' married. Mary even helped me with my makeup." She blew her nose. "I didn't know where we were going at first. Then when we got here, he told me if I didn't do it he wouldn't ever marry me. He said he didn't want a baby dragging us down and messing up our marriage."

He ought to know all about that, I thought bitterly, *with four children already and his wife expecting.*

"He told me we'd be staying at Mary's 'til the divorce came through."

The divorce that had never begun. The divorce that never would begin.

She started crying harder. "He said he was almost certain promised a good job so we could have an apartment like Mary's, only with a swimming pool."

She smiled through her tears. "I knew how excited Corrine and the boys would be about that."

"Why didn't you call me before they started?" Mrs. Kitchens asked. "You didn't have to go through with it."

"I didn't know he would leave me." Her words came out in sobs. "I only did it for him. I didn't want to kill my baby."

"Hush now. Hush now." She held Trina close and patted her back.

But Trina would not be quieted. Once she started to talk, she wanted to pour out everything she had held back. "Mama, he made me keep quiet and let him do all the talking. He told that doctor I was only two months gone," she cried, wiping back her tears. "He told him I was his wife, and this was *our* decision since I'm so young. Bill said he wanted me to have time to grow up myself before I had his baby." She was crying so hard that for a moment she could not continue.

"Well, he got that part right, Trina," Mrs. Kitchens said gently. "You *are* just a child. You didn't know what you were doing. And you couldn't have been much more than three months gone. Two months or three months, it don't matter, baby." She spoke softer and softer as if she *were* soothing a baby. "He's a married man, and he took advantage of you."

"Mama, the doctor was real nice," Trina said through her tears. "He said I come through it fine." She held out a card. "I got to go back for a checkup in a few weeks. To make sure it all heals up right." She winced. "Every now and then I feel this little cramp." She cleared her throat. "But the worst part was the shot. They make you lie down on this table and they put this white sheet over you so you can't see the needle. And then they give you this awful shot. Then you don't feel nothin'. Except you hear that tube working. It's *scary*. It sounds like a vacuum only soft—"

"Stop it!" Mrs. Kitchens jerked upright. "I don't want to hear anymore about it."

Trina covered her face in her hands. "You think I'm a murderer, don't you, Mama?" Her sobs came out louder and harsher. "You don't love me anymore. And Bill don't love me either. Nobody loves me." She hurriedly opened the door when we stopped at a light. "Good-bye, Mama. You'll never see me—"

Mrs. Kitchens pulled her back into the car and locked the door. "Now that's enough foolishness, Trina Kitchens. Nobody called you a murderer. But now that Bill Matthews," she spat out his name, "I don't know what to call him. Hanging's too good for him."

"Oh, Mama." Trina leaned against her mother, rubbing the tears from her eyes, her innocent face wretched with betrayal. "He said he'd be waiting for me. He even gave me this ring." She held out a dime store rhinestone ring. "He put it on my finger before we went in there. He wrote our names down on the form as Mr. and Mrs. William Matthews." She started to cry again. "He said just to think of it as practice for when we really would be. And he told me not to worry 'cause we'd have plenty of time to have other babies." She wiped her eyes again. "Then he hugged me like he wasn't never gonna see me again. I told him not to worry so much. That I'd be fine. He said he knew that, and he'd be waiting for me.

"But when I came out, he was gone. At first, I figured he'd just gone to the restroom. But the receptionist was watching for me. She said my husband had to run out for a while and left me a note.

"After I read it I tore it into little pieces and threw them on the floor. Everybody was watching me, but I didn't care." She wiped her nose on a crumpled tissue. "The note said he was sure it wouldn't work out for us. And one day I'd find some nice boy my own age. He said I shouldn't look for him 'cause he was goin' away to start his life over." She burst into louder sobs. "I was gonna have a baby. This morning I had a husband. I mean he *almost* was. And now I don't have nobody."

I fought hard against my own tears thinking of Trina reading that note, standing deserted in that waiting room with her dime store ring and her bleeding body. And sick, humiliated Candy, now pregnant again and left all alone with her four children. Then I became aware that my name had been called several times.

"Could you take us back now please, Miz Bauer?" Mrs. Kitchens asked again. "We're both wore out and we're ready to go."

"Back to the apartment?"

"I want to take Trina home. She can't face Mary and those children now. I'll get her things later on."

"Do you feel well enough for the drive, Trina?" I felt shy actually addressing her though I'd been thinking about no one else for hours. "I can get you a motel room if you need to rest. You can go home tomorrow."

"I can make it home OK, Laura." She sounded more cheerful. "It's not like I'm really sick or nothin'." She giggled self-consciously. "But I'm real hungry. We didn't have breakfast this morning."

"We'll stop somewhere on the way back." I was glad she felt well enough to be hungry. "What do you feel up to?"

"Anything's fine with me. Long as there's plenty of it." Her mood was brighter. "I wouldn't want to put you to no special trouble."

CHAPTER 15

A Little Lie

"I don't know about the rest of you," Mavis said, making no attempt to hide her disgust, "but I sure don't want nothin' suckin' on me."

We were seated in a circle on the floor of the Project living room leaning back against big, colorful pillows after watching a film about breastfeeding.

When the lights were turned back on, I'd tried to read their faces. Mavis looked bored and contemptuous. Mandy seemed noncommittal. Nell was silent and open-mouthed. I couldn't imagine her nursing, but it was also impossible to think of her having sex.

"It is hard to picture her with a fella, idn't it?" her mother had said when I'd asked about the father. "She never went anywhere except the superette, and she sure didn't do it there." She threw up her hands. "She don't even want to go there anymore. If it weren't for the Project, I reckon she'd never leave the house."

I looked out at the captive faces of the new girls. There were several I knew only as names on an enrollment list. They sat, as resigned as children in church, waiting silently, yawning and fidgeting, until finally freed by the last "amen." I did not delude myself that all our clients valued the classes we gave them. I realized they wanted a doctor's care and to have their babies delivered in a hospital and accepted that a certain amount of boredom and irritation came along with these services. Even the ones who were not as vocal about their displeasure as Mavis.

"I know all I want to know about this nursing bit," Mavis said testily, handing Susan back her pamphlet. "You may as well give this to somebody else. I already bought me a bottle set at Sears. It's got two sizes of bottles, nipples, brushes, and everything."

"Let's save that for when we talk about bottle feeding, Mavis," I interrupted, despite her smoldering eyes. I could not allow her to sabotage the class. I handed the pamphlet back to her. "Please follow along with us."

She was silent, though she'd gladly have annihilated me with a stare.

"My mama nursed all of us," Mandy said simply, as if suggesting a brand of scouring powder her mother had used. "We all turned out real healthy. We never had any bad sickness except the chicken pops and measles and stuff like that."

"I bet it messed up her figure," Mavis claimed. "I'm not gonna go through the rest of my life with droopy ole boobs when that little sucker can get all he needs right out of a bottle."

"There's not a thing wrong with my mama's . . . well, you know." Mandy blushed. "She even got her figure back a whole lot faster than some of her friends that didn't nurse."

I couldn't help beaming like a first-grade teacher handing out gold stars. "Mandy's right. Breastfeeding is good for the mom, too. Let's read about how it helps the baby." I stopped short. Even Susan's usually encouraging eyes looked glazed.

"How about a volunteer?" I asked. "I know you're sick of listening to me, so let's take turns reading this aloud." I sat back and waited. "Who wants to start?" Everyone looked down at the floor. They each seemed to grow smaller.

I smiled, hoping someone would smile back. But they all looked away.

"All right, then I'll pick somebody." I quickly looked around the circle. "Mavis, please get us started with the first paragraph."

"I don't want to read *this*," she said sullenly.

"I didn't ask what you *wanted* to do," I answered, mustering my sternest voice. "Please begin."

"You better let somebody else start," she said standing up. "I have to go to the bathroom." She stared at me as she passed by with a look that silently bored into me, daring me to stop her.

"OK. How 'bout somebody else?"

Finally, Mandy raised her hand. "I'll give it a try." She sat up straight and pushed her bangs out of her eyes. *"Breast or Bottle Feeding: How will you choose?"* She read as haltingly as a young child. "This bro-brochure is de-designed to provide you with facts to help you decide what will be best for you and your baby. Re-mem-ber. No matter what ap-proach you use," her flat voice struggled on, "con-con—"

"Consistency," Susan prompted. "You know, doing the same thing all the time."

"Consistency is the most important part of feeding your baby. Your baby's matu-matu—"

"Maturation." I wanted to tell her to stop but there was no way to do it without humiliating her. I could see the perspiration on her forehead as she concentrated. "It's just a big word for growth," I said, stopping her.

She nodded and went on. "Your baby's maturation is linked to the nour-nourishment he receives." She paused as if deliberating over this information.

"Do you have a question?" I was surprised she'd find so much to debate in that simple statement.

"No, but could somebody else read now? It kinda wears me out."

"Of course. Thank you, Mandy. Nell, how about you?"

She shook her head and cleared her throat. "I have a sore throat."

"Rita?" I looked hopefully to the new girl Susan had just enrolled. She was thin, almost to the point of illness. Her blonde hair was stick straight and not much thicker than corn silk. She didn't look as if she possessed sufficient energy to eat an apple, much less read out loud.

"I can't read in front of anybody," she said softly, hanging her head. "Ever since I was little, it makes me throw up." She fiddled nervously with a high school ring on a chain around her neck. I wondered where the boy was who had given it to her. Susan had asked, but Rita wouldn't talk about him.

"I'll take a turn, Laura," Susan said enthusiastically, like she'd won a weekend in the Bahamas. "I enjoy reading aloud." Then she effortlessly read a section in her strong, ex-teacher's voice. "What do y'all think about all this?" she asked when she came to the end. "Raise your hand if you're going to nurse your baby. Keep your hand down if you're going to bottle feed."

"Wait a minute," Mavis said. "Are you gonna pay for it?"

"Pay for what?" I asked.

"The formula."

"No. We're not budgeted for baby formula."

"It costs a whole lot," Nell said. "They got it at the superette. Cans and powder you have to mix up with water. It takes a whole lot of money to feed a baby."

It was startling to hear so many words come out of Nell's mouth at one time. The other girls looked surprised, too, yet they listened attentively.

"It don't seem fair you won't pay for it," Mavis said irritably. She patted her abdomen. "I guess I'll have to let that thing suck on me, just 'cause I can't afford not to."

"You can get it with Food Stamps," said Gladys, a small, muscular black girl from Carrollton, whom none of the others had met before. "Formula's food just like anything else. But it's real expensive. All that baby stuff is."

"How about Pampers?" Mavis asked. "Can you get them with stamps?"

"Nope. You can't get diapers or soap or anything like that," Gladys told them, appearing to speak from experience. "It has to be stuff to eat."

"What about cigarettes?" Mavis's tone was bold and challenging, claiming with every word that *nobody* could make rules for her.

"Nope. No beer or wine either," Gladys answered.

"Can you at least get Cheetos and a Coke? I got to have something for all this trouble." Mavis patted her stomach again and all the girls laughed.

"Sure you can," Gladys reassured her. "You can get anything you want so long as you can eat it. My mama cooks real healthy, but she always gets cookies and popsicles for us when she gets her stamps."

"I used t'know this lady," Rita said, "who had this card they gave her down at the welfare office. And when she showed it at the store they gave her all kinds of things. Milk and cheese and eggs. She didn't pay anything for them neither."

"Then this baby better get used to drinking milk and eating cheese real fast," Mavis said. "I'm not wasting my money on a lot of canned formula that stinks so bad I don't see how anybody can drink it."

"Some of it's made from soy beans," I explained. "You're just not used to the smell. But let's not get into that now. It's not what we're here for."

"What *are* we here for?" Mavis looked me in the eye, cold and hard. She was ready to pick a fight.

"To learn more about pregnancy and childbir—"

"Girl, the only reason we're here is 'cause you say we got to be or you won't pay for nothin'," Mavis said. "We got no choice about it."

"Well, isn't that just too bad," Susan said sharply, standing up. She was taller than Mavis and accustomed to putting down insurrections back when she taught high school. "These classes are required. If you want the free services, you have to put up with the rest of it. And I promise you it won't be the last time in your life you have to do something you don't want to. Is that clear?"

"Maybe I have to do what you say *now*." Mavis's eyes flashed angrily. "But after this baby's born, ain't you or nobody else gonna tell me how to raise him or what to feed him or anything else. 'Cause you won't have nothin' to hold over me. I'll raise him up however I want. I'll give him a bottle full of Coke if I want to."

"Now, calm down. Hold on a minute." Susan's voice was suddenly conciliatory and soothing. She put her arm around Mavis, apparently unaware when the girl recoiled from her touch. She looked totally sure of what she was doing. "Nobody's going to push you into anything." She smiled and turned from Mavis to face the group. "Who'd even want to try?"

A few girls laughed appreciatively and Mavis's shoulders relaxed.

"It *will* be your baby. Laura and I won't be breathing down your neck. If you want to feed him pizza and Nehi Grape, it'll be up to you."

We all looked at Susan in amazement.

"I thought that'd get your attention." She laughed and sat down. "But you know, seriously, I got to tell y'all a little story on Mavis here."

The room became immediately silent. Mavis looked distrustful, and I wondered what in the world Susan was trying to do.

"Mavis talks real tough, and she *is* tough," Susan admitted. "I wouldn't want to tangle with her over anything. But I'll let y'all in on a little secret." Susan leaned forward and whispered dramatically, "When it comes to children, she's a pussy cat. You should see her with her little brothers and sisters. She's practically raised them all 'cause her mama and daddy are so busy with their church. And those children look up to her. Every one of them's healthy as the pictures of children in those parenting magazines. If one of them starts to cry, Mavis snatches them up for a hug in two seconds flat." She smiled and shook her head. "I'm not worried about that baby. Not one bit."

Afterwards while we were cleaning up, Susan looked at me accusingly. "I knew you were making a mistake when you asked them to read. *Especially* Mavis."

"Then why didn't you stop me?" I asked angrily.

"You're the boss." She shrugged her shoulders. "It's not so easy to go against the boss, Laura."

"I've always asked you to speak your mind. I'm not so hard to talk to."

"You wouldn't have listened." Her first words came slowly, but then she got up her nerve and her feelings poured out. "You've got all your big-city ideas about education and women's rights and 'taking control of your life.'" She couldn't help laughing. "See, I've listened real well. So have all these girls. But you're not getting through to them. They all tell you exactly what you want to hear. Except Mavis.

"They're shy, Laura. Some of them are only thirteen and fourteen, and you're asking them to read about breasts and nipples and nursing babies. How do you know if they can read if you try them out on something like that?" She sighed. "Though most of them probably can't. And they have to listen to us talk about nutrition when they never get enough to eat."

I was embarrassed Susan had stepped in to handle a situation I could not. I turned on the vacuum cleaner and began vigorously attacking the crumbs left from our refreshments. My thoughts jumped all over the place as I cleaned and finally settled on my own memories of seventh-grade health class. Some girls had not been clear about what sexual intercourse involved, and we were embarrassed when the teacher pulled out her diagrams of vaginas and penises and stages of pregnancy and childbirth. We giggled in discomfort when she got to the part about breastfeeding, and we weren't even pregnant. And all of us *could* read, though even our inept health teacher had possessed the sense not to make us read out loud about it.

I couldn't shake the feeling of my own cloddishness, free-associating more embarrassing examples as I straightened the meeting room, dating back to when I was five and my great-aunt Leah, a tall, heavy woman came to visit. Several neighbors had recently given birth, and I had watched their pregnancies progress until it seemed they had watermelons under their dresses. Although Aunt Leah, with her bouffant-styled grey hair was much older than the pregnant neighborhood women I had observed, her protruding abdomen so resembled theirs that I had innocently inquired, "When are you going to have the baby?"

My mother, always polite and gracious, was mortified. Yet there was nothing she could do to lessen my mistake other than quickly engage Aunt Leah in relaying all the news of the Dallas cousins. The awkward moment had passed by the time we retrieved Aunt Leah's suitcase from the baggage carousel, yet later that evening, when I overheard the adults discussing my unfortunate remark, I felt ashamed to have hurt the feelings of this kind aunt.

"I'm sure she's forgotten all about it now," my mother said gently, when she came up to kiss me good night. "Besides, you just didn't understand that it's not a question you ask someone long past the age to have babies. But it's all right." She leaned over and kissed me so that her soft curls touched my cheek, and I could smell the delicate sweetness of her perfume. "You just didn't understand."

Only this time I berated myself for not knowing better. I had grown up but was still my awkward child-self when it came to reading people. When I got home and told my mother what had happened, she would encourage me to consider all the good I did for our clients instead of focusing on one mistake. But hard as I tried not to, over the whir of the vacuum cleaner, I heard their halting, humiliated voices in my head.

When Rita Washburn came back inside the office, Susan and I had not heard her, occupied as we were in cleaning up. She seemed very nervous as if someone had frightened her. "I waited outside 'til everybody was gone, she explained, looking shyly at Susan and me. "I was just wondering . . . if you don't need it all . . . and if you could spare it . . . could I please . . ."

"What is it, honey? What can we do for you?" Susan asked tenderly.

"I'm just so hungry." Her eyes filled with tears. "Mama and Daddy can't help not having enough for all of us since Daddy got laid off. There's never enough with so many little ones. And now that you told us," she said, holding out her pamphlet, "how it can hurt the baby if the mama doesn't get the right things to eat, I'm *so* scared for my baby." She wiped her eyes with the back of her hand. "I don't mind so much for me, but I can't let *him* get messed up. I know it's going to be a boy. I'm sure of it. I can't never see his daddy again, but I want my baby to be strong just like him." She started to cry uncontrollably.

Susan quickly enfolded Rita in her arms and held her tight in a silence that was so deep and compassionate it seemed to stop time. Rita gradually stopped crying as Susan stroked her back, much as she might have soothed a baby. Then Susan led Rita over to the couch, still murmuring softly. This gave me a chance to run into the kitchen, where I fixed Rita a thick ham and cheese sandwich and filled a plate with the remains of Nadine's three bean salad. I set the plate in front of her on the coffee table along with a glass of milk. Rita quickly pulled away from Susan and ate so hungrily she hardly took time to chew.

"Could I have please have some more?" Rita asked, setting down the empty plate and taking a long drink of milk.

"Sure you can." Susan quickly filled another plate with fruit and cheese and crackers. "I'm going to pack up something for you to take home with you, too." She began placing boxes and containers into a large shopping bag.

"Could I come back tomorrow instead?" Rita asked shyly. "If I take this home now, I'll have to share it with the others. I couldn't eat in front of them. It wouldn't be right."

"Take some home *and* come back tomorrow," I said, pouring her some orange juice.

"Would you like a ride home?" Susan asked solicitously. "It's dark out there."

"It's not too far. I'll be fine."

"It's at least two miles. And it's late." Susan sounded concerned. "I'll take you if you can wait 'til I finish up here. I've got a client coming by as soon as she gets off work."

"Come on, Rita. I'll drive you now," I said, handing her the bag of food.

She followed me silently to my car. Once she was settled inside, she leaned back and closed her eyes. I was happy to see her relax, even if it might only be for a short car ride. But then she sat up and watched me anxiously.

"There was something else I came back for, Laura," she said finally, talking to the floor. "I have to tell you something. I'm afraid you're gonna be pretty mad 'cause I told you a lie."

"I don't see how *anybody* could be mad at you, Rita. I bet it's only a misunderstanding, not a real lie," I told her, wondering if this had to do with the father of her baby whom she had just mentioned for the first time.

"No, I *lied* to you."

I couldn't imagine what terrible secret she was concealing. I kept driving and waited for her to tell me.

"I told you I'd only missed *two* periods when I signed up. But I was three months gone when you came by the first time." She looked at me tearfully, begging for forgiveness. "I did it 'cause I was scared you'd turn me down. But last week when I saw the doctor, he figured it out and said he'd have to tell you. *Please* don't throw me out, Laura," she pleaded. "It was just a little lie. Please don't kick me out. I don't know what I'd do without the Project."

"Nobody's kicking you out." I squeezed her arm and handed her a tissue as we approached her house. "One month more isn't *such* a big deal," I said, trying to convince myself and praying it wasn't actually longer than that.

But I worried what Mrs. Cremins *would* do if her calculations showed that Mavis was overage and that both she and Rita were past the eligibility date when we enrolled them. Or if she discovered Vernon was an alcoholic who had set his desk on fire. "Come on, Rita," I said, trying to tease away her sadness and my own fears. "Pull yourself together. Or your folks are going to wonder what we do to you at these classes."

She laughed weakly and collected her heavily packed plastic bag.

"It's going to be OK," I told her. "Stop worrying."

"Thank you, Laura. God bless you." She walked around to my window and looked in solemnly. "I promise I won't lie about anything else *ever* again. Cross my heart and hope to die."

CHAPTER 16

The Right Thing

Susie was wearing her Sunday shoes and a pink skirt with a flowered blouse instead of her usual jeans and T-shirt. Her long, coal-black hair was carefully tied back. She looked purposeful, as if this were an important occasion like a wedding or a funeral.

I shut my office door behind her, though I knew you could hear right through the thin walls. I waited for her to explain what was troubling her, but she seemed to need special encouragement. I smiled, but she blushed and turned away. Then finally she got it out. "I've got this friend Cathy. She idn't in the Project, but she was due same time as me. Only her baby came early for no reason the doctors can figure out. They had to put it in the incubator, and they don't know for sure what's wrong with her." Her lower lip trembled. "It might die. It's the tiniest little preemie, and something might be all wrong inside her. Her heart or her lungs. I don't know what all it could be."

I handed her my box of tissues, wishing I had the nerve to dry her eyes. I was afraid my touch would embarrass her. Yet when our hands touched, she took mine and held on.

"I been at the hospital all day. Cathy was all alone 'til I got there. See, when she went into labor she got a neighbor to drop her off, but that lady couldn't stay with her. And then she was so scared she called me. I'm close as she comes to kin, 'cause she don't know where her mama and daddy are, and she don't get along with her grandma even if she does live with her.

"When she called me, I couldn't let her down. Only I didn't feel real good, and my ankles have been swelling up something awful. But I kept thinking of her down there all alone. How it could be me. Lying there all alone—" She broke off in tears.

"You won't be alone, Susie. You'll have *us* and your family. No one's going to leave you by yourself."

"But it could be my baby. I've done everything I'm s'posed to. I been eating right and hardly smoking at all, but it could happen to *my* baby." She sniffed and wiped her nose.

"It *could* happen," I admitted to this fragile girl, her pallor more striking than usual, in her agitation, with her dark hair drawn back from her face. "But the doctor says you look fine. If you're following his directions, that's all you can do." I squeezed the hand that remained in mine.

"Lord, I'm trying hard as I can." She looked past me. "But I *am* all alone. I 'preciate all you and Susan and Mama and Daddy are doin' for me. But it's not the same. Mickey walked out on me. I can't figure him out. Seemed like he loved me a whole lot 'til he found out about the baby."

"I know you thought he'd be there for you, Susie." I relaxed my grasp on the hand that clung so desperately to mine. "I'm so sorry he's let you down."

"It's 'cause of those fellas he hangs out with in Steel Vulture, Laura," she told me, holding back her tears. "He wouldn't do me this way if they didn't come around all the time talkin' about the band. How he's got to write more songs real quick so they can play at some festival up near Ball Ground and be famous. WQRL already played 'Love You 'Til I Die' on their Rock Cavalcade. They say he don't have no time for babies since they're goin' on tour. They even put his name on the drum set. Mickey Osgood and Steel Vulture. It's gone to his head."

I knew the kind of guys she meant, driving around in a broken-down Chevy van with a Grateful Dead bumper sticker and the dark-tinted glass you can't see through. Custom wheels and extra chrome, but they have to empty all their pockets to come up with gas money. They practice in somebody's parents' garage or basement and play for beers and spare change on the weekends. But they know they're going to make it big so they don't need to finish high school, much less go to college or technical school. They stay up all night drinking and smoking cigarettes and grass if they can score it, feeling high on their own genius.

"They're really going on tour?" I held on to my suspicions, yet in case I was wrong and Mickey had actually written the next number-one hit single, I wanted to encourage her to get him to pay her child support. WQRL was strictly local, but if the station was playing Steel Vulture, maybe the band *was* going somewhere.

"It's only local festivals and craft fairs so far, but the garage where Mickey works part-time is sponsoring the Steel Vulture T-shirts and giving them a free tank of gas for the tour van," she reported proudly.

"But they're with a record label?" I was starting to feel slightly impressed despite my initial skepticism.

"Well . . . not exactly. But Mickey knows this guy who has a recording studio in his parents' garage. So they made them a few records, and this other guy who does tattoos came up with a design for Steel Vulture. I heard it looks real cool. It's silver and gold so it looks great on black T-shirts. I wish I had one," she said longingly.

I didn't say anything, but I decided my original impression of the band had been correct. Mickey wasn't headed for stardom in the near future. The only thing Susie would likely receive from him would be a copy of the "hit" single after it had sat moldering for a while in his garage. She shouldn't expect much from a boyfriend who didn't even give her a free T-shirt.

"I still don't get it, Laura." Susie shook her head and sniffed, starting to cry again. "How could he write those songs for Steel Vulture if he didn't mean 'em? They're really loud and the bass feels like it's goin' right through you sometimes, but they're still mostly love songs," she reminded me. "And Mickey said I was his inspiration."

A week later I drove Susie home after our sewing class. We stopped at the drive-in before we got to her house because she wanted to talk to me alone. She was afraid she'd know somebody inside, so we sat in the car talking over our milkshakes.

"I know Mickey walked out on me, so I'm supposed to hate him. But I want him back." She smiled hopefully. "Don't you think once he sees this little baby that's half his, he'll stop runnin' from me?"

"Susie," I asked as gently as I could, "then why did he run away when you told him you were pregnant?"

"He just got scared," she said defensively. "I was, too, at first. When I missed the second month, I didn't know what to do to save my life. I knew Mama had to wonder why I felt sick all the time. I'd seen other fellas run off when their girlfriends told them. But I knew it would be different for me and Mickey."

"Were y'all together a long time?"

"More than a year," she said proudly. "We started goin' out when he was a junior and I was in tenth. That whole year. Even after he dropped out.

"He got him a job and moved into a trailer with a couple of his buddies. They got on real good when they was all workin' and they had time for their music. Then Mickey's hours got cut back at the garage 'cause they weren't busy enough. And he couldn't find nothin' else and him and Gary and Larry started gettin' on each other's nerves something awful. None of them was working except odd jobs, so they got behind on their rent.

"And right then's when I had to tell him about the baby. We had driven out to this place in the country we used to go to be by ourselves. It wasn't much, but there was a little creek and a few big shade trees. He wanted to do it, but I didn't feel like it. But he kept trying to make me want to. He wouldn't keep his hands off me. So then I told him. Real quick. I'd been trying to think what to say to him, but then it seemed like I couldn't wait. I just told him straight out he was gonna be a daddy.

"I wanted him to say it'd be all right. That we'd make out OK. Only he just sat there like somebody had died. It would've almost been better if he'd yelled at me, but he just kept on staring at me 'til finally I was so nervous I apologized to *him*. Told him how sorry I was and I didn't mean for it to happen.

"Then I got to thinkin' it was as much his fault as mine. But he wadn't saying nothin'. So I said, 'Mickey, what are we gonna do?' I knew what I wanted him to say. Only he just sat there with his jaw going. He's always got a mouthful of bubble gum.

"Finally, he said he didn't know. Started telling me how expensive trailers and furniture and utilities are. Didn't once mention the baby or me. So I said, 'Take me home, Mickey. I can't sit here with you actin' like all this is about is money.'

"Then he kissed me. Like that would make it better. He sat there chewing his gum and saying, 'What are we gonna do, Susie? Baby, what are we gonna do?'

"Next morning I felt so miserable. I got out this number my friend Carolyn gave me to this place in Atlan'a helps girls out if they're not too far gone. I knew I had to hurry.

"So I told Mama I was going shopping. Then while I was getting my things together, there was this loud knocking at the back door. Mama called out, 'Susie, get that door! It must be Mickey. His car just pulled up in the yard.'

"He was all dressed up. I mean good pants and a nice shirt his mama gave him for his birthday, and his hair was combed back so it wadn't in his face. It didn't even look so long the way he'd brushed it, and it looked like he'd trimmed his beard." She smiled at the memory. "His hair's blond as mine is black, but his beard's strawberry blond. Anyhow, he put his hands on my shoulders and talked real serious just like we was grownups. 'Listen,' he said. 'I don't know when I'll get a real job, but I wanna do the right thing. Let's get married.' He put his hand on my stomach. 'You don't show, but it's our baby in there. The three of us belong together.' He kissed me so gentle it was like it was the first time.

"It felt just like something out of the movies. We drove right into town. Mickey couldn't afford a fancy engagement ring, but he bought me a pretty little birthstone ring. We told Mr. Rittenberg, the man owns the jewelry store, that we were getting married. Then we went home and told Mama and Daddy and Mickey's family.

"Both our mamas married real young, but everybody was still real surprised. Mama said, 'Ain't that something. Just when I thought you two was having lovers' quarrels you come and tell me you're getting married. Mickey's mama didn't say too much. She was fixing lunch for all the kids when we came in. But she hugged and kissed me real quick and said she could understand why Mickey was so fired up to marry me 'cause she couldn't wish for a nicer daughter-in-law.

"Mickey took me home and went on to Marietta to see if they'd take him on in this new garage over there. So Mama and me sat and talked all afternoon. We made lemonade and Mama told me about when she and Daddy were courtin'. How he brought roses the night he asked her to marry him and played her a song on his guitar. Then we talked about the kind of wedding dress I wanted.

"'Cause Mama can sew anything. She can see something in a store and make you one so's nobody could tell the difference. And the whole time, Mama never even asked me if . . . *you know*, "she said blushing, "why me and Mickey was in such a hurry to get married. I reckon it's why most people get married. But even if she thought it, Mama never said a word to me.

"Mickey and me set the date two weeks off so I'd know for sure I wouldn't be showing. I figured by the time the baby came it'd be too late for anybody to say much about it."

She sighed wistfully. "Looking back, that was the happiest time in my whole life. Like it was Christmas every day. I even started feeling happy about the baby. Mickey hadn't found a job, but it still seemed like things would work out.

"Mama had a fancy bridal shower for me right before the wedding. She made little bitty san'wiches with cucumber and mayonnaise and pimento cheese that looked like the pictures in magazines. She borrowed the punch bowl from the church and made this real fancy punch with ginger ale and Hawaiian Punch. All the kids' toys got put away for once, and she put fresh flowers on the table.

"It was a party just for ladies, but towards the end, Mickey was s'posed to come over. The ladies brought us all kinds of presents. Dishes. Towels. Cookbooks. A crock pot. Tupperware. A fancy nighty with real lace on it. All the things you need when you're starting out. Everybody had such a nice time 'til it was getting late, but Mickey hadn't shown up.

"'Where is that boy?' Mama whispered to me.

"'Where's your honey, honey?' Miz Akins asked. She was laughing, but she looked concerned.

"After a while they went on home. I knew he was hurt in a car wreck or something just as bad. 'Cause I knew he wouldn't miss that party knowing what it meant to me. So I went over to the trailer. I walked over in my party dress, sweating in the sun and getting my new sandals all scuffed and dirty. I was crying. I knew he must be hurt awful bad.

"When I got there, Larry was sitting in the front room. He's got an awful beer belly and this great big ole tattoo of a naked girl right on his chest. He called out, 'Mick, she's here. Better come out now!'"

Then Susie turned to me. Sister to sister. Sharing it all.

"Guess I should have known then. Guess anybody but *me* would have known. But I was so worried I was blind. 'Is Mickey sick?' I asked Larry. 'Is he gonna be all right?'

"Right then Mickey came out to face me. His hair looked dirty and he was wearing old jeans and a torn T-shirt like he'd never planned on coming.

"'Guess I'll go out for a walk,' Larry said, drunk as a dog, belching like he was proud of it.

"So we stood there eye to eye like boxers. I still kept waiting, thinking he'd explain it. He'd say something to make it all right. But he just kept chewing his gum, making me pull it out of him.

"'Mickey, talk to me.' I was getting scared. 'What's going on?' He looked at me like I was the teacher and he'd been made to stay after school.

"I was crying. I couldn't hold it back any longer. 'Why didn't you come? Mickey, tell me!'

"'Susie, I'm real sorry.' He wouldn't look at me. 'I couldn't come 'cause . . . it's not gonna work. We can't get married.'

"He said it like it was nothing. Like he couldn't take me to the movies or a football game.

"'We're gettin' married,' I reminded him. 'We're getting married next Sunday.'

"'I don't have a job, Susie. Where we gonna live? We can't afford a doctor and all that baby stuff.'

"'I'm having our baby, Mickey! I can't stop it. It's *your* baby. We're in this together.'

"'But it ain't gonna work, Susie.' He turned away from me. I never felt so alone in my whole life. 'I'm sorry I didn't come to your party,' he said. 'It just seemed too weird me coming over and us not getting married. Maybe we can later on when I'm working again.'

"'You can't walk out on me!' I didn't care who heard me screamin' at him. 'Not after everybody thinks we're getting married. Mama already made my dress. Everybody we know will be at church on Sunday. And the *baby*, Mickey. I can't go put it on layaway. That baby's *coming*. You can't leave me now. I thought you loved me.'

"'A course I do, baby.' He actually put his arms around me, but then he said, 'We can't make it now. We'd fight all the time. We wouldn't have enough to eat. That's no way to start out. You'll be better off just staying with your folks.'

"I don't usually lose my temper. I hold it back like you hold your breath under water. Only I was so mad I took that birthstone ring he gave me and threw it right in his face.

"But soon as I walked out that door, I broke down crying and couldn't stop no matter how hard I tried. My face was so puffy you wouldn't have believed I was s'posed to be a bride. I wished I could find me a hole to swallow me up. I couldn't stand to see Mama's face after she'd made my dress and given me this big party.

"So I lied. I walked into the house smiling like there was nothing wrong in the whole world. Mama came rushing out of the kitchen to meet me. Her hands were still dripping with dish water.

"'Well?' she asked, her face all set for bad news.

"'Mickey's real sick, Mama. He's got one of those stomach bugs. He was up all night throwing up so by accident he slept straight through this afternoon by.'

"Mama didn't say nothin'. She was drying the punch bowl and acting like it took all her concentration to work on that.

"'I'm so tired, Mama,' I said. 'All that running around just about did me in.'

"'Then you best lie down. Or first thing you know, *you'll* be getting sick,' she warned me.

"Mama looked so serious I was scared she'd guess the truth. I ran up to my room quick as I could. Soon as the door closed behind me, I cried like to never stop. The pillow was soaked before I was done.

"Then I pulled myself together. I got out my savings. It wasn't much, but I knew I had to leave. I couldn't stay home and shame Mama and Daddy like that. I figured somehow I'd have to make it on my own. Then I was so worn out by all that had happened, I lay down on the bed and slept 'til morning.

"When the sun came up, I knew what I had to do. I waited 'til Daddy went to work and Mama was out front walking the little ones down to the school bus. I left her a note saying I was going shopping downtown for wedding stuff. Then I stuck the real note under Mama's pillow where she wouldn't find it 'til after I was gone. I wrote: 'Dear Mama, I'm sorry. I guess you figured I was having a baby what with me and Mickey getting married so quick. But now he's changed his mind. I can't stay here and shame you. So I got me a place to stay. Don't worry. I'll be all right. I love you. Please don't try to find me.'

"Then I went across town where Mama and Daddy never go and got me this crummy old trailer. I could rent it by the week 'cause it was so run-down. Roaches ran around like they owned the place, and there was dust so thick you could write your name in it. But I got busy cleaning it up. At least that gave me something to do.

"I was trying not to spend any money, so all I ate was peanut butter sandwiches and Kool-Aid. And I slept a lot. I didn't know what I was going to do at the end of the week when my money ran out. 'Cause nobody would hire me.

"See, I tried to get work doing housework for people. But I couldn't ask anybody that knew me and might tell Mama, and all the strangers turned me down cold.

"My third night, when I was coming back from the store, I saw Daddy's pickup parked by my trailer. Mama saw me and came running out to meet me. She was crying and then I started, too. Neither one of us could get a word out.

"Mama took my face in her hands. 'Baby,' she said, 'why'd you run off?' She hugged me so hard I could barely breathe. 'Darlin', we don't care what you done. If that boy ain't man enough to stick by you, that's on *him*—not you. You don't have to come live out here.' She kept hugging me. Then she wiped both our eyes with a corner of her apron. 'If you're ashamed, maybe you got some cause to be. But that don't mean you don't have a family. You're coming home right now. Let the neighbors talk 'til Kingdom come. But you come back where you belong.'

"My wedding dress is still up in the attic. I go up and look at it sometimes," she admitted sadly. "I still feel kinda funny when people come over.

III

But mostly I try to think about my baby. He's comin' out of all of this, and he ain't gonna be messed up by it."

Two weeks later Susie stopped by to see me again. She was wearing jeans and showing more, but she looked painfully thin everywhere else. Her dark hair was loose and wild. Her eyes were red and she seemed so exhausted, I wished I could put her to bed.

"Mickey's gone and done it," she said, crying before she made it into my office. "Sharon, this girl I know who goes out with Larry, ran into Mickey this morning. He's workin' more hours now at the garage. And . . . and there's this girl living with him at the trailer. Mickey and Larry think she sings every bit as good as Grace Slick, and Mickey's got her singing with Steel Vulture. He even wrote a song just for her."

Then she was in my arms, clutching me, her head buried in my shoulder, as if the last part she had to tell was so terrible she couldn't stand to look at me.

"Sharon says she's gonna have a baby. And Mickey gave her my ring."

CHAPTER 17

Nothin'

Their food logs were filled out as carefully as income tax returns or entries in family Bibles. The forms came back stained from kitchen mishaps, wrinkled and refolded from time spent in back pockets. They were turned in every two weeks baring the sweat and crossed-out words of self-conscious writers.

"You wait and see," Mrs. Cremins had predicted when she explained the requirement. "They'll write down all these balanced meals to impress you. But they won't eat them. They're teenagers. They'll keep wasting their money on junk, and they'll never tell the truth about what they *really* eat. But we must maintain our records."

My mother was disturbed when she saw me reviewing the logs one night as I sat working at the dining room table while she and my father drank their coffee. We had just finished a good meal composed from all four basic food groups with ample portions for all. I watched her study the forms that had been completed in isolation and ignorance by those who didn't know how meager the meals they described would seem. No one had lectured them about protein. Milk was too expensive to buy, and most were too poor to own or feed a cow if there had been anywhere to keep one on a tiny trailer lot. The logs I read showed no attempt to impress us with make-believe meals as Mrs. Cremins had expected; our clients were too busy every day simply finding something to eat. They painstakingly reported their meager diets, and we maintained their logs in a growing number of large binders, exactly as directed.

"This foolishness makes no sense," my mother said disdainfully to me and my father. "Only in America would they have people document their starvation." She ran her fingers through her thin hair, tinted dark brown to hide the grey. She had told me it had been thick and wavy when she was a girl, but after her head was shaved when she entered the concentration camp, it had grown back with some of its curl but had never regained its original thickness and luster. She rarely spoke of those days, but even after years adjusting to her American life, she could not understand American ways.

"Why does she make these poor girls write down their pathetic meals?" my mother asked, knowing I was following Mrs. Cremins's instructions. "She already knows they live in poverty. Laura shouldn't be required to ask these poor girls to turn in those horrible charts filled with their suffering."

My father, always the peacemaker, tried to explain bureaucracy. "Molly, it's the way they run government programs. Filling out these forms proves Laura's staff monitor their clients' daily diet. There's probably a whole department in Washington to receive them from all over the country," he said with a little bit of his own disdain.

"Then it's indecent, Mike," my mother protested. "Laura says many of the girls are practically starving. Why don't they just give them something to eat? Nobody needs to *prove* they're hungry. Laura says you can see it in their eyes." My mother's tone grew bitter with indignation. "Even the Nazis, who documented *everything*," she insisted, looking at the number tattooed on her arm, "didn't waste their time proving their victims were starving. They just starved us."

"Could we just get through one discussion without bringing up the Nazis?" my father demanded, abruptly getting up from the table.

"That's not fair, Mike," my mother called after him. "I only meant America should be better than this. What kind of government *proves* people are starving instead of ending their hunger?"

I closed up my files, wishing I had not set out my evening's work on the dining room table and touched off an argument between my parents. They rarely even raised their voices at each other. I watched my mother, elegant even in her lavender sweat suit, look regretfully after my father. She sat quietly for a few moments, and then when it seemed he would not be coming back to finish his coffee, she got up to take one of her long evening walks. Ever since I was a small child, she had widely traversed our neighborhood to maintain both her figure and her composure. But I knew no amount of walking would soothe her when he was so agitated.

We were both accustomed to my father's strong opinions and his intensity, yet we worried that he continued to ignore his doctor's caution to reduce his long days. When he insisted he must keep working six days a week at his jewelry store, my mother feared he would have a heart attack. To appease her, he sometimes came along on her walks and reluctantly gave up his evening cigar. My mother's appearance no longer revealed her brutal past, but my father had become so afflicted with arthritis that he no longer stood as tall as he had when she arrived from Poland to stay with cousins in Atlanta and fell in love with him. He still found much amusement in daily life but had to see it behind thick glasses, and his blue eyes were often bloodshot from frequent, sleepless nights.

"Molly, I'm sorry I said what I did," my father said remorsefully as he came back downstairs to join us. He had heard my mother calling to her old golden retriever, Marigold, as she prepared to leash her up for their walk, and would not let her leave without apologizing for his angry words. "But these girls aren't victims of this program. Laura and the others *are* helping them. Only there's just so far they can go."

"Don't you think I know that?" she answered angrily, ignoring his conciliatory tone. "If people are going hungry, *no one* should keep a record of how badly they're starving." She threw the leash down on her chair. "I was there, Mike. Maybe if every day you'd watched little children and teenagers starving, you wouldn't accept this sor—"

"I don't accept anything!" he shouted, abandoning the loving voice he always reserved for her. "Don't *you* forget I was there to see the walking skeletons when we liberated the camps. People too weak to even eat the food the soldiers held out to them." As he spoke, his words seemed to break inside of him, and he grabbed his chest, in physical pain. "Go get my nitro," he called to me. "Quick. Get it from the bathroom."

I rushed up the stairs with Marigold hurrying after me. When I returned with the bottle, my mother frantically seized it and knelt before him, carefully placing the pill under his tongue. He tried, as always, to make a joke of it, even as tears shone in my mother's face from her fear of losing him and her memories of other losses that hovered painfully just beneath her skin.

"Why is it, do you think," he mused, "your mother is the one whose heart is broken, but I'm the one whose heart keeps trying to stop?"

After we all calmed down and my parents had gone up to bed, I returned to the logs, which Mrs. Cremins would be examining in our office to prepare her quarterly report. I knew she would criticize the handwriting and the minimal entries. Each log I examined was unique in its misspellings, but their meagerness was very similar:

Breakfast: corn muffin and black coffee
Lunch: squash from the garden (I guess a half a cup)
Grape Kool-Aid
Supper: Bologna sandwich, Tater tots, Coke

Breakfast: Coffee and a biscuit
Lunch: Roll with gravy and Coke
Dinner: Half a turkey TV dinner and R.C. Cola

Breakfast: Grits an gravy
Lunch: didn't feel like nothin'
Supper: Co-cola and peanut butter crackers

When I came to Annie Simmons's file, I remembered Susan's recent visit to Annie's house, where she had found an entire family existing on a starvation diet. Usually when Susan returned to our office, she placed food logs in my mailbox, but this time she had personally presented me with the form revealing nourishment worse than any prison diet:

Breakfast: Toast and water
Lunch: White bread and mayo sandwich and water
Dinner: White bread, coffee

Breakfast: Saltines and coffee
Lunch: White bread with mustard sandwich and Coke
Dinner: Biscuit with molasses and water

"We have to *do* something, Laura," Susan had implored me, sitting down at my desk. "When I got to Annie's house she was sitting at the kitchen table bawlin' her eyes out. So I asked her, 'Honey, what is it? What's the matter?'

"At first she was cryin' so hard she couldn't tell me. She could hardly catch her breath. So I just sat there with my arm around her. Then I thought maybe a cool drink of water would make her feel better. I knew she always keeps a bottle of ice water in the fridge so I told her I'd get it for her.

"But she begged me not to. At first I didn't understand, but then I realized she didn't want me to look inside her fridge. Because that bottle of water was the only thing in there. There was *nothing* else. Not even one egg or an apple or a piece of cheese.

"I know you think I'm prejudiced 'cause I don't hold with blacks and whites goin' to school together and livin' side by side. But that doesn't mean I don't believe everybody ought to have a decent place to live and enough to eat. And when they come into this project, I treat all my girls the same. I don't care what color they are."

"I know you do, Susan. You're wonderful with them," I had answered, hoping to placate her. "It has to be terrible seeing what you do. But there's nothing you can—"

"Laura, Annie was *starving*. And what bothered her the most was for me to see it. She couldn't even look at me, but she told me, 'We finished the last piece of bread yesterday. I been waitin' for Tommy t'get paid this afternoon. The landlord's been by twice after the back rent. I'm just hopin' they'll be enough left to get us somethin' to eat after we pay him.'

"Laura, I don't have the stomach to stand in front of our girls preaching about nutrition, while they're so hungry. Annie felt worse about turning in a blank food log than she did about having nothing to eat. She actually apologized to *me*." Susan wiped her eyes and got up to go. "I know we have to do these logs because the Project manual says so. But it sure feels wrong."

Mavis's log was next in my stack. It wasn't signed, but I recognized her precise handwriting. The printing was in bold black letters that didn't waver even enough to slant in either direction. She often wrote in all capitals:

Breakfast: Coffee
Lunch: Coke and a doughnut
Supper: Nothin'

Breakfast: Coffee
Lunch: Ice tea and doughnut
Supper: Don't feel like doing this anymore. Not tonight and not
tomorrow.

That was her last entry.

When I came to Susie's log I stopped to admire the rounded, even penmanship any schoolteacher would have praised. Her logs were always folded neatly in a white envelope, and some of her vegetables, like *glazed carrots* and *broccoli with Hollandaise,* had at first surprised me. Until I learned the truth. And then I hadn't had the heart to discard her logs or ask questions about them.

My own family never ate Hollandaise sauce. It was fattening and easy to ruin, often coming out runny, burnt, or full of lumps. The thought of Susie mastering Hollandaise made me smile, and then I felt ashamed for feeling superior. Maybe she had taken home ec in high school or her mother had taught her to make it, and they had it for Sunday dinner.

I learned the truth a few days after I received her log, when Susie called the office to talk to me about it. She sounded frightened and anxious, as if she were calling to confess a horrible sin.

"Laura, I hope you won't think I make things up all the time," she began tremulously. "'Cause I never made anything up before. Y'all said just be honest and let you know what we eat each day. But I got tired puttin' down the same old things. So I made up the glazed carrots and the brockly with Hollandaise." I imagined her hanging her head and could hear the actual tears in her voice.

"See . . . last week when I was in the doctor's office, I saw this magazine with all kinds of recipes in it. I already knew about glazed carrots. But we didn't have any honey or brown sugar to spare to put on carrots," she said sadly.

"When I saw that recipe for brockly with Hollandaise, it sounded so pretty. So far away and fancy that I loved to think about eatin' it. So I wrote it down, and I *meant* to fix it.

"But then I felt so silly. Mama had never heard of it, and I figured they'd all laugh if I tried it. And if I messed it up, well, we don't have any eggs or cream to waste. But I *wanted* to eat it. I hope you're not mad."

The following Monday when I took Rita Washburn to tour the hospital maternity ward, she asked if I would let her cook the meat for the next family gathering.

"If you buy the meat, whatever you want to have, I'll fix it however you say. But Laura . . . I was hopin'," she said with longing, "'cause it would mean so much to the little'uns, if you could just spare me a small piece for them. We hardly ever have meat at home with so many mouths to feed.

"I *promise* I wouldn't let 'em have any before the Project dinner. But we always have food left over so I was just hopin' you could let me take a little somethin' home. The little'uns would be so excited.

"But it's okay if you can't. We get by. Mama tries to save *me* a glass of milk every day. And Mr. Whitfield down at the diner—I do a little cleanin' for his wife—he saves the old rolls for me. They're real nice Brown 'n Serve rolls. There's usually enough for the little'uns, too.

"Brown 'n serve might look kinda fancy when I write it down on my log since all we mostly have is biscuits and cornbread. But I really eat 'em when I say I do, Laura. Every single time."

CHAPTER 18

Just One Night

"Hello?" I forgot to answer officially when the office phone rang in the in the middle of the night.

"Is this the Project office?" The woman's voice was stern, almost irritated. I'd heard this voice before but could not immediately place it.

"Yes. This is Laura Bauer. Who's calling?" I pulled my red plaid bathrobe tightly around me. Even though no one could see me, it was disconcerting to receive a work call in my pajamas.

"This is Miz Landrum, Lisa's mother."

"Is something wrong?"

"I wouldn't call you in the middle of the night if everything was all right, would I? She's spotting something terrible. I don't see how she's going to hold on to this baby."

"When did it start, Mrs. Landrum? How heavy is it?" I got a pad and pen off the table to start taking notes before I called the doctor.

"It wasn't heavy at first. A few days ago it was just a tiny spot I'd see on her panties when I did the wash. Now it's getting heavy like she's having a period. I didn't want to bother you so late like this, but I reckon somebody'd better see her right away."

"Take her to Kennestone Hospital immediately," I directed her, realizing this was an emergency. "I'll call her doctor and meet you in the emergency waiting room, OK? I'll tell them to expect you."

"I can't possibly leave here now," she complained. "I've got the boys in bed with a bad stomach virus. They've been up and down all night and they just got off to sleep. If I wake 'em now, they'll start throwing up all over again. And my car's been acting real funny. I can't risk having it break down on the way."

"I can call an ambulance. That's probably best anyway."

"Please don't do that. Last time Miz Warrell down the road called one, they took near an hour to get here. They don't like coming down this old bumpy road. And it would scare poor Lisa something awful to hear that siren and see those flashing lights."

"I'll come get her. As fast as I possibly can." I hung up before she could complain about anything else. I dressed quickly, feeling like a fireman rushing out after an alarm and drove off into the night, for once unconcerned about speed limits.

If she was bleeding as seriously as Mrs. Landrum had described, I'd have to take Lisa to the county hospital, which wasn't equipped for high-risk pregnancies. They might refuse to admit her since we didn't have an account. She could hemorrhage to death. I felt furious with myself for listening to her mother when I should have called an ambulance.

I turned on the radio to distract myself. Olivia Newton-John bubbled through a sweet, vapid song. I sang along as loud as I could, trying not to think about miscarriages and death. When I pulled into the parking lot outside the old grocery store where the Landrums lived, I was shocked to find Lisa waiting outside.

"Lisa, you shouldn't be standing up." I jumped out to help her. "Did you think I wouldn't come in for you?"

"It didn't bother me none. I wanted some fresh air. Besides, Mama didn't want to have you wake the boys blowing your horn."

Damn her mama, I thought. *She knew I wouldn't blow my horn. But even if I wake up the entire neighborhood, she has no right to make Lisa stand outside like a stray dog.*

"Let's get going," I said, trying to sound calm and in control. "We'll be there in twenty minutes. Maybe even sooner." I got her settled and fastened her seat belt.

"I sure am glad you came," Lisa said gratefully. "And don't you worry. I got a towel wrapped around me so I won't mess up your seat."

She was hemorrhaging, maybe even losing her baby, but she was worrying about my car seat.

"How heavy is it, Lisa?"

"At first it wasn't so bad. But tonight it got real heavy. I had to put on my sanitary belt before I went to bed. And I still had to get up to change the pad." She turned to look at me. "Laura, what's happening to me?"

"I'm not sure, Lisa," I answered, though I didn't see how it could be anything but a miscarriage. "I'm taking you to the hospital to check everything out."

"You think I'm gonna lose my baby?" she asked tearfully.

"Try not to imagine the worst." I felt myself stalling, uncertain of how much this child could take. "Let's see what the doctor says. Do you feel any pain now?"

"No. Except when the cramps come every once in a while. But I don't care how bad it hurts long as I don't lose my baby."

I felt relieved when we entered a dark stretch of road where she could not see my concern or sense my disloyalty, since I believed if she lost the baby, it really was for the best. Then I felt ashamed to so easily eliminate her baby, even if only within the confines of my mind. I grieved silently, imagining the future of this baby if it did survive.

When I explained the situation, the doctor on duty examined Lisa ahead of the people waiting with broken bones and earaches. She would not release my hand so I stood beside the examining table. When the doctor finished, he asked me to step out in the hall with him.

"Don't leave me, Laura," Lisa called out. She pulled herself up and started to get down from the table.

"Don't you worry, baby," the motherly nurse told her. She adjusted the sheet around Lisa. "You lay back now and rest. I'll stay right here with you 'til your friend comes back."

The doctor whispered to me, "I'm afraid it's bad news." He was a tall young man with solemn dark eyes and thinning blond hair. "She's going to lose it. I'm about ninety-nine percent sure." He massaged his neck and leaned wearily against the wall. "I've seen some terrible birth defects in the babies of these young girls. Even if I had a way to keep her from miscarrying, it would be a mistake to try. We'll just have to wait and let nature run its course."

"Are you going to tell her?" I asked uneasily, hoping this responsibility would not fall to me. I could imagine Lisa's despair at this news.

"Only if she asks me. It won't help to frighten her more than she already is. Maybe she can get a few hours of rest. I'll give her something to help her sleep."

"I'll stay with her. In case something happens, I don't want her to be alone."

"What about family?" he asked. "Isn't there someone who can come stay with her?"

"Her mother's home with her little brothers. Her father's dead."

"What about the baby's father?"

"He couldn't help her," I said, shuddering to think of him. "She's really all alone."

"It's a damn shame," he said, glancing at her chart. "But she's only thirteen. Maybe she can get her life back together when this is over."

I felt certain there was no way to put Lisa's life back together. Even if they saved the baby, there was still its father to consider. If she lost the baby, I would still be taking Lisa home to her mother and Bert. People always claim things will seem brighter in the morning light, but I knew daylight would not help this situation. Lisa's young life was battered.

"We'll get her up to a room," the doctor said wearily, making a few notations on Lisa's chart. "There's nothing more we can do right now. I'll put her in a double so you can have a bed." He patted me on the back. "Looks like you could use it."

"It's so pretty in here," Lisa said happily once we were settled in the hospital room. "All this space just for us."

At first I thought she was trying to make me feel better about being stuck in a hospital in the middle of the night. But when I thought about the hot ex-grocery store where Lisa lived, with the sealed windows and the partitions still in place, I realized our hospital room seemed like a lavish hotel room to her. Even the hospital bed with the thin, plastic-covered mattress and the ill-fitting white sheets felt luxurious to her after nights spent on a narrow camp cot, where she slept without a mattress.

"Look, there's even a closet for each of us," she marveled. "And a place to put your toothbrush and your makeup. And look here! We've got our own bathroom. We can take a bath whenever we want to. You think they got bubble bath?"

"You can't take a bath when you're spotting, Lisa. You can take a shower, though. Would that make you feel better? I'll help you get ready."

"No thanks, Laura. I'd just like to lie down on that nice bed," she said wearily, her voice suddenly very small. "I'm *so* tired."

I turned down our beds and took off my shoes. "You sure you're not hungry or thirsty? I'd be glad to get you something."

"No, thanks. I don't need a thing." She lay back and pulled the covers up to her chin. "This sure feels good."

"Try to rest then. They'll be in pretty soon to take your blood pressure and your pulse and all that kind of stuff."

"Even if you're asleep?" she asked, closing her eyes.

"Sure. They'll be looking after you all through the night."

"And they'll watch out for my baby?" She sat up again. "They won't let anything go wrong, right?"

"Honey, I guess you know why we're . . . I mean, there's a chance . . . a *strong* chance, you could lose the baby," I whispered, afraid myself to say the words aloud. "The doctors and nurses are trying their hardest, but we have to be prepared. It *could* happen."

"I knew soon as I started bleeding heavy, it might happen. I guess it's really up to God," she confided in the darkened room lit only from the hallway. "I've tried so hard to be good and do the things y'all said to. I know I'm young, but I'd still be a good mother. You know I would."

"Don't worry about that now, Lisa." I tried to soothe her. "Just close your eyes and try to rest. I'll be right here if you need me," I promised her. Lying down on the other bed, fully clothed, I heard the sounds of the nurses talking as they walked from room to room, carts rolling down the hall, toilets flushing, and the whine of generators.

"Laura? You asleep yet?" Lisa's voice called out, soft and gentle.

"Do you need something?" I sat up quickly, afraid something was happening.

"No. But I should have told you earlier . . ."

"What is it, honey? What did you want to tell me?"

"I was real scared before, but I felt better soon as I saw you."

"I'm glad, Lisa. Don't give it a thought."

"Lots of people would've been put out with Mama callin' in the middle of the night."

"That's what I was on call for. Besides, *anybody* would want to help you, Lisa. You're a very special girl."

"You really think so?" she asked with obvious surprise.

"Of course I do."

"That's funny." She sounded puzzled, yet very pleased. "Mama's a real good judge of people. She said she could tell you were getting fed up with me same as she does." She sighed and yawned. "I don't reckon anybody's ever fooled Mama before."

In the morning Lisa lost the baby. They gave her something to ease her pain, but she still knew what was happening, and nothing could stop the sorrow she felt over her loss. When they took her away for the D&C, I called Mrs. Landrum. She had not called to inquire about her own daughter's condition, but I was required to let her know.

"The Lord giveth and the Lord taketh away," she intoned, without a trace of emotion, as if we were discussing a total stranger.

"I don't think the Lord had anything to do with this." I felt bitter and was too tired to conceal it.

"What do you mean?" she asked warily, as if she sensed a coming accusation.

"I don't think the Lord gave a thirteen-year-old girl a baby. This has been horrible for Lisa."

"I couldn't agree with you more." She spoke very reasonably. "And I can't picture Lisa as a mother. She's just a child, of course, but still, she's always been so flighty." Her tone was steely. "If I ever find out what boy did this to my little girl, I'll horsewhip him."

"It's no mystery," I said, spurred on by my own anger. "Lisa told me. I'm sure she'll tell you." I wanted her to know that I knew.

"What did Lisa tell you?" she asked tensely.

"I can't tell you, Mrs. Landrum. Lisa talked to me in confidence." I didn't want to say more until I had a signed statement from Lisa that could be investigated by the Department of Family and Children Services.

"I'm her mother. I've got a right to know what lies she's spreading around," she declared angrily.

"I don't think Lisa lies. She seems a very honest girl to me."

"Now I believe you're misunderstanding me, Miz Bauer. I think the world of that child," she went on in a syrupy tone. "I just know she *exaggerates*. Like any young girl. They don't mean nothin' by it."

"When are you coming to see her?" I asked. "She'll be back in her room soon. I know she'll want to see you."

"I'd love to come. But I can't leave my little boys so sick. And Bert's coming down with it, too. To tell the truth, I don't feel so good myself. I'll call her later, but it'll be tomorrow before I can get there."

Mrs. Landrum didn't call, and even when an infection delayed Lisa's return home, her mother did not come to visit. The first time she saw Lisa was when I brought her home two days later. Mrs. Landrum was on her way to the grocery store, and even then, with her daughter just arriving home from the hospital, she didn't interrupt her plans.

She hugged Lisa, hardly breaking stride, and said, "Darlin', you just go lie down and rest. I'll be back in a jiffy. I have to run get more Maalox for the boys. And I'm gonna get you some Co-cola. I know how much you like it when you're feelin' puny."

She wouldn't meet my eyes. "I'll be right back," she said, hurrying to her car. "Now, Lisa, don't you worry about the boys. I told them to stay out your way. They're gonna play outside with their G.I. Joes." She looked back at me smugly, having regained her composure. "Miz Bauer, please don't feel like you have to wait. Bert'll be back in a few minutes. He can stay with Lisa until I get back." She hesitated a moment, waiting for my departure.

"I'll be all right, Laura," Lisa said under the pressure of her mother's scrutiny. "You don't have to stay. I know you got a lot to do." She seemed like a little girl, hoping to convince an adult she was old enough to stay home alone. Yet her face looked pale and troubled.

"Good-bye, Miz Bauer. Thanks for helping out," Mrs. Landrum said. "I imagine you'll be gone before I get back."

I carried Lisa's green Rich's department store shopping bag inside. This was as close as she could come to a suitcase.

"I think I'll sit up a bit," Lisa said, sitting down at the greasy Formica table. I propped the door open and switched on the large fan, the unprotected kind children lose fingers in. It was so close in that room you could come in feeling cool and start sweating in minutes.

I couldn't leave her. I had to reach her before her mother returned.

"Lisa, I know it was awful losing the baby. But you're so young. In a way, you're getting a second chance."

"That's right. I'll have lots more chances to have a baby. I guess something must have been wrong inside like the doctor said."

"I wasn't talking about chances to have babies."

She looked at me blankly, as if I were speaking a foreign language.

"You have a chance to finish school. You can be all kinds of things. You don't have to become a mother now."

"But I wanted my baby." Her face crumpled. "More than anything in the whole world. It would have been a beautiful baby."

"Don't you realize all kinds of things could have been wrong with it?" I felt myself trembling as I said the words. "You're not supposed to have a baby with your own brother. It's even against the law. You can't do that again."

"I know." She began to fidget with the propeller of a child's airplane she had picked up off the table. "Let's not talk about it anymore. It's not like we always did it. It was just one night. It was an accident."

An accident. Like tripping on the stairs or losing your lunch money.

"What about other boys, Lisa? Thirteen's awful young to be having sex. Getting pregnant is very serious."

"I guess so," she said dejectedly. Then she smiled and looked up at me brightly. "But Laura, I would have loved that baby *so* much."

"I'm sure you would have." I was touched by a conviction in love from someone who'd known so little of it. "Only love isn't enough. You're still growing up yourself. Take some time to enjoy being a teenager."

"Cindy didn't like being a teenager."

"It might be different for you. Wait and see for yourself."

"All right." She hung her head.

"Lisa, what is it?"

"Nothin'." She wouldn't look at me.

"Come on. *Tell* me," I coaxed her. "Maybe I can help."

"It's just with Daddy dying and Cindy gone, it don't seem like our family anymore."

"I'm sorry." I squeezed her hand. "You must feel very lonesome without them."

"It's even worse for Bert 'cause he worshipped the ground Cindy walked on. If you gave him a piece of candy, he'd turn right around and give it to her. He gave her everything he made in school. Even the shoeshine kit that was meant for a boy." She looked off dreamily into the distance. "He still watches for her. He waits down at the end of the road hopin' she'll get out of somebody's car. He's prob'ly down there now. Waiting for *nothin'*. But of course you can't explain that to him."

My thoughts scared me. But I didn't know if I should speak. I needed someone to advise me, but I was on my own.

"Lisa, do you . . . do you think Cindy and Bert had the same kind of accident before Cindy ran off?"

"Of course not!" she answered in a startled, frightened voice. "Cindy's older than me so she got her own bed. She never had to double up the way I did," she said, pleased she could put my mind at ease. "Besides, I got my own cot now. I don't have to share it with anybody."

I tried to keep my face immobile, but my fear and disgust felt volcanic.

"Don't worry, Laura. It won't happen again. It wouldn't have this time if we didn't have to double up when the little fellas got the chicken pops. Bert had to give up his bed for them. He's got a real weak chest so he couldn't sleep on the cold floor. Now I got Cindy's cot since she's gone. So there won't be no more accidents."

"Lisa, I need you to help me with something before I go."

"Sure. What do you want me to do?" She wiped her sweaty face. "I'm sorry it's so hot in here. You want some ice water?"

"No thank you. But I'd like you to sign this paper for me before I go." I placed it in front of her, hurrying to finish before her mother returned.

"Is this the same paper you brought to the hospital when my stomach hurt too bad to look at it?"

"That's right. It's real simple. It just says, 'My brother Bert Landrum is the father of the baby I lost through miscarriage on October 13, 1973.' And you sign right here."

"Why?"

"So I can take you somewhere else to live. Where you'll be safe and this won't ever happen again."

"Away from my family?"

"At least for now. You need a home where nobody can hurt you. Where you won't have to share a bed with your brother or anybody else. Where there won't be any more 'accidents.'"

"I'm fine living here with my mama," she said protectively. "She *loves* me and so do Matt and Dan and Bert. You got no cause to break up our family." She began to cry and pulled away from me as if I were her dreaded enemy.

"I'm so sorry I upset you." I handed her a tissue and pulled my chair closer, realizing how badly I had frightened her. "Don't worry about signing now. We can talk about it later."

"Lisa, don't you sign nothin'!" I hadn't noticed Mrs. Landrum's car pull up, and unexpectedly she stormed heavily across the room. I tried to grasp the statement, but she intercepted it.

"You two, stay out in the yard," she said sharply to Matt and Dan, who had run inside when they saw her car. She held the paper close, examined it quickly, and crumpled it into a ball.

"Where did you get a crazy idea like that, Miz Bauer?"

I wanted to run, but I couldn't leave Lisa. Mrs. Landrum stood over me threateningly, waiting for an answer.

"Lisa told me who the father of her baby was. She *had* to tell me," I added hurriedly, not wanting Lisa to be blamed.

"Maybe you weren't listening so good. Or maybe Lisa misunderstood your questions. She does that all the time. Idn't that so, Lisa?" She leaned over the girl as she spoke.

Lisa nodded, her eyes on the floor.

"It's real easy to get confused when people have the same names, Miz Bauer." Mrs. Landrum gained confidence as she talked. "See, my son's name is Bert, but that's short for Albert after his daddy. Now the boy Lisa here fooled around with was also named Bert. But his is short for Herbert. And he don't live around here anymore. His folks moved away a few months ago. Nobody knows where they went."

"That's not what Lisa said, Mrs. Landrum," I said firmly. I was determined not to back down. I was prepared to come back with another copy of the statement *and* the sheriff if that was what it took to get Lisa away from there.

"But it's what you *meant* to say, idn't it, honey?" Mrs. Landrum demanded, her arm wrapped firmly around Lisa's shoulders. A threat didn't come through in her tone, but it showed in her eyes, and watching Lisa's face, I could see that she understood her mother's message as well.

Lisa's answer came out in a whisper. "Yes ma'am," she said, looking only at her mother as if I were no longer in the room.

"It's a shame you had to worry for no reason." Mrs. Landrum smiled at me. "Busy as you are. In fact, I reckon we won't be needing to take up more of your time since Lisa's not pregnant anymore. We 'preciate all the Project has done for her though. Idn't that right, Lisa?"

"Yes ma'am," Lisa said, getting up and coming towards me, her eyes full of tears. "Thank you, Laura. I'm gonna miss you."

"But I'll be coming back soon," I said, naturally as I could. "Lisa still needs her follow-up exam with the doctor. And counseling. We have other girls who haven't carried babies to term. There's a progr—"

"That's real nice of you," Mrs. Landrum said. "But I can carry Lisa to the doctor. And I know what to tell her about birth control. Though I can promise you she won't be needing it. She's not gonna make the same mistake again." She motioned to Lisa. "Come on. Let's walk Miz Bauer to her car, and then you can sit out on the glider where there's a breeze." She smiled victoriously. "We been through a tough time, but we'll be fine now."

Just as we were about to part, Bert appeared. "Lisa's back. Lisa's back," he cried out joyfully, running towards her.

Lisa hugged him tenderly as if he were Dan or Matt. Then he ran into the house and came back with a birdhouse. It was painted green and white with a little smiley face above the door.

"I made it for you," he said, rocking back and forth in his excitement. "I missed you." He glowed like a puppy overcome by his master's caress.

"It's real pretty, Bert." Lisa kissed his cheek. "It's the best one you ever made."

"One day I'll make a house for *Lisa*." He gestured grandly with his hands. "A big ole house."

"Come sit down now in the glider," Lisa said. "You're all sweaty." She mopped his face with a tissue. "We'll get you a Coke. Mama just came back from the store."

Mrs. Landrum put her arms possessively around Bert and Lisa. "Matt! Dan!" she called sharply to the little boys. "Y'all come have some Coke."

Lisa smiled and her face relaxed. "It sure is good to be home. You want some Coke before you go, Laura?"

I wanted to stay with her, yet one look at Mrs. Landrum's face told me I'd better leave. I didn't want Lisa to pay later for her mother's obvious displeasure.

"Lisa, honey, I think you've already taken up *more* than enough of Miz Bauer's time. She must be exhausted after all you've put her through."

I tried to soften the hurt that ran across Lisa's face. "It was no trouble, Lisa." I squeezed her hand. "You take good care of yourself, OK?"

"I will. And Laura, will you tell everybody 'good-bye' for me?" Despite her mother's watchful eyes, she hugged me and whispered, "Come see me if you ever come up this way."

As I got in my car, the others went inside for their Cokes. Lisa watched for a minute as I started my car. Then she ran cautiously to my car window, glancing carefully over her shoulder to be certain her mother wasn't looking. She leaned in and whispered, "I didn't get confused before, Laura. It *was* Bert. But since I lost the baby, it don't really matter so much, does it? Mama always says, 'All's well that ends well.'"

CHAPTER 19

Your Dan-Dan

Rita Washburn tiptoed slowly down the stairs, stopping each time they creaked, and then crept silently, shoes in hand, through the dark hallway to the kitchen. Smokey, the black, mostly Chow dog, followed excitedly after her, expecting Rita to take out something to eat. She could hardly see him in the dark but felt his cold nose against her calves. He began to yip excitedly.

"Shh! Hush, Smokey." She tossed him a chunk of Velveeta cheese to quiet him. She slipped on her blue Keds as she started out the door. Smokey immediately began to whine.

"Hush, right now!" She stepped back inside to quiet him, but when he continued to whine, she tossed him a slice of white bread. He took it gingerly in his soft mouth, a retriever's mouth as her daddy had described it, and began to nibble at it. While he was occupied, she ran quickly out the door.

Danny had pulled in behind the pine thicket and dimmed his lights. He opened the door on the passenger's side when he saw her coming. "Hey, baby," he whispered as he pulled her across the car seat almost into his lap. "How's my girl tonight?" She could smell beer on his breath as he kissed her. She shivered in the cold November wind.

"You better get out of here quick," she said, snuggling close to him. "Smokey's gonna start barking any minute."

"Let's go," he said eagerly, scattering gravel as they scratched off down the road.

"I didn't mean like *that*." She fell back against the seat. "You know Mama's a light sleeper. I bet you woke her up."

"Aw . . . come on." He pulled her close and kissed her lightly on the nose. "Even if she heard it, she wouldn't know it was us. Lots of people come down this road."

She turned the dial on the radio trying to find some music she liked. "Daddy will kill me if he finds out."

"How's he gonna find out? By the time he gets off his shift, you'll be safe in bed." He winked at her. "Besides, I'm the one who should be scared. If he finds out, it's my butt that's gonna get kicked." He kissed her deep and hard. "Now *stop* worrying. I said I'd take care of you, didn't I?"

He waited for her to say something.

"Didn't I?"

"You said you'd stopped drinking, *too.*" She slid back over to the passenger's side.

"Well, I practically have." He reached for her. "Now come on, baby. Don't be mad. This is our last night together for a long time. Don't be mean to me," he pleaded in baby talk. It was their special game, made even funnier by how big he was. "Don't be mad at your Dan-Dan."

"I'm not mad." She moved closer to him and pressed her cheek against his. She was pleased to find it smooth, another sign of his love for her. He'd shaved late at night and put on English Leather cologne. She loved the smell of it, first on him, and afterwards on herself.

He lit a cigarette. "You want one?"

"Not now," she said, watching him exhale. "Maybe later."

"I thought we'd drive up behind the drive-in. Nobody'll be out there this time of night." He laughed slyly. "Unless they're doing what we're doing."

"Danny, I'm not staying if there's anybody back there."

"Nobody's gonna be there, Rita." He stroked her cheek. "Why can't you take a joke? I wish you'd have some of this." He took a beer can from between his legs. "It'll help relax you."

"I don't want any," she said, pushing the can away. "I wish you wouldn't either."

"It don't hurt me none." He took a last drink and tossed the can out the window. "I never get drunk. I just have a good time. Why are you such a worrywart anyway?"

She didn't answer him because it did no good. They had argued about his drinking ever since they started going steady. She turned up the radio and closed her eyes to the gentle sound of Gordon Lightfoot singing "If You Could Read My Mind." She loved that song and the way Lightfoot reached the high notes but still sounded so husky and masculine at the same time. She wished she was in a car with him.

"Don't go to sleep on me," Danny said, giving her a nudge.

"I won't," she said dreamily. "But if I do, you can wake me up."

"I'll wake you up all right," he said with a gruffness that excited her.

Soon they reached the turn off for the drive-in. It was scary with all the lights off. "I don't know about this, Danny," she said.

"I told you, Rita." He was getting impatient. "Nobody's gonna bother us. Besides, this is the last time for I don't know how long. I've *got* to be close to you." Then his play voice returned. "What's a matter? Don't you want your Dan-Dan?"

They parked and Danny cut the lights, plunging them into a blanket of darkness. It was too cloudy for stars, and Rita couldn't see the moon. It was so deserted she felt a shiver run through her and was almost sorry there were no other cars around.

"Hey, what's the matter?" He put his arm around her.

"I don't know. Guess I'm just a little jumpy. It's so dark here."

He nuzzled her ear and whispered, "Let's get in back where I can hold you. That's all you need."

He folded down the back seat of the station wagon and spread a blanket. He got an extra one out to use as a cover. They lay down together and he rolled on top of her, careful to keep his weight from crushing her. He'd been a football star his senior year, and even a year later looked as if he'd just stepped off the field.

"Jeez, I'm gonna miss you," he said.

"Not half as much as I'll miss you." She felt tears coming on. "At least you're going somewhere."

"I'm going in the *army*, Rita. It's not a vacation."

"But that's why I wanted to get married." She buried her face in his neck. "Then I could go with you."

"Not to basic. You got to finish school anyway. After I get my orders, there'll be plenty of time to get married."

"You sound just like Daddy." She pulled away from him.

"I'm sorry, baby." He stroked her hair. "I wish I didn't have to go. If I hadn't wrecked my knee, I would've got a football scholarship for sure. I could have seen you every weekend like we planned. But that's the breaks." He lit a cigarette. "The army don't think I'm too broke up to be useful. I'll get through basic, and then once I get leave, we'll get married."

"You promise you'll come back for me?"

"Of course I will." He kissed her forehead and offered her a drag from his cigarette. "You think your Dan-Dan would leave his baby?"

They undressed quickly and slid under the blanket. She was glad of the darkness since she couldn't help feeling shy in front of him. He always watched so hungrily. She shivered until she was in his arms.

He hugged her tightly to his muscular chest. She felt safe and warm, but also frightened. "Danny, it's not the same with you going away."

"What's not the same?" he asked her, but she felt he wasn't really listening. His hands were moving over her, and he seemed far away.

"You know. Doin' it." She turned on her side. "If something happens you'll be so far away. I'll be all alone."

He stopped caressing her and looked down at her intently. "Now wait a second. Has anything ever gone wrong before?"

She shook her head "no."

"Am I careful?"

"Yes."

"Do I love you?"

"Yes."

"Do you love me?"

"You know I do." She threw her arms around his neck.

"Then let's make love. I don't know when we'll get another chance."

"It just don't seem right sneaking around and doing it in the back of a car."

"You never made such a big deal about it before," he said insistently. Then his face softened, and he spoke tenderly, "But I sure don't want you doing nothin' you don't want to. You know I'm not that kind of guy." His eyes and voice beseeched her. "Baby, you *know* I love you, and I'm gonna marry you just as soon as I can."

"I'm scared, Danny." She spoke into his chest. "You might never come back, and I can't live without you." She started to cry.

"Nothin' will keep me from coming back to you." He kissed her nose. "You're my girl. We're gonna get married and have our honeymoon." He wiped away her tears. "You want me to take you home? Maybe this wasn't such a good idea."

"But it's our last night."

"Well, what do you want to do?" He smiled tenderly down at her. "I'm not gonna twist your arm."

"Love me," she said. "But be careful."

They began to move together. She breathed in his English Leather and let herself get lost in their heat. In the darkness. In the power of his body. Suddenly he pulled away from her. She heard him gasp. Then he was quiet. She kissed the back of his neck.

"That was close," he said. "You felt so good I almost forgot to—you know—"

"Danny, you didn't . . . ?" she asked, horrified.

"Of course not. What kind of fool you think I am? I love you," he said, gently holding her head in his hands. "Don't you know your Dan-Dan loves you?"

Three weeks later he was dead.

"The drill sergeant was amazed," his mother said tearfully when she called. "Said he'd never seen such a fine physical specimen. He told me everybody liked Danny, and he would have been a good soldier. But he never got the chance." She blew her nose. "It happened with no warning. They were doing calisthenics. Just routine exercises they do every day. All of a sudden Danny collapsed. They thought he'd fainted from the heat. That happens time to time.

"So they tried to revive him. The medics tried CPR, and then they rushed him to the hospital. Three different doctors worked on him. But he was already gone. They think it was a heart attack. After doing all those stadiums and playing so much football, you'd never think a few calisthenics would have hurt him." She began to cry again. "It's just not fair. He had his whole life ahead of him. Now there's nothing left of my Danny. And there'll never be another boy like him.

"I always figured y'all would marry," she said in a trembling voice. "But now he's gone, honey. You and me'll just have to get used to it." She broke down again. "I don't know how. I got a letter he wrote right before he died. He said to be sure and give you his love and tell you he'd call you Friday night. That's tomorrow night," she sobbed. Then the connection was broken, and Rita was left standing there, stunned, holding the horrible receiver in her hand.

She ran outside. She had to get away. She couldn't stay in the house with the dreadful news that he was dead. She sat on the porch swing where they had rocked on warm summer nights. She pushed Smokey away angrily when he tried to jump up beside her.

She tried to comprehend *never*. He would never sit beside her again. She would never marry him. She would never marry anyone. She knew it. Not for her whole life. She would wear his high school ring on a chain around her neck even when she was an old lady.

She would attend other people's weddings. She might even catch a bridal bouquet. Those who didn't know about Danny would see her pretty face and youthful figure—because she would never let herself go—and wonder why she'd never married or even dated. Until the word would get around. "You know, she loved a boy who died," people would whisper. "She still wears his ring. She won't even look at nobody else."

She would go to their baby showers and smile and later coo over and cradle her friends' newborns in her arms. Everyone would say it was a shame she didn't have babies when you saw how good she was with them. But she never would.

Unless. She hadn't thought about it while she was missing him so much, and he hadn't been there to love her. But she did feel kind of funny. Her period had always come on like clockwork before, but now it was two weeks late. She had figured she was just upset from missing him. But now she didn't know.

She felt like she was about to jump in cold mountain water. Her daddy would yell and her mama would cry. She didn't know what his mother would say. She might never speak to her again.

Rita put her hand on her stomach. It felt the same as usual. Danny had always loved how flat and smooth it was. And he'd been positive he knew what he was doing. But she pressed harder. She could feel nothing beneath her hand except her own body. But she knew, just as certain as if a doctor had told her. She figured it was one of those things a woman just *knows*. Like when you first feel womanhood stir inside you when a boy touches your hand. Before it would have been just a sweaty hand holding yours, only suddenly something moves through you and you know he isn't just a boy and you're not just a girl anymore.

She accepted Danny was dead, but he wasn't really gone. She kissed his ring on the chain around her neck and felt that he was living inside her. He had always called her his baby. And now, she guessed, he would be hers.

CHAPTER 20

The Sampler

"Here's a dollar," Nell's mama said. "Go buy yourself a movie magazine or anything you like."

She was wearing blue stretch pants and a tight blue knit top. Her hair was fresh from the beauty shop, frosted and sprayed. Nell's stepfather jammed his hands into his pockets, jingling the car keys inside. He didn't understand why they couldn't just give the kid a dollar and get the hell out instead of discussing it all afternoon.

"Now don't you sit around all afternoon," Nell's mama told her. "The kids'll be at that party so you don't have to fool with them. Go out and get you something. Do you good to get out of the house." Nell's mama smiled nervously. She wished Nell would say something, but she hardly ever did unless you asked a question she had to answer "yes" or "no."

Nell kept on brushing her hair. She'd heard somewhere that if you brushed it one hundred strokes it would grow quicker. Ever since the last haircut her mama had given her, Nell's thin, dark hair had hung in limp strands around her face. It was just long enough to tuck behind her ears. She had wanted to refuse to let her mama cut it but had been afraid of making her angry. Anything—even looking horrible—was better than making her mama angry.

"I sure wish she'd make some friends," she heard her mama say to her stepfather as they were walking out. "Since we moved up here, she hasn't met nobody. 'Course she never had friends back home either. She just don't mix."

"Like folks say you can give somebody lots of chances," he answered, "but if they're not willin' to take 'em—"

"Oh, she's willin' enough. She just ain't a pretty child. There's no way to make up for that."

After they were gone, Nell sat for a long time examining her dollar bill. She decided she wanted to buy something to make her hair curl up. But she figured that would cost more than a dollar. If she saved the dollar, then maybe sometime her mama would give her another one and she'd have enough. Only she knew her mama would get mad if she didn't spend this one today. She might even take it back. So Nell walked down to the superette to see what she could buy. It was a small store with a gas pump out front and inside they had groceries, cigarettes, candy, Cokes, beer—all kinds of stuff. The home ec teacher had said not to shop there because you paid much more than you would if you went to a larger store. Nell figured this lady didn't know it was too far for most folks to get to a supermarket if they didn't have a car. Even if somebody could catch a ride to a big store, they'd have no way to get back home with all their bags.

When she went inside, the counterman was talking to a man who was buying some B.C. powders. Nell strolled over to the corner with the shampoos and conditioners, but there wasn't anything for a dollar. She guessed she'd have to buy candy or a magazine or maybe a little jar of hand lotion.

"What're you studyin' over there? Is there somethin' in that corner I don't know about?" the counterman asked playfully after the other customer left the store.

Nell laughed. She'd learned if she laughed, people didn't push her to say anything. They left her alone. She prayed somebody else would come in so he wouldn't ask her anything else.

But he called to her. "C'mon over and talk a minit." He leaned back against the counter. "Business is slower than Heinz catsup. So I guess I'll have me a cup of coffee. You want one?"

She had to go over. She knew he would keep talking to her until she answered.

"You drink coffee?" He was preparing to pour her a cup.

"No, sir."

"Well, here. I bet you'll like this better." He reached in the glass case and brought out a huge jar of stick candy. "You take whatever kind you like."

She chose a cherry one. She thought it was real nice of him to give her a ten-cent stick of candy for free so she didn't have to break her dollar. Even if he was a grownup, he smiled so friendly and watched her so carefully, she felt like somebody real important. She guessed he was about her stepfather's age. He had brown eyes like hers; only his didn't look like mud. Her mama said any eyes but blue came out looking that way.

"You live close by, honey?"

"Up there." She pointed to the hill.

"I figured you did. 'Cause I've seen you come in here lots of times. Sometimes with your mama. Sometimes with a bunch of kids. Your brothers and sisters?"

She nodded "yes," too shy to say anything more.

"Yeah, I thought you was the big sister. The one in charge."

She smiled again. It was all she could think to do.

"You got such a pretty smile." He looked at her real hard. "I bet you got a whole string of boyfriends."

She looked down. *Why did everybody have to bring up boyfriends,* she wondered. *Why were they always harping on that?*

"Well, if you don't now," he said, taking in her downcast eyes, "you take my word, you will soon. Sometimes fellas are slow gettin' started, but once they do—" He smiled at her. "You'll have so many to choose from, it'll make you dizzy."

"Nell has cooties! Nell has cooties!" She remembered how girls used to chant that at recess. They ran around her shouting the hateful words, and nobody would sit next to her in class.

"Didn't nobody ever tell you to take a bath?" one girl asked contemptuously, holding her nose.

Nell knew she didn't really smell. She took a bath every day.

"Y'all don't be so mean," Brad Berry admonished. He was class president. "She cain't help the way she is."

"Fifteen years old in the seventh grade," Mary Lou Pickens exclaimed. "I'd be too ashamed to show my face."

They always laughed when she read aloud. By herself she could read the words just fine, but in front of them, knowing they were all listening, waiting for her to trip up, she stuttered and missed every other word. She started skipping school and hid down in the woods. Then the truant officer called her mama, and her mama gave her a licking with a green switch. When that did no good, her stepfather beat her with his belt. But that was still better than going to school.

"Hey, what you say we go in the back?" The counterman pointed to a door in the rear of the store. "Don't look like folks are shoppin' right now. It's much nicer back there. We could sit an' talk instead of standing here in the middle of the store."

She walked behind him. He was such a nice man, and he really liked her. She couldn't believe her good luck. He wanted to talk to her just like she was a grown woman.

He shut the door behind them and pulled the chain on a single light bulb, which hung from the ceiling. She looked around the small storage room filled with crates and boxes and a metal table right in the middle. She didn't think it looked like such a nice place to talk.

"Just boost yourself up on that table, Nell." He smiled again, staring at her real hard. "Now ain't that more comfortable? I *sure* would like to get to know you better, honey. Would you like a Coke or something?"

Nell shook her head "no." It made her nervous trying to carry on a grownup conversation, and she worried if she drank anything she might throw up.

He climbed up and sat right beside her. "Yessir, I sure do like talking to you," he said. He slipped his arm around her real gently and squeezed her shoulder. "I like a woman who ain't always jabberin'."

Nell thought he was friendlier than any grownup she'd ever known, and she was sure he liked her. He kept smiling at her and then all of a sudden he started kissing her on the cheek and the forehead, and then he held her in his arms. In her whole life, no one had never whispered to her that way or even wanted to hold her hand. She'd always thought it would feel awful being with a man that way, but she felt comfortable being close to him.

"You sure do feel nice!" he said softly. She felt his hand slip under her shirt. When he unhooked her bra, she thought maybe she shouldn't let him, but it didn't seem to matter with just the two of them there.

"You're *all* woman, Nell," he told her excitedly. He touched her breasts with the tips of his fingers until she tingled in a way she hadn't known she could. "I want to see all of you, Nell." His hands caressed her. "You wouldn't mind if we slipped that. . ." He eased her shirt off and then, smiling, hugged her to him. She could feel his heart beating fast and strong. Then he lay back and pulled her on top of him. He pressed up against her holding her real tight. Then he moved one arm from around her and reached down and unbuckled his belt. When she heard him unzip his fly, she started to feel embarrassed. She didn't want to look, but he said, "Look here, Nell. Look what you do to me."

She looked down and saw it was sticking straight up. She'd never seen one before except her little brothers' when she took them to the bathroom to pee. And theirs were so tiny. But this one was big and ugly, she thought.

"Go ahead, touch it," he whispered. "It won't hurt you."

She felt scared. She knew she shouldn't touch that big ole thing.

"Here," he said, taking her hand. "Just put your fingers right here." When she hesitated, he eased her hand around it, all the while smiling like it made him real happy. "Now feel the end of it."

She felt scared, but she did as he said. A few drops of something came out. She thought he was going to pee in her hand. She couldn't believe he'd really do that, but she didn't know what else it could be.

"That's only love juice, Nell," he said, laughing at the concerned expression she thought she had concealed. He kissed her cheek. "Don't you fret. It can't hurt you." He kicked off his pants. It was the first time Nell had ever seen a naked man.

"You've never done this before, have you, Nell?"

She shook her head. She wasn't sure just what he meant by "this," but she'd never done anything like what they were doing.

"Don't you worry 'bout a thing, Nell. Everybody's gotta have a first time, and you're a whole lot better off with me, instead of some fool boy who don't know what he's doing. Don't you worry. I know what I'm doing."

Then she was on her back and he was on top of her. "Just relax," he said. "I'll take care of everything." He took it in his hand and rubbed it against her, then into her just a little. "Now this might hurt at first, Nell. I'm not gonna lie to you. But what comes after'll sure be worth it." Then he raised himself up and pushed it into her harder and harder.

She wanted to cry out and tell him to stop because it sure didn't feel *good*. She knew there wasn't room for that big ole thing inside of her. She was going to tell him so, but then he leaned over and kissed her. All of him was pressing and moving into her. He was panting and gasping until she was afraid he was having some kind of attack. There was a sharp pain like something tearing inside of her. She tried to draw back. "Easy, easy. There now," he said. "We done it, Nell. We done it." There was victory in his voice. "It won't never hurt you no more." She felt him thrust deeply. She wondered where it went.

He moved up and down, pounding into her until he grunted real loud and suddenly pulled out. She felt something gooey on her leg. He lay real still for a moment. Then he reached down and pulled a checked handkerchief from the pocket of his pants. After he wiped himself off, he wiped her. He held it out so she could see the blood.

"Don't let that scare you," he said. "It happens the first time." He cleaned her thigh where it was messy. "See, just like I promised. Pulled out just in time." He pulled on his pants and gathered her clothes for her. "I sure wish we could stay here for a while, but I got to get back out there. Boss would fire me right off if he walked in and I wasn't there." He kissed her. "How're you doin', honey? You gonna come see me again?"

Nell could feel herself blushing. She was embarrassed to still be naked in front of him, and couldn't think of a thing to say.

"You know how much I want you to, don't you? Any night you want. You come by 'bout an hour after supper. That way they'll already have come in for their cigarettes and won't be back for beer 'til about ten o'clock. You'll come back, won't you, Nell?"

"Yes," she said, but she looked away from him. She was afraid he was laughing at her like all the rest of them and didn't mean any of it.

"Say, Nell," he said, walking her to the front, "what did you want when you came in here, anyway?"

"I dunno. I was just lookin'." She didn't want to tell him she didn't have enough money for what she really wanted.

"Now come on. There must've been something you needed."

She didn't say anything, but wondered if he could guess what she wanted by looking at her stringy hair. She hung her head to avoid his eyes.

"Well here," he said smiling. "You take these." He opened the counter and took out the candy jar. He put a bunch of the many-colored sticks of candy in a brown bag and handed it to her. "There you go. You gave me a little sweetness, so here's some for you."

That night she lay in bed thinking about him, the candy stashed beneath her bed. Several times during the night, she reached down as quietly as she possibly could so the little ones wouldn't hear the rustling of the plastic wrappers. She'd pull a candy stick out and suck on it, not knowing until it was in her mouth what flavor it was. After a while she reached down to touch herself. She never had before. It hadn't seemed like there was any reason to.

It was sore. She guessed it was supposed to be the first time. She closed her eyes and wondered how long it took before they told you they loved you more than anyone else in the world. And you knew it was settled that you'd always be together.

The next day she couldn't go see him. Her mama was home all day, and Nell made her angry first thing in the morning.

"What did you get with that dollar I gave you?" her mama asked at breakfast. "Did you buy a magazine?"

"No ma'am."

"You get somethin' t'eat?"

"No ma'am." She tried hard to think of something that would please her mama. She didn't want to show her the candy sticks. There were so many of them her mama would know she couldn't have gotten them for a dollar.

"Did you buy *anything*?"

"No ma'am," she admitted, since she had nothing to show her.

"I declare, you won't even *try* to cheer yourself up," her mama exclaimed in exasperation. "So you hold on to that dollar, Nell. It'll be a coon's age before I give you another one." Then there was warning in her voice. "You better shape up, girl. Tonight's Tupperware. I don't want you mopin' around my customers. You keep goin' around with that sour look on your face, it'll freeze on you."

The next night her stepfather worked late, and her mama and the kids went to a concert at the high school. She waited until right after suppertime to get ready. She brushed her hair and washed her face. She put on a tiny bit of her mama's perfume, as much as she dared use without her mama noticing, and then she walked slowly down the hill. She'd never had a fella to go see before so she felt nervous. He might laugh at her and say he hadn't really wanted to see her again.

She felt silly for worrying once she saw his face. He smiled real big the second she walked in. "Boy am I glad to see you, Nell!" he said.

No one else was in the store. She felt a warm circle of happiness just like the first time.

"I was afraid you weren't coming back," he said, looking at her in a hungry way she had seen only in the movies. "You want a Coke?"

She was glad to have one. She wasn't thirsty, but it made her feel more comfortable having something to hold.

"Yessir," he said, reaching for her hand. "It sure is good to see you."

When they went in the back, it was easier. She didn't feel scared of him this time or of *it*. He pulled a sleeping bag and a blanket out from beneath one of the crates. "I figured we'd be more comfortable this way," he said. He locked the door behind them. "We'll just pretend we're campin' out."

As they lay down, she wondered if this would be the time he would tell her. If he would look down at her and say he loved her and he always would.

"You make a man feel like a man, Nell."

She felt herself blushing.

"Damned if you don't make me feel like I'm twenty again," he said hungrily.

They were just getting started when they heard the bell ring, signaling that someone had entered the store.

"Hell," he said. "Prob'ly all they want is a nickel's worth of bubble gum. Fool kids." He pulled on his pants and quickly fastened his belt. He smoothed the blanket over her. "You just close your eyes, honey. I'll be back before you have time to miss me."

She could hear him talking and the sound of girls' voices. Then the register rang, and she heard the bell ring again as the door closed.

"I wish we could have reg'lar time together," he said, when he took her in his arms again. "Instead of stealin' it this way. Maybe we will one day."

Nell smiled because she knew this was it. *This must be how they told you. Before they actually said they loved you, they led up to it like this.*

She was only slightly tender as he entered her. She wasn't sure what she was supposed to feel, though she could tell she didn't like it the way he did. She figured maybe having it stick out that way made men feel more, since from the way he carried on, she saw how much he enjoyed it.

"You're my little apple dumplin'," he said, kissing her throat. "You're my girl."

I wonder why he wants me, she thought. *He's so nice. He could have one of those girls with all the pretty blonde hair. Why does he waste his time on me?*

"Sweets for my sweet," he said after they were back out in the store. From under the counter, he took out a big red satin heart inscribed in fancy letters: *Valentine Chocolate Sampler.* "It ain't Valentine's yet, but you're still *my* valentine."

She couldn't believe it. This was close. The next time she knew he would say he loved her out loud.

"Good night," he said. "You hurry home before your mama misses you. There's lots of t'morrows."

Nell couldn't sleep that night. *He loves me,* she thought. *Mama don't know nothin' about it. She figures nobody can love me. But he does.*

When the breathing in the room sounded deep all around her, she reached under the bed and touched the satin heart. She traced the red velvet design with her fingertips, conjuring him up, remembering the tenderness of his voice. He'd said, "There'll be plenty of t'morrows." *He will tell me that he loves me,* she thought. *Mama and everybody else will hear him. If they don't believe him, he'll say it again.*

A few days later, Nell was washing the breakfast dishes when her mother returned from shopping.

"How come you're just gettin' to those now?" her mama asked irritably, setting down her shopping bags. "You been actin' awful dreamy lately. Make sure you scrub those good." She poured herself a cup of the last breakfast coffee and sat down at the kitchen table.

"They got a new man workin' at Bradshaw's," she reported matter-of-factly. "I didn't go in there today, but I heard all about it at the drugstore."

I must not show it, Nell thought. *If I ask too much, she will know.* Though her hands trembled, she began to scrub another egg-encrusted plate.

"You remember the fella who worked there?"

Nell nodded "yes," still careful to look down at the dishes and away from her mama's questioning eyes.

"Always seemed like such a nice fella, but they fired him." Her mama laughed her hard, sharp laugh. "Looks like he had everybody fooled. You know T. K. Bradshaw, the old man? Well, he went by the store yesterday to look things over. The ole tightwad's always checkin' fifty times a day on folks that work for him. Well, about seven o'clock in the morning, I reckon he got more than he bargained on. That counterman of his was in the back room lying there with some young girl. Both of them naked as the day they was born."

Nell sat on the toilet waiting. *It will come,* she thought. *It must come.* She wiped hard. Then harder. *It must come. He promised he took care of everything.*

"You got some kind of bladder infection?" her mama asked when she came out. "I'll have to carry you to the doctor if you don't stop spendin' so much time on the potty. It's gettin' where nobody else in the house can have a turn."

Nell tried not to, but she couldn't help blushing. She worried all day and tried not to spend as much time in the bathroom. She couldn't afford to make her mama more suspicious. *It's got to come,* she told herself. *It's prob'ly just missin' him that's making it late.*

She ate the chocolates one by one, flattening the foil and putting the smooth gold wrappers in the bottom of the candy box. *It's all I have left of him,* she thought. She lay in the dark, never biting the candy, but sucking it slowly until it finally dissolved.

He will write, she told herself. *When they fired him he had to leave quick before he had a chance to tell me. Whoever she was they caught him with, he didn't love her. He was just with her because it was one of the days when I couldn't get away to see him. It sticks out and so they have to do it. They can't help it. But he didn't love her. As soon as he can, he will write and send for me, and I'll marry him. Mama won't believe it. She says nobody with mud eyes can get married. But he will come for me. He said there'd be lots of t'morrows.*

"Where'd you get this?" Nell's mama walked into the living room holding the candy sampler. "You heard me," she said angrily, when Nell didn't answer. "Where'd it come from?"

Nell was sitting on the floor helping her little sister with her paper dolls. She kept her eyes on the dress she had been cutting out. *I won't talk,* she thought. *If I look away, maybe she will just hit me right away. She will hit me hard a few times, and then it will be over.*

"There must be something wrong about it or you wouldn't be hiding it under your bed!" Nell's mama's voice grew louder. Her sister ran out of the room. "Did you steal this?" Mrs. Walton grabbed Nell by the shoulders, pulling her up from the floor and shaking her back and forth. "Did you? Did you shame the whole fam'ly?" She slapped Nell across the mouth so hard she tasted blood as one of her front teeth cut her bottom lip. "Answer me, you little thief!" She slapped her again, leaving a red mark on Nell's cheek.

"No. He give it to me." It slipped out before she could stop it. *Now she'll know,* Nell thought. *She'll spoil everything.*

"Who gave *you* a box of candy?" Her mother slapped Nell again. "I never seen nobody come by the house for you. You been sneakin' off somewhere to meet some boy?" Her voice turned shrill when Nell wouldn't answer. "Answer me!" she screamed in Nell's ear.

Nell said nothing and lowered her head to prepare for more blows. *If mama hits me hard a few times, she will stop,* she thought. *She will have enough.*

Her mama opened the box and dumped it out on the floor. There were just a few candies left. Nell snatched them up, clutching them to her like jewels. "So you *have* been sneaking out," her mother accused, kicking the red box and scattering the precious, gold wrappers Nell had lovingly saved. "When I'm so busy I don't know what to do, you been runnin' out to meet somebody who can't even come get you at the house like a decent boy."

She slapped Nell harder, her rage driving her on. "Now you tell me who he is. I don't intend to ask again. You tell me right now!"

"He's gone," Nell said, choking back her tears. "But he's gonna send for me."

"Who, may I ask, would send for *you*?" her mother asked cuttingly.

Nell tried to answer, but no words would come out.

"Don't you stare at me with those mud eyes." Her mother kicked the empty candy box across the room. "For the last time, who is he, and why did he give you this big box of candy?"

"Because he loves me," Nell managed to whisper.

"Who loves you?" her mother asked disdainfully. "Have you been fooling around with somebody?"

Nell stared at the floor.

Mrs. Walton picked up the box and examined it. She couldn't understand why anybody would give Nell such a large box of candy when there were so many pretty, popular girls around. Though it was just old Valentine candy left from the year before. She could see the box was faded from sitting on the shelf so long.

She stared down at Nell while she fit the pieces fit together. All the time Nell was spending in the bathroom. How she'd started sneaking off. The way she was always mooning around like a fool. She stood over Nell and looked her straight in the eye. "When did you have your last period?"

Nell bit her lip but couldn't keep from crying. Before she knew it, she was sobbing. *Whatever she says, whatever she does,* she told herself, *it doesn't matter. He will come back for me.*

"Are you pregnant?" She studied Nell, looking her up and down and side to side. "You answer me! You little whore. You—" Mrs. Walton grabbed Nell's shoulders and shook her back and forth. "After I did *everything* for you. Tried getting' you to mix with the young folks at church. Invited girls over to the house for you.

"Even though it was like driving a mule. But still I kept trying. Only you couldn't act right. You had to go sneakin' out. Nice girls know better. Or at least if they do it, they get them a husband. They don't sell themselves for a box of old stale candy." She shoved Nell away in disgust. "You're nothin' but a nasty little whore. You ain't no daughter of mine. You ain't nothin'. Nothin'!"

Nell ran out of the house. The screen door slammed behind her. She went down the hill, across the road, running hard, breathing so fast it hurt. She didn't stop until she was safe in the woods. She hunkered down behind a big poplar tree, hugging it, trying to hide herself.

He will write, she consoled herself. Mama will be sorry. *When we are married, I will never call her. Not even at Christmas. I will get my hair done, and one day we'll come back here. We won't call ahead or nothin'. We'll just drive up one day in a big car and bring Kentucky Fried Chicken for everybody. She won't have nothin' to say. She'll have to admit how wrong she was. About him. About me. About everything.*

It started to get dark. Night was falling fast. The wind cut through Nell's sweatshirt. She had sat stiffly for hours, only getting up one time when she had to pee. In the darkening twilight, the shadows came down all around her, but they didn't frighten her. They were covering her, protecting her. *I won't go back,* she thought. *They won't find me here. But he will find me. Soon as he can. He will come back. He will come back for me.* She closed her eyes and bowed her head and tried not to hear her mama's voice piercing the darkness and her sanctuary.

. . . .

CHAPTER 21

Something Borrowed

As I parked in front of the plain white church the morning of the wedding, I considered how little Mavis had to look forward to in marriage. "At least it'll get me out of *here*," she had told me when we talked it over weeks earlier as I dropped her off at her parents' house. "I won't have to listen to Daddy preaching all the time, and I'll have a place where I can do what I want."

But as it turned out, Mavis would not be getting a new home after she got married. Instead, Willie would be moving into her parents' home. Since Mavis shared a bedroom, and actually a *bed,* with a sister, it seemed likely she and Willie might not even get to sleep together.

"It won't be easy," she'd told me. "But it's better than going to his mother's. You wouldn't believe that place."

Mavis's house was so hot and airless it made me feel faint. Palmetto bugs bigger than my thumb scurried out of the closets and over our shoes as we sat talking. There were always so many people around, we seemed to be competing for oxygen. I'd shuddered, wondering how bad Willie's home must be if she preferred her own.

And Mavis ran Willie down whenever she talked about him. "All he's really good at is football," she told me before she had made up her mind. "He don't know nothin' else. Why would I want to marry somebody like that?"

"You don't have to do it if you feel that way, Mavis," I had advised her. "Getting married is supposed to be something you're happy about."

"For people like you," she said acidly.

I could understand her bitterness. Living in her parents' house with a new husband, without even a room to call their own, sounded miserable. And being stuck at home with a baby was far from the free life Mavis had hoped for when she dreamed of seeing the world in the army or living in an apartment with the city of Atlanta unfolding before her with countless, imagined attractions. Instead, her future would be confined to washing mounds of diapers while she cared for her baby and other children in the household, as well as performing whatever cleaning duties at home or the church that her parents demanded. She might still have a night out with Willie at the café where he had defended her honor, but she would not be visiting upscale clubs with exotic, icy drinks or spending her weekends at Atlanta's newest shopping malls with her friends.

"Being pregnant turns you into an old lady," she had announced at a group session in the Project office. "Your clothes don't fit. It ruins your figure. Everybody wants you to rest like you're sick or dyin' and you're s'posed to eat all this food you can't stand. But *nothin'* changes for your boyfriend," she went on angrily. "He can keep eating whatever crap he wants to and stay out drinkin' all night. Not that *you'd* know anything about that." Her mocking tone had all the girls staring at me, wondering how I'd deal with her disdain. "Since you never want to do anything. Except read all your old books."

"You don't know what I *know*, Mavis, or what I deal with at home," I snapped at her, my anger bubbling up like a pot on the stove with the heat set too high. "But I don't mind telling all of you what I *believe*." I was so worked up I even got up from the circle, propelled by my frustration.

The girls watched me in surprise since I usually ignored Mavis's outbursts in front of our group. Susan looked worried, as if I were an actor who had suddenly gone completely off script.

"Life isn't fair," I admitted. "It never has been and it never will be. And Mavis isn't the first person who's felt angry about it," I continued in a calmer voice. "Why do some people get cancer or get struck by lightning?" I asked them, not expecting an answer. *Or get sent to concentration camps where everyone they love is murdered?* I thought to myself.

"There's no answer. So we keep going no matter what comes at us." I stopped, reading the distress still evident in their faces. "I'm sorry. I shouldn't have yelled. But Mavis, y'all aren't the only ones who've made bad choices or got stuck with someone else's. You're right. Men don't get pregnant. But they still put up with their share of sh—you know what I mean."

I stopped just in time. But they all laughed. They knew what I'd been about to say.

"You don't understand, Laura," Mavis said brokenheartedly as I drove her home later that afternoon. "I had no choice about getting married. I see the way you look at me sometime like you think I'm selfish. But I'm stuck. And you don't get that I always have been. I can't let this baby run around with no daddy and everybody calling it a bastard. The preacher's bastard grandbaby."

"I'm so sorry." I didn't know what else to say. It was much too late to talk about other options.

"Laura, I wanted more than Willie." Mavis looked more disappointed than angry. As if she'd opened a Christmas package that was supposed to hold a stereo and instead found a vacuum cleaner.

"What *did* you want, Mavis? It's not like you won't get another chance. You're smart. You can go back to school and train to be—"

"No, I can't! It's all over. I'll *never*—" She stopped, and went silent. She had seemed ready to tell me something important but had changed her mind.

"Go on, Mavis," I tried to encourage her. "What is it?"

"I wanted to get the hell out of here and never come back. And now a broken rubber's messed up my whole life." She pounded her fist into the hot car seat between us. "I wasn't gonna be like Mama, marrying young, having so many babies she can't keep all our names straight. And here I am startin' out just like her."

"Then talk to the doctor about birth control. Go back to school. Train to be whatever you want to be," I pleaded with her. "Your life isn't over."

"Please don't start another one of your sermons. It's too hot for that," she protested, fanning herself with a magazine. "I get enough of them at home anyway."

I took the hint and stopped talking. I turned up the air-conditioning and tuned the radio to an R&B station Mavis enjoyed. I kept my eyes on the road.

"Maybe later on, I might try being a police officer," she confided after a few minutes. "I'm good at makin' people listen and breakin' up fights." She smiled playfully. "Not just startin' them."

"That's good to know. I was worried you wanted to take me out earlier." I smiled to let her know I was only teasing. "I do see the leader in you, Mavis. The other girls all look up to you."

"You really think so?" she asked gratefully. Then she turned down the radio. "I'm sorry about before. Those classes make me ornery, but I didn't mean anything by it. If I didn't know better, I'd think I was getting my period."

The church marquee admonished, "Let Jesus In, and Fear Not Sin. From a Christian Heart, He Will Not Part." I tried to make myself as inconspicuous as possible walking up the steps, smiling as I imagined how the congregants might feel about having a Jew in their midst.

Mavis had assured me I would be very welcome. Though when she first invited me, she had examined me critically, studying my hair with particular interest. "Only you better be ready for questions about what's under all that curly hair."

"What are you talking about?" I reached up self-consciously to see if anything weird were on my head but felt nothing unusual.

"No, you're cool," Mavis said quickly, laughing at my concern. "Nothing's wrong with your hair. You'll just be the first Jew most people at my daddy's church have ever seen. So somebody might ask to see your horns."

I couldn't think of a comeback or one I could make without cursing. I had believed better of Mavis.

"I'm *serious*. Somebody's gonna think it's so wavy on top to cover up your horns."

"That's a ridiculous stereotype. Jews don't have—"

"*I* know the dumb thing with the horns got started 'cause people thought Michelangelo put them on Moses's head. 'Cause I saw the slides in art class. I sure know you're not Moses." She laughed out loud. "But most of the old folks at Daddy's church had to take wood shop instead of art class. If they even got the chance to go to high school."

Green and purple light came through the loud stained glass windows. The pews were dark wood with a high polish. There was red carpeting down the aisles but none between the rows, as if church dollars could be stretched only so far. The altar was covered in white linen embroidered in gold, and a massive roughhewn cross stood behind it.

I closed my eyes. I would try not to look at anyone, I decided, and hoped they would forget about me or think I was praying. Then no one would disturb me.

The choir hummed softly in the background. I breathed deeply and felt myself easing into a more peaceful mood. I might be the only white person present, but they didn't care. They weren't even thinking about me.

"Miss? Miss?" a man's voice invaded my repose. I looked up into the grave eyes of a young man. His dark face was solemn, and he wore a dark suit with a thin blue-and-gold-striped tie.

Oh my God, I thought. *Without knowing it, I've offended some honored custom. I sat in the wrong place or they thought I'd fallen asleep. Now he's going to ask me to leave. I'm going to be thrown out.*

"Excuse me," he continued. "You're Miss Bauer, aren't you?"

I nodded and felt relieved when he smiled. He was not coming to chastise me, nor was he scrutinizing my head.

"I'm Deacon Roberts. We're real happy to have you with us today." He shook my hand gently and glanced apprehensively at his watch. "We were ready to start—in fact, we were lining up the procession—but Mavis says she *has* to talk to you first. So would you come with me out to the vestry?"

I rose quickly, feeling all eyes on me as we left the sanctuary. I feared Mavis had had a fight with Willie, or even worse, with her father. Or she had changed her mind and wanted me to help her call off the wedding at the last moment.

The vestry was a tiny room where the minister's robes hung on the wall. Extra prayer books and hymnals were stored on shelves across from cleaning supplies and Christmas ornaments. For the wedding, a dressing table had been improvised from a desk fitted with a mirror. As soon as I walked in, Mavis pushed her mother and sisters out. "I told you," she said impatiently, "I need to talk to her *alone*."

"Mavis honey, everybody's waiting," her mother said in a conciliatory tone I'd never heard her use with her daughter. "You don't want to start late. It's bad luck."

Mavis shut the door and sat down at the dressing table. She admired herself in the mirror. "These folks are making me crazy," she said. "Being a pregnant lady and all, I don't need the aggravation."

"Do you feel all right?" I worried that all the stress was making her sick and that was why she'd wanted to see me.

"I feel fine." She stood up and faced me. "Don't I look fine?"

"You absolutely do. That dress is perfect for you." I couldn't get over her transformation. I was accustomed to seeing her in jeans and smocks and faded sun dresses. She looked stately in her white lace dress despite her pregnant body.

"Aunt Evelina did herself proud this time," she said. "Of course it's not real, handmade lace, but it's real enough for me." She showed me the fine detail of the yoke. "This is all hand stitched. It took her hours to do it."

"It's lovely, Mavis." I moved towards the door, hoping to hurry her. "What did you want to see me about? They're all waiting."

"Let 'em wait. They can't have a wedding without the bride. They're not goin' anywhere."

I sat down. I could tell she was going to take her time working up to whatever she wanted to talk about.

"I got a problem," she said.

"Is something wrong between you and Willie?"

"No. Willie and me are fine. Willie's so happy it's sickening."

"Then what's bothering *you*?"

"Just seems kinda funny, me walking out there pregnant in front of all those people."

"They're your friends and neighbors, Mavis. They know you're pregnant. They wouldn't be here if they didn't care about you."

"Oh yes, they would. They came to look at me walking down that aisle big as a cow."

"Honey," I said, shocked at having the nerve to call her an endearment. "This is your father's church. You've known these people all your life. You don't have to be embarrassed in front of them."

"I wish they were strangers I'd never laid eyes on. I may be pregnant, but I still got my pride."

"You can call it off if you want to and go to a justice of the peace," I offered hesitantly. "But I don't know how Willie's going to take being stood up. And you know your parents are going to feel *terrible*." I was chilled by the thought of Mavis's father standing alone and furious at the altar.

"I'm gonna do it," she said. "Just wish I had something to help me." She sighed. "I know you won't do it, but I sure need a drink."

"Even if I would—which I won't—it's Sunday. There's no place to buy liquor. But do you believe in good-luck charms?"

"Sure. Like that thing they say, 'Something old, something new, something borrowed, something blue.'" She held up her dress to show me a blue garter. "And I got on new panties and this bracelet is real old. My granddaddy gave it to Mama when she turned twelve, and she gave it to me when I was baptized."

Suddenly she looked horrified. "You know what? I forgot to borrow something. Let me look around here fast." She poured over the dressing table. "I got to find something before we get started."

"Here, take this." I unhooked my gold beads and handed them to her. "But I need them back after the reception."

She nodded solemnly and hooked them around her neck. "Thank you, Laura. They're so pretty. Are they real gold?"

"Yes. They were my grandmother's. I loved them when I was a little girl. When Grandma died, my father gave them to me. I only wear them on special occasions. That's why I wore them to your wedding."

"It's really OK if I wear them?"

"Of course." *What can happen if they're on her neck?* I thought. I arranged them against her lace collar. "They look beautiful with that dress, Mavis. Think about my grandmother as you walk down the aisle. She wasn't scared of anything. She was the first woman driver in Atlanta. And she loved weddings."

There was an impatient tapping at the door, and then Mavis's mother looked in. "I'm sorry to interrupt," she said, acknowledging me. "But Mavis, the time for talking is *over*. Everybody's fidgeting. Willie's looking nervous and your daddy's getting mighty impatient. So you come on out and get married like you're s'posed to."

"All right. I'm coming." Mavis took a last look in the mirror and started towards the door. "Thank you," she said, touching the beads at her throat. "I'm proud to wear them."

"Please take all the time you need getting back to your seat," Mavis's mother told me. "We won't start 'til you get set. Miz Mitchell can play "Eternal Love" one more time."

"Good luck," I said, giving Mavis's hand a squeeze. "I'll see you when it's over."

"And you wait right here for your Uncle Joseph," her mother said firmly, pushing Mavis through the door. "We don't have time for any more foolishness."

Then she led me back through the sanctuary past the many faces watching us with curiosity. As I turned into my pew, she whispered, "I don't know how you did it, but thank you. We couldn't budge her. I was just about ready to get her daddy to come give her a licking."

I realized Mavis's mother didn't mean this literally, but I knew Mavis had received "lickings" in the early months of her pregnancy. She and Willie would be married, but they would be under her father's roof. I didn't know if etiquette would allow her father to still hit her with his belt, or if he would expect Willie to do it. I couldn't believe Willie would dare try it. *It will end, I told myself. He wouldn't want to do it. Not Willie. He would never raise his hand against Mavis.*

My thoughts were broken by Mrs. Mitchell's pounding rendition of the "Wedding March." With all the others I looked back up the aisle to watch the three bridesmaids coming towards us, and then finally Mavis, on the arm of her Uncle Joseph. She looked proud and determined as she approached the altar where her father and Willie waited for her.

She touched her throat as she passed by me. To anyone else it would have seemed a nervous gesture, a bride's anxiety with so many eyes upon her. To me it was an intimate sign, like a wink or a smile or a final embrace, made all the more special by its rarity.

CHAPTER 22

This Bounty

When each girl brought in her casserole, salad, or dessert, everyone crowded around to admire it. Nadine had set the table with her own fine white cloth, and Vernon contributed an arrangement of orange marigolds and red zinnias for a centerpiece. The room conveyed the festivity of a Thanksgiving gathering.

Nadine collected all the recipes so she could include them in the New Families Project cookbook. Mavis had obviously written hers on a scrap of paper as she and Willie were driving in because the handwriting was wobbly and hard to read. Mandy's recipe for baked squash was neatly printed on a card titled in pink letters, "From the Kitchen of Mandy Barfield." She presented it as proudly as if it conveyed membership in an exclusive club. James placed her casserole on the table and retreated to a corner. He was wearing a white dress shirt and dark slacks and looked slightly self-conscious, like a young man on a first date. He motioned in a friendly way for me to join him, his earlier hostility clearly set aside. "How you doing? You look a little puny." He regarded me sympathetically and insisted I take a seat.

"Just a little tired. Kind of a rough week," I confessed, wanting to change the subject. "Nothing some sleep and a long weekend won't cure."

"You sure that's *all* it is?" he asked with what seemed like real concern, his blue eyes inescapable, first in their intensity and then in their friendly sympathy.

I hadn't said a word to Susan or Nadine and was trying to keep doing my job without missing a step so no questions would be asked. Yet suddenly I felt susceptible to telling James Barfield, a client who had bitterly opposed his wife's joining the Project, a man I hardly knew, exactly what was troubling me.

"Can I get you something to drink?" he offered when I didn't answer. "Even a drink of water?"

"Thank you, James. I don't need a thing." I smiled up at him, and though I couldn't, of course, see my own face, I knew my smile must appear unconvincing, since I felt nothing like smiling.

He rested his big hand on my shoulder in a companionable way. I expected the weight to feel heavy, but was surprised when reassurance emanated from him in the same way that energy always followed him into a room. He did not pressure me as he watched me, but inclined his head slightly and asked so that no one else could hear, "Something is on your mind. What's worryin' you, Laura?"

"I'm just a little concerned about my father," I answered, the words slipping out, violating my own wish for privacy as well as Mrs. Cremins's admonition to avoid personal disclosures to clients. "We've been through a rough time. He hasn't been well, James." I retreated again into the safety of understatement.

"I'm *real* sorry to hear that, Laura," he said kindly. "You *know* we can manage things here just fine. Wouldn't you feel better if you went on home?"

"Actually, it feels good to be here with everybody. I love these dinners, James." I could feel myself smiling with pleasure. "I wouldn't want to miss one."

It would also have felt disloyal to express my relief at an evening away from the hospital. For over a week, I had shared shifts with my mother, trying to keep my father, the former master sergeant of an infantry unit, from yanking out his tubes and fleeing the hospital to return to his store, where, except for funerals and rare vacations, he had not missed a day since he opened it twenty-five years before.

"They can't do a damn thing for me here," he had complained when he was admitted for chest pain, "except run tests I don't need that make my blood pressure go up. So then they can run more tests. They're going to *make* me have a heart attack!" he had shouted when I'd visited him earlier that afternoon.

I felt Barfield's breath against my cheek as he leaned over to whisper in my ear. "I wish I had something better to offer you, Laura. 'Cause it sure looks like you could use a good drink." He smiled courteously, offering me comfort. "I do have a couple of beers out in the cooler. Suppose I get you one?"

"I'd love one. But somebody might report it to the Feds, and we'll get written up for consuming alcohol on government premises. Over *one* beer. But thanks for the offer." I looked up at him, enjoying his friendly attention, and smiled across the room at Vernon, who was pouring lemonade for several of the fathers.

Barfield patted my arm in a friendly way. "I know you're worryin' about your daddy, Laura. And I can tell you don't like folks pryin' any more than I do. So I won't do that. But I want to thank you. You folks have taken good care of my Mandy. You've done everything like you promised." He gently squeezed my shoulder before he moved his hand. "You sure there's nothing I can do?"

I realized he meant something he could do for *me,* and I clung to the moment. After months of tiptoeing around his resentment, I treasured his support.

He nervously cracked his knuckles. "I hate standin' around like this."

"OK. You want something to do, James?" I was eager to divert his attention from my troubles, self-conscious to have already shared so much with him.

"Sure. What you got?" he asked eagerly.

"We've got chicken ready to go on the grill. Feel like barbecuing?"

"You're talkin' to a pro." He took my arm. "Lead me to it."

When we came outside a few moments later, I saw Susie sitting on top of a car, her head in her hands.

"What's with her?" James asked Mandy who was standing nearby.

"Mickey won't have nothin' to do with her," she whispered. "Seeing girls here with our husbands and boyfriends made her feel *real* bad."

"Well, where is he?" James stood up straight and hitched his hands in his pockets. "You want me to talk to him?"

"If you can *find* him. He sure don't get in touch with Susie. All he cares about now is Steel Vulture," she said angrily. "And some girl sings with them. Thinks they're gonna make it big."

"So big I never heard of 'em. Sounds like kid stuff," Barfield said dismissively. "A *man* gets somebody pregnant, he marries her."

"He's a lot younger than you are, honey." Mandy proudly put her arm around his waist. "Not ev'rybody's lucky as me."

"Well somebody better talk to that boy. May as well be me." He spoke with so much determination, I thought he might leave the chicken to go hunt Mickey down.

"Honey, please let's have a good time tonight," Mandy cajoled him, sounding more like an old married woman than the young girl she was. "Maybe you can catch up with him this weekend."

"All right. But see if you can cheer her up." He gestured towards Susie. "We can't have her sitting there crying." He tried to make a joke out of it. "She might get me so distracted I'll burn the chicken." He poured more sauce over the pieces of chicken before putting them on the hot grill. "Y'all go on in. This is making an awful lot of smoke." He looked affectionately at Mandy. "Please make her sit down, Laura. The doctor told her not to stand around since her ankles started swelling. But she forgets if I don't stay on her."

"I'll watch her." I pretended to be stern. "Don't you give me any trouble, Mandy Barfield." Then I went over to Susie. "Come inside with us and get out of this smoke. Would you like some lemonade?"

"Y'all don't have to worry about me," Susie said dejectedly. "I heard y'all talking, but I'm all right. I don't need anybody talkin' to Mickey."

"I'm sorry. I guess we spoke too loud, Susie," I apologized quickly, seeing Mandy's awkward expression. "Mandy just thought James could talk to Mickey man to man."

"*Please,* Mandy, don't let James say nothin' to Mickey," Susie answered, appealing to both of us. "I don't want him coming back to me 'cause somebody talked him into it. That's no kinda love. I want a love that don't have to be forced." She looked enviously at Mandy when James blew her a kiss as we turned to go inside.

Once we got near the serving table, Nell's mother approached me. "I want to talk to you about these beans," she announced, her displeasure visible.

"Hello, Mrs. Walton. How are you feeling, Nell?" I didn't see how anyone could look more pregnant.

"The doctor says it could be any day," Nell said shyly.

"Thank you for coming tonight, Mrs. Walton." I had hoped to steer her away from a fight, but she didn't return my greeting, and I read the apprehension in Nell's face.

"There's no point mincing words, Miz Bauer. I don't like being told how to cook beans I been putting on my table longer than you been on this earth!"

"No one was instructing *you,* Mrs. Walton. Nell's just practicing what she learned in our Cooking and Nutrition class."

"How do you expect Nell to cook anything? She can't even make a decent cup of coffee."

"Looks like she did just fine." I turned approvingly to the greatly depleted serving dish of green beans.

"Nell had nothing to do with those beans. I can promise you that," she said with authority. "Just one look at that recipe, and I knew it was no good. I couldn't have Nell shame our whole family serving everybody half-cooked beans. So I fixed 'em how we always fix green beans. The recipe I raised five children on. I guess that ought to be good enough for everybody else." She stirred and rearranged the remaining beans to make them look more inviting.

"Looks like everybody enjoyed them," I answered agreeably, determined, no matter what she said, not to argue with her in the middle of a Project dinner. "Come with me, Nell," I urged. "I could use some help bringing more things out." I whisked her out to the kitchen before her mother could respond. I still felt Mrs. Walton's eyes boring through me.

"I'm sorry 'bout what Mama did to my beans," Nell whispered anxiously. "I *tried* to stop her, but she put these great big ole ham hocks in and lots of salt. She made me cook 'em forever. I tried to make 'em healthy, Laura. Honest I did." She hung her head. "I know you're mad 'cause I messed them all—"

"It's all right. They're fine." I put my arm around her. I hoped the damned beans wouldn't get her so agitated she'd go into labor. "I know you wanted to make them the way we did in class, but I understand how mothers can be. I've got one of my own."

Nell smiled with relief. "Next time," she said, revealing a glimmer of new-found dignity, "I'm not gonna let her know what I'm making. I'll come fix my dish over here." She looked defiantly at her mother as we approached the table. "I won't even taste them, messed up like they are."

Then James came through the door holding a platter of barbecued chicken in front of him like a trophy. "Ladies and gentlemen," he said grandly. "What you've all been waiting for!"

Everyone hurried over to the crowded table with their paper plates held out expectantly. The air was full of, "Look at that!" "Don't those sweet potatoes look *good!*" "Susie made that Jell-O mold. I don't know how she got it to come out so perfect." "Rita's ham looks just like the ones you see on TV."

When I heard the praise for Rita's ham, I watched her smile with pleasure. She had told me she got the idea to do pineapple slices alternating with cloves out of a magazine. "I think it turned out even better than the picture," she whispered to me. "Thank you for letting me do it. I hope they leave a little bit for me to take home."

Then the gaiety stopped when I became aware of Mavis's father at my side. I had watched his heated conversation with Mavis as the last food was brought to the table. Willie, self-conscious in white shirt and tie, had moved away from them. I assumed I was witnessing a family conflict until Reverend Williams addressed me. He usually orated, as if he were speaking from the pulpit, but this time he spoke softly.

"We ought to say grace," he said. "Young lady, we need to stop and bless this table before it's too late." Proud as he was, he was afraid to make this request to an integrated group, for fear of being ignored or, even worse, attacked. In his own setting, he would simply have directed us to pray.

"Excuse me, everybody. Could I have your attention?" I clapped my hands until the room grew quiet. "Reverend Williams just brought to my attention that we forgot to bless this food. I apologize for our mistake, and I've asked him to say grace."

There were murmurs of approval from respectful, attentive faces and then shocked silence from a few as they discovered the black man standing beside me was Reverend Williams. They were ready to offer up grace for the feast before them but not under the guidance of a black minister. I feared I had made a terrible mistake. I should have offered a blessing myself, even if all I could think of quickly was, "God is great, God is good. Let us thank Him for our food."

Nadine's eyes flashed concern. I knew she was wondering why, with everything going so well, I was risking a confrontation. Mrs. Walton nudged Nell towards the door, leaving behind their plates of food. I wished I could undo my foolishness, however well meaning my wish to be inclusive. I looked apologetically at Reverend Williams, a guest whom I risked dishonoring. His face was impassive.

"Let us bow our heads," he finally began with just the right balance of command and respect. "Our Heavenly Father: We thank You for this food we are about to eat and for the loving hands which prepared it. We think of those less fortunate who cannot enjoy this bounty. We thank You for this blessed opportunity to share with our families and new friends. We are grateful for Thy wisdom in bringing us together and for giving these young people a chance to better their lives and the lives of their unborn children."

I heard the restless feet and sighs of those who wanted to start their meals. I hoped he couldn't hear them. I was moved by his words but also fearful someone might be rude if he didn't finish soon.

"Thank you for this beautiful table and an evening when no one must go home hungry. When everyone will have food for the body and fellowship for the spirit. Dear Lord, please accept our thanks and grant Your blessing to all who are about to receive this bounty. In Jesus's name we pray. Amen."

Then "amen" echoed around the room in many voices. Nell looked uncertainly at her mother, who had stopped near the doorway once the Lord's name was invoked.

"That was a mighty fine blessing, Reverend Williams," James Barfield said. I hadn't realized he was standing close by. "You did us proud." He extended his hand to Mavis's father.

"Thank you sir." Reverend Williams shook James's hand.

"I'm James Barfield, and this is my wife Mandy."

"I'm pleased to meet you," Reverend Williams said formally. "And Mrs. Barfield, too."

"Please call me, Mandy, Reverend Williams. Ev'rybody does."

"I've heard Mavis speak of you," he replied politely, yet carefully avoiding a term of personal address that might be considered too familiar. "She says you're a very good cook."

"She's right about that," James said. "Mandy learned most of it right here." He smiled at me and then served Reverend Williams a helping of Mandy's squash casserole. "You tell me if that idn't the best baked squash you ever tasted."

Reverend Williams took the plate James offered and started to move down the line.

"No, sir, I meant right now," James said. "Just take a little bite and tell me what you think."

"James, *stop.* Don't fish for compliments for me. With you carryin' on that way, Reverend Williams only took some so's not to be rude."

"That's *not* true, Mrs. Barfield. I happen to love baked squash." Reverend Williams took a taste and seemed to be debating a serious point for a moment. "Your husband is absolutely correct. This couldn't be improved."

"There now," James said to Mandy with pride. "Maybe now you'll believe me." He beckoned to Reverend Williams. "Now come try some more of *my* chicken. I've got some ready to come off the grill right now."

"Isn't that nice?" Susan observed as we stood back like chaperones. "They're having a ball." She took a bite from her own modest portion. "Everything's so good, I might have to go off my diet."

"Not *you.* You sure don't *need* to, but you'll probably be dieting on your deathbed."

She laughed, but I could see there was something she wanted to tell me. "Don't get me wrong," she said hesitantly. "I'm no great liberal—I guess you already figured that out—and I didn't think it would work when you first brought up having these dinners." She looked around and smiled. "But this is nice. Just folks being folks. Enjoying good food."

"Then come on. Have some more." I pointed to her nearly empty plate. "The girls feel so proud when we like what they've made."

"You go right ahead. But I'm stuffed. Unless that's an order?" she asked playfully.

"Of course not. But I need to go try Rita's ham," I said, walking back towards the serving table. "She's asked me three ti—"

Susan made a quick sign to be quiet and pointed to the nearby corner where Susie and Mandy stood talking over their iced tea.

"Reverend Williams sure loved my squash," Mandy said proudly. "It means something when a total stranger likes your cooking. James goes on about how good it is 'cause he has to. But Reverend Williams didn't have to go back for thirds."

Susie laughed. "I can't believe you were counting. Besides, you shouldn't put too much store by what *he* thinks." She began to whisper. "He may be a preacher, but don't forget, he *is* colored. It's not the same as if one of us—"

"Susie Richards! I'm ashamed of you. Talking that way about Mavis's daddy," she scolded. "Besides, James works with a real fine colored fella. James says he acts just as nice—maybe *nicer*—than some of the white men on the crew. How can you say things like that?"

"Where do you get off actin' so high and mighty all of a sudden?" Susie accused her. "You used to carry on about how much you hated going to school with 'em. How they dragged the school down. You know you did."

For a moment Mandy was silent. Then, meeting Susie's critical eyes, she admitted, "You're right, I *did* say it. It's what Mama and Daddy always said." Her quiet voice gained courage. "But they were wrong. Bein' white or black don't make a person good or bad. And girls like Mavis and you and me. We're pretty much in the same boat."

"No we're not. James is crazy about you. And Willie married Mavis. I wouldn't call that the *same* as the boat I'm in."

"I'm sorry, Susie." Her face looked truly regretful. "I was talkin' about gettin' pregnant before we got married." She tried to encourage her. "Please let James talk to Mickey. It's not too late. I bet he can turn Mickey around."

"I *told* you before. I want Mickey to come around on his own, not 'cause James twists his arm. Besides, his new girl's already pregnant. That's how much he cares about me."

"I'll tell James to forget it," Mandy said gently as they watched the convivial flow of families circulating around the room. Then Mandy pointed to the corner where James and Reverend Williams stood talking together. "I never heard a better grace. Mavis's Daddy sure has a nice, deep voice."

"I don't have nothin' against Mavis's daddy, Mandy," Susie said crossly. "And I shouldn't have said what I did before. I know better. But don't keep sayin' how wonderful he is just 'cause he ate a lot of your ole squash." She smiled good-naturedly. "He ate a big helping of my cole slaw, too. You think I should run out and join his church?"

Susan and I lost the rest of the conversation in their laughter and the loud electric guitar break on an Allman Brothers tape somebody had just slipped into the tape deck.

Susan took another bite of squash. "It really *is* good," she said. "And we're lucky Reverend Williams ate three helpings. Lord help us if he'd just pushed it around his plate."

"I wasn't worried. He's too smart for that."

"You could stand to take a lesson from him," Susan said, glancing over at Mrs. Walton, who had led Nell back to the serving table. "You didn't even *taste* her green beans. Don't think for a moment she hasn't noticed. And when they get home, you know who she'll take it out on."

I thought about Nell's sad eyes and knew Susan was right. I set aside my exasperation with her mother and walked over to present my plate.

"I thought you'd change your mind," Mrs. Walton said triumphantly, dishing me up a large portion. "You're always gonna find that the old ways are the best ways."

CHAPTER 23

Michelle's Daddy

"Thank you for coming," Mrs. Richards whispered at the door of Susie's hospital room. "She's got herself all worked up over a bouquet of flowers."

As I approached the bed, Susie turned to face me and pulled the sheet up to her chin. She looked at me so shyly it was hard for me to believe she was someone I knew well.

"I reckon I'll leave you two alone," Mrs. Richards said, shaking her head. "Don't know what I might say if she starts carryin' on again about that Mickey." She hurried out, calling back to us, "If you want me, I'll be in the cafeteria."

Susie looked tired but very pretty. Her dark hair was thick and luxuriant, covering the white pillow. Her blue eyes were highlighted by shadow and mascara, but she had been crying long enough to make black streaks beneath her eyes. I wondered what had upset her so badly.

I ran water in a vase for my daffodils and set them on her tray table. "How are you doing?"

"Fine, now that Mama's gone." She sighed in frustration. "She just won't leave me alone. She keeps trying to interfere between me and Mickey. And she hovers over me like I'm about to die or something."

"She's trying to look after you. *Remember,* you just had a baby."

"It's not that. She knows I'm OK. But she's trying to keep me from seeing Mickey. Only let's not talk about her. Did you see my baby?" she asked proudly.

"I sure did. She's beautiful. She's the prettiest one in the whole nursery."

"You really think so?"

"Of course I do." Watching her face brighten, it saddened me how much she needed my reassurance.

"I thought she was kind of funny looking," she admitted hesitantly. "She sure don't look like the pictures in those baby books."

"Those aren't newborns."

"You sure her head'll be all right?" she asked, clearly afraid of my answer. "It looks kinda mashed on one side."

"She'll be fine. Think of all she went through to get here. And speaking of looks, you look *great*. Are you doing OK?"

"Yeah. Just a little sore."

"You'd have to be. I mean, eight and a half pounds!"

"I guess that's 'cause Mickey's so big."

"How big were your mother's babies?"

"None of us was even seven pounds. I only weighed about five. Mama said she was real worried about me. But the doctor started me on cereal right away, and I started growing just fine. And I been eating and growing ever since."

We both laughed. Susie had gained almost nothing during her pregnancy. We had to push her constantly to eat.

"It's not because she's pregnant," her mother had told me. "She's never been much of an eater. Barbie's only eleven and she already weighs more than Susie."

When Susie got up to go to the bathroom, I could see she was as thin as ever. If she hadn't been on a maternity ward, no one would have guessed she had just given birth.

"Thanks for the flowers," she said as she came back to bed. "They're real pretty."

"We have a baby present for you, too. But Susan picked it out, and I want to let her give it to you when she gets back from vacation."

"Where'd she go?"

"Jekyll Island."

"We went there once when I was little. I got stung by something in the water and my whole leg swole up."

Even her vacation memories were difficult. I wished there were something I could do to make her feel better.

"Do you need anything, Susie? I could run out for it."

"No thanks. They give me everything I need." She glanced away shyly. "Mama feels kind of embarrassed about me nursing the baby. Most ladies she knows use formula."

"Do *you* feel OK about nursing?"

"Everything we read said my milk's better for her. So I'm gonna keep it up, "she said resolutely. "And I've been walking a whole bunch to help me get stronger. But the nurses told me to rest more."

"You *should* listen to what they say."

"I try to, but I don't think they read the same books we did," she reported thoughtfully. "They got put out with me this morning 'cause I didn't want to eat breakfast. It was fried eggs and bacon and white bread toast and grits just *dripping* with butter. They thought I was crazy when I asked for oatmeal and orange juice and skim milk."

"You'll be home soon. Then you can eat whatever you want."

"It's gonna be strange," she said wistfully. "I thought I'd be going home with my husband to our own place. Not back to Mama and Daddy's."

"You've had a big disappointment," I acknowledged, actually thinking *betrayal,* yet incapable of expressing such a thought to someone so forlorn. "But you'll have your own place one day. And a husband, too, if you want one. It's hard for you to believe now, but you'll get over Mickey."

"You sound just like Mama," she said reproachfully. "I don't *want* to get over Mickey. And now, I don't have to." She pointed happily to the arrangement of pink and white carnations he'd brought her. They were clustered in a plastic vase shaped like a stork, and the smiling bird carried a baby in pink swaddling in its beak.

"Mickey walked out on you, Susie," I reminded her, thinking of the sad history she seemed able to erase with a few flowers.

"He didn't *want* to leave me. But he couldn't find a job. And then he was so busy with Steel Vulture," she happily explained, once again Mickey's champion. "He's wanted to cut a record his whole life. He's been so sweet. He came to see me this morning, and he'll be back this evening after rehearsal." She smiled dreamily. "He dedicates all the songs he writes to me."

"But you said his new girlfriend's pregnant and they're getting married," I reminded her, understanding completely her own mother's despair at Susie's faith in Mickey. "What's he going to do?"

"She lost the baby," Susie reported matter-of-factly. "So they don't have to get married. She stopped singing in the band and she's already moved out. So Mickey can be with me."

"You're actually going to see him again?" I asked, forgetting professional objectivity in my amazement.

"He's Michelle's daddy!" she protested, shocked I could ask such a question.

"So that's her name. I was going to ask you."

"I decided early this morning," she said yawning. "When Mickey gave me this." She pointed to a small gold heart at her throat. "And those beautiful flowers. He's such a proud daddy." She smiled contentedly. "I decided on Michelle 'cause it's the closest name to Mickey I could think of. Don't you think it's a pretty name?"

"Very pretty."

"It's French."

"Yes, I know."

"Just think of that. My baby has a real French name. She's gonna *be* somebody. Mickey took a whole bunch of pictures when she was in here nursing. He's going to get some baby announcements with her picture on them to send to all our family. And he's going to put our wedding announcement in the paper."

"Susie, don't you want to wait until you've been home awhile to decide about getting married?" I asked. "After all, he walked out on you one time."

"But I've always wanted to marry him, Laura," she insisted. "I love him."

"What makes you think he won't change his mind again?"

"Because he won't," she said defiantly. "Mickey loves me no matter what you and Mama think."

It was my turn to beseech her. "Please wait a little while. He *abandoned* you, Susie." This time I did not hesitate to use the word.

"I *am* gonna wait, Laura," she said, smiling charitably, willing to forgive me my doubts. "'Cause, it'll take a little while 'til I get my figure back and get my hair done. I wouldn't want to get married lookin' like *this*." She checked her watch. "I'm sorry, but you're gonna have to go. They'll be bringin' Michelle in to nurse. Nobody can be in the room but the mama and daddy or the grandparents."

"OK. I'll check back later. Call if you need anything." I gave her a quick hug good-bye.

"Don't you understand, Laura?" she asked almost tenderly. "You don't have to worry about me anymore. I've got Mickey to look out for me. I'll be fine." She smiled dreamily. "I'm so happy. My baby's got a daddy again."

CHAPTER 24

When Nighttime Shadows Fall

I told Nell first. Her eyes followed me like a scared puppy's when I said there was something I needed to tell her. She looked so frightened I wished I had scheduled visits with a few others and gradually worked my way up to her.

"Don't worry. Nothing's the matter." I forced my voice full of good cheer. "I wanted you to know I'll be leaving the Project at the end of the week. It won't change *anything*. Susan will come see you and Charlie. She'll take you to the pediatrician, and you can call her whenever you need to."

We were sitting outside on her porch where mosquitoes hummed around us. Although they were biting, Nell didn't stir. She stared straight ahead, still as a doll.

"I'll miss you, Nell," I said, hoping to soothe her by expressing my own loss. "I'm so proud of how well you're managing. You're doing a great job with Charlie."

She hung her head and pulled her knees up tightly against her chest like a position in an old civil defense drill. While we talked, Charlie slept in the infant seat the Project had given her as a baby gift. He had brown eyes and brown hair. At one month he was already a very big baby.

"But you won't be here to see Charlie grow up," she said with both accusation and remorse.

"Susan and Vernon will be here for you," I offered hopefully. "And I know, Nadine'll invite me back for one of the family dinners. So I'll see you then."

"It won't be the same."

"No, it won't." I reached out and patted her hand. My words seemed empty and comfortless. I wanted to reassure her, yet felt myself pulling away from the soft, child-like hand beneath mine. "Nell, good-byes are always terrible. I'm sorry this one makes you feel so bad. But it's time for me to do something else now." I stood up, hoping to get by with this vague explanation.

"But I thought you liked working here, Laura," she reminded me, speaking up more forcefully than I'd ever known her to do. "What do you wanna leave for?" She wiped away tears with the back of her hand. "You said you looked forward to seeing us every week."

She said "us," but I knew her heart was really saying, *"me."*

"I *do* like it." I hadn't intended to tell her, but my resolve crumpled under the intensity of her distress. "My father had a heart attack, Nell. He'll be all right," I assured her, hoping he would continue to recover, "but my mother needs my help in Atlanta taking care of him and running his jewelry store."

"I'm real sorry, Laura," Nell said. "I sure hope he feels better soon." Her face brightened for a moment. "Couldn't you just take some time off for a while 'til he's ready to go back to work?"

I had to laugh. "You'd have to know my father to understand why that won't work, Nell." I tried to make light of it. "If my mother and I don't watch him every second, he'll sneak out of the house and go back to work even though he's exhausted." I handed her some more tissues. "He's taken care of me all my life. Now it's my turn to help him and my mother."

I wondered how Nell might imagine my mother, based on her own harsh and dominating one, and perhaps comparing my running my father's business with her own servant-like attendance at her mother's Tupperware parties. I did not share how desperately frightened my mother was that she would lose my father and with him her entire world. She had survived the camps but no longer had a mother or father or brother or cousins. My father was her joy and her life raft, as in a different way she was his, sitting beside him at the end of each long day, while they exchanged stories and he ate the dinner she had kept warm for him. Sometimes they held hands, even when this made it difficult for him to cut his meat, each of them still tender towards the other.

"So this is it? This is our last visit?" Nell's eyes grew wide with fear.

"I'll be at the dinner Friday. But I didn't want to tell you in front of everybody."

That was my gift to her, a few extra words to convey that she was not *everybody.* That my departure might mean more to her than to others. And that she meant more to me.

"And after that you won't be around anymore?" Her face truly looked afraid of my answer.

"No. I'll be in Atlanta."

"You don't really think you'll come back to visit, do you?" She asked, her voice hurt and raw. "You won't be coming to a family dinner."

"I don't know," I conceded softly, admiring her honesty in accepting my unlikely return.

Charlie began to cry harshly. He started at full power, not even taking a few seconds to work up to it. Nell picked him up and stuck a bottle in his mouth. He sucked furiously, his fists unclenched, and his eyes closed. His little body relaxed in her arms.

"He lets you know when he wants somethin'." She smiled with pride and admiration. "Nobody's gonna step on him."

"He gets that from his mother."

She looked at me in disbelief as if I were flattering her or describing someone else.

"I mean it, Nell," I assured her, enjoying the light in her eyes when she understood my praise was genuine. "You've gotten *so* much better at telling people how you feel and standing up for yourself. When I first met you, you wouldn't say a word."

"Sometimes, I still can't get the words out," she confided. "And then people always hurry me. 'Specially Mama. But it's real hard for her," she added sympathetically. "She never had a child like me before."

I waited, wondering what dreadful pronouncement her mother had made. It was my turn to stare at the floor, afraid of what she might see in my eyes.

"You know what I'm talking about," she said sadly, turning away. "Slow and ugly, *too*. Bein' pretty and smart like Mama is makes it hard for her to put up with me."

"But you're *not* slow or ugly. I wish you could believe me."

She smiled modestly. "You really don't think I'm ugly?"

"Honest to God. Especially those big brown eyes."

"You got 'em, too," she said, obviously pleased.

"Me and millions of other people. You shouldn't worry so much what you look like," I tried to convince her. "You need to think about your future."

"It'll just be me and him." She looked down tenderly at the sleeping baby.

"What do you think you'll do?"

"I reckon I'll help Mama out for a while. She says we can stay here long as I pitch in with the housework and the garden and stuff like that."

It grieved me to think of Nell continuing as her mother's Cinderella. I could picture Mrs. Walton lying around watching soaps while Nell cared for Charlie and all her mother's other children, cooked and cleaned, and tended a half-acre garden.

"Don't you want a life away from your mother?"

"I got nowhere to go," she said in a small voice.

"Maybe not right now," I agreed. As mean as her mother was, Nell wasn't ready to manage on her own. "But later on when you get a job. After you finish at the vocational school the way you wanted."

"I got Charlie to think of now," she said proudly. "Besides, Mama don't hold too much with school once you get to be my age. She says Charlie ought to be my whole world now." She kissed his tiny nose.

"How'd you decide on Charlie, Nell? I always meant to ask you."

"I was gonna call him Larry or Laura if he'd been a girl," she answered softly. "But Mama said it wasn't right to take a name outside of the family when nobody'd been named for her daddy."

"Thank you for wanting to do that for me. I'm honored, Nell." I hugged her, touched by her desire to give so much to me. And I grieved that her mother took everything—even the right to name her own baby—away from Nell.

"D'you think he's doin' all right?" Nell asked nervously.

"Look how he's growing!" I wondered at her anxious expression. "Hasn't the doctor told you how great he looks?"

She nodded. "But I wondered what *you* think."

"You both look great, Nell."

"I wish you'd been there when he was born," she said regretfully. "Mama bossed everybody around something awful. I always counted on you being with me."

"I'm sorry I was out of town. I couldn't know when you'd go into labor."

"It didn't really make no difference," she said quickly, more concerned for my feelings than her own. "I just always figured you'd be there." She shook her head sadly. "I can't believe you won't be comin' around anymore."

Then Mrs. Walton drove into the yard, scattering gravel, setting off the dogs, and ending our intimacy. I had wanted to reach out, to give Nell a last word, something more than our hug. But it was too late.

As I stood there fumbling, Nell reached out to me. Before her mother was in hearing range, she said, "I *never* let Mama hear me. But sometimes, when it's just me and him, I call him Larry, anyway."

Susan insisted on taking me to Barnett's for a good-bye lunch.

We'd spent many lunch hours there together, alternately agreeing and arguing in the privacy of its old wooden booths.

"You really don't need to do that," I'd assured her when she'd suggested the farewell lunch.

"I know I don't *need* to, but I wanted to." She laughed as we placed our orders. "All you ever get is vegetable soup. I can handle that even on my salary."

"I'm going to miss you." I felt myself tearing up as we waited for our food.

"Don't start getting mushy. If you start me crying, I'll never stop."

"OK," I agreed, sniffing back a few tears. "But can I ask a favor?"

"Sure. Ask away." She looked curious and willing.

"If you ever find out what happened to Lisa Landrum—whether it's good or bad—will you let me know?"

"Of course I will. It *was* weird how they disappeared. And Lisa never going back to the doctor." Susan shook her head incredulously as she took a long drink of sweet tea. "It'll be awful hard on Bert, too, wherever they ended up. Folks around here saved odd jobs for him. In a new place, he won't find anything to do," she sadly predicted.

"But I guess Mrs. Landrum moved because of him."

"Because he was . . . you know." Susan struggled to say it. "The father?"

"She must have been scared people would gossip. She had to know she couldn't keep Lisa quiet for long," I told her, recalling Lisa's friendly chattiness. "I wonder where her sister went. You really think Bert got them *both* pregnant? Lisa didn't say so."

"I'm sure she wanted to tell me," I maintained, picturing the unselfconscious way Lisa had conveyed her story, until my distress and her fear of her mother's wrath had silenced her. "It was hard to believe she *was* pregnant. She looked like she should be playing with dolls."

"She *was* much too young to be looking for love. Probably most of them would have had more fun playing with dolls." Susan shook her head ruefully. Then, so she wouldn't be heard in the crowded restaurant, she whispered, "'Cause they don't even get a good time out of sex. They don't even know they're supposed to."

For the first time, I was excused from bringing a dish to the Project supper. It had sometimes been an awful bother after a long day to prepare chicken or string beans for thirty or forty people. Once, a large container of my homemade barbecue sauce leaked all over the back seat of Rob's car, a red Mustang with a pristine black interior, which I had borrowed at the last minute when my battery died. Months afterwards, when we were out together, I could still detect the hickory-smoked smell. Another time late at night, I'd knocked a carton of eggs off the counter in the Project kitchen as I reached across it to grab the ringing telephone. Yet instead of being relieved by having no obligation to cook or potential messes to clean up, I felt isolated. Everyone else had helped prepare our meal, while I, the honored guest, was an outsider.

I watched Susie's proud face as she placed Michelle in the baby swing and arranged parsley and tomato slices around the platter of turkey she'd prepared. Nadine was slicing a gigantic carrot cake covered with cream cheese icing. "I know it's full of fat, Laura," she said, "but for once I didn't use low-fat cream cheese. We're going to eat it the way it's *s'posed* to be eaten."

Susan gave a final stir to a rice salad which was being examined suspiciously. "That's all right," she said, undaunted by those who passed by it or took very small helpings. "Nobody *has* to try it. I made it for Laura to show her we'll keep trying new things even after she's not around to make us."

"What's it got in it?" Mavis took a tiny bite and swallowed gingerly as if she'd detected ground glass.

"Nuts, pimentos, olives, celery, onion, cucumber, green peas. And, of course, lots of rice. The dressing has a whole bunch of different spices in it, and in Laura's honor, I used yogurt instead of mayonnaise."

"I never heard of eating cold rice with all kinds of stuff chopped up in it," Mrs. Walton said. "I'm sorry. That may be the latest thing, but I guess I'm just a country girl. When we eat rice up here, we eat it hot with plenty of gravy."

"I like it, Mama." A small voice spoke up behind her. "It tastes real good with the turkey." Nell was actually talking in front of the whole group and daring to disagree with her mother.

"Thank you, Nell." Susan's eyes flashed encouragement. "I'm glad we've got at least one adventurous spirit around here."

"You want to try one of our homemade rolls?" Nell held out the basket to Susan. "It's Mama's recipe. I made *these*. They're good, but they're not as good as hers."

I couldn't tell if Nell had intended this as a peace offering to her mother, but it worked. Mrs. Walton smiled at her daughter for the first time I could recall. "They look mighty good, Nell." She took a roll and tasted it thoughtfully. "They taste fine. Just next time, I'd use a little less milk. And don't handle your dough quite so much."

A few new girls came out of the kitchen with salads and bowls of lima beans, black-eyed peas, and sweet potato soufflé. The table was barely large enough to hold it all. Everyone loaded my plate and waited expectantly for me to taste their creations. I didn't want to hurt anyone's feelings, yet felt too overcome on this last evening with them to eat more than a few bites.

Rita Washburn came toward me with a tall, older woman I didn't recognize. "Laura," she said, "I want you to meet Mrs. Moore. She's my—well, if Danny and me could have got married, she would have been—"

"It's all right, honey." The grey-haired woman put her arm around Rita and took over. "It *is* a little awkward. My son Danny was Rita's boyfriend." She started to get teary. "They would've gotten married if he hadn't died so suddenly." She pulled Rita closer. "My boy loved this little girl, and he'd have wanted me to stand by her so Rita's staying with me right now. It's real crowded over at her mama and daddy's. I got plenty of room, and I been real lonesome with Danny gone." She wiped her eyes. "This way we can get ready for the baby together just like Danny would've wanted."

"I'm glad you could come," I said, trying not to look too long at Rita, who blushed when anyone spoke to her. Though each girl concealed some secrets, I recognized the immensity for Rita of finally naming the boy who had given her the high school ring she always wore.

"I think she's feeling a little shy," Mrs. Moore said, reading my mind. "Rita didn't want to come at first, but when Nadine called to remind her, I thought it'd do us good to come together." She turned to Rita. "Now, honey, you got to stop worryin' what folks are gonna say. I'm just the same as your mother-in-law. You *know* Danny would've married you."

"Yes ma'am," Rita said softly.

"I told you not to ma'am me, honey. Call me Peggy."

Rita smiled shyly.

"Come on, let's get some supper, honey. My grandchild's hungry," she said, leading Rita away to the serving table.

Without warning, my throat tightened so that I feared I would be unable to say even a few simple words of farewell. And then my tears could not be held back, like the kind that come over you in shopping malls before Christmas, amid the lights and Salvation Army music, when you are supposed to feel festive and yet you are weary, sad, and reminiscent. I blinked hard and prayed my tears would stop before somebody noticed.

"Something the matter, Laura?" Susie was by my side, watching me with concern.

"No, sometimes my eyes just get a little irritated when I'm tired. I'll be fine." I tried to smile.

"I'm glad that's all it is," she said kindly. "I thought you were crying." She watched me carefully for a moment, and then, satisfied, she asked, "Do you know where Mandy is?" She wound up the baby swing to keep Michelle in motion. "When I talked to her yesterday, she was planning to come. She said she was bringing you a surprise."

"It is just about her time," Mavis said, overhearing us. "Maybe she went on and had that baby." She set down her plate and looked at Susie curiously. "But you two are so close she would have called you if she was having it."

"I guess so," Susie said. "Unless her labor came on all of a sudden."

"Wouldn't the hospital call you?" Mavis asked me.

"I bet they wouldn't if it happened in the middle of the night," Lindsey said. She was a tall, serious new girl who took notes on everything we said in class, as though she feared either we or she might forget something important.

"We have an answering service," I assured her. "And they're not afraid to wake us."

Susie ran to the window when we heard a vehicle pull into the lot. "It's James's truck," she said. "But he's by himself."

"I bet she had it," Mavis said, "and he's come to tell us. Willie, what you think she had? Boy or a girl?"

Willie rubbed his powerful neck and said thoughtfully, "James wouldn't have a girl."

Everyone grew quiet when James walked in. It was obvious from the smile on his face and the important way he held himself that Mavis had guessed correctly.

"Ladies and gentlemen," he said, pausing as if there had been an actual drum roll, before holding out a Polaroid snapshot. "Allow me to present Loretta Sue Barfield. She was born this afternoon at 2:14. She's eight pounds, two ounces, twenty and a half inches long. Blue eyes. No hair to speak of and the sweetest little feet you ever saw."

There were cheers and handshakes. Susie kissed James on the cheek. She stopped the swing and held Michelle up to him. "That's a brand new daddy, Michelle," she said. "He's got a little girl just like you. Only littler."

"That's right," James said proudly as Michelle lunged wildly for the snapshot. "Look at the right on that girl. Her daddy been teaching her to box?"

"He is silly with her," Susie said. "He's set on having her walkin' before her first birthday."

"So he's coming to see her regular?" James asked, tempering his voice so everyone wouldn't hear.

"Often as he can," she said protectively. "He's been real busy since Steel Vulture cut their record. He's in Atlan'a right now settin' up this gig for the grand opening of the Pizza Magic restaurant."

"He ought to be seeing that baby every week," James scolded. "Even if he is working on this music thing." He looked skeptical. "Has he been helpin' you out some?"

Sensing Susie's embarrassment, I stepped away. I hoped James would stop grilling her, though I shared his distrust of Mickey. I wouldn't have bet money Mickey would return from Atlanta. If that was even where he had gone.

"He brings me Pampers sometimes. But James, he don't have much money." Her voice, still audible to me, begged for his understanding. "He can't help if all he can get is part-time at the garage. And he *has* to put money into the band. At least until their record takes off and the sales start comin' in."

"He's just throwin' good money after bad, Susie. I better sit that boy down and straighten him out," James said. "I know you don't want me to, but somebody needs to make him act like a man. The headliner at *Pizza Magic*," he muttered derisively.

Then Willie came running up to James. "I want to know what *you're* doing here if Mandy just had a baby." Willie's voice was challenging, but his eyes were smiling. He loved to ride James. "I never would've figured you'd duck out after she had the baby. I thought an older man like you was s'posed to set a good example for the rest of us."

"You're picking on the wrong fella." James answered good-naturedly, but sounding tired. "I been at that hospital so long I feel like I live there." He sat down. "We got there about midnight yesterday, but that little girl just didn't want to come out. Mandy and me was ready—we been ready—but that baby wouldn't drop. Then all of a sudden, she was crowning." He smiled at me. "You would have been proud of me. I remembered all the exercises and the breathin'. And Mandy did real good. She liked to walk my legs off."

"Were you with her when the baby was born?" Nell asked. I wondered if everyone else noticed the wistfulness in her voice.

"I sure was. They handed her right to me."

"Congratulations, James." Vernon shook his hand. "I wish I could offer you something better than tea. But you know the Project rules."

"I sure *do*. 'Cause I heard 'em enough from Laura," he said, feigning annoyance but smiling in a friendly way. "I got to be going. I just wanted to let y'all know everything was OK." He glanced at his watch. "I already stayed longer than I meant to. Mandy was taking a nap. I promised to be back before she wakes up."

"I'll get by to see her first thing tomorrow," Susan said. "I'm sorry we didn't know she was in labor."

"I would've called," James said apologetically, "but Mandy wanted to wait 'til it was over. She didn't want to worry nobody." He turned to me. "We appreciate all you did for us, Laura." He turned down the plate of food Nadine brought him. "No thank you, ma'am. I couldn't eat a bite." Then he turned to me as if no one else were in the room. "You know we couldn't let you go without saying good-bye, Laura."

I felt myself choking up again. "I'm glad Loretta's here safe and sound, James. Tell Mandy I really missed seeing her tonight. And congratulations."

"She felt real bad she couldn't be here." He smiled awkwardly as everyone watched us. "There's a special cake she wanted to bake for you. She fixed it for me one time for practice, and it came out real good. She was gonna make one yesterday afternoon, but it just wasn't meant to be." He smiled again as he carefully placed Loretta's photograph back in his pocket.

"Can I have a rain check?" I asked.

"Any time you say. And listen here. Take good care of yourself, Laura. We'll miss you around here." He made one of those gestures somewhere between a pat and a squeeze of the shoulder. A handshake would have seemed too formal and a hug might have overstepped our relationship. "I'll be seeing the rest of you real soon," he called out. "Y'all come see Mandy."

Then he hesitated in the doorway, looking back at me. I could tell there was something else he wanted to say.

"I'll walk you out, James," I said. "I could use some fresh air."

He held the door for me. As I passed him, I could smell wintergreen breath mints and aftershave. Even his casual clothes looked ironed. He was a very careful man.

"I reckon this is good-bye," he said when we reached his truck.

"I wanted to tell you something." I could hear the uneasiness in my own voice.

"I figured you did." He smiled. "I reckon you knew I could find my way to my truck by myself."

"I wanted to tell you. . . ." I stopped short, rattled by the return of the choking feeling. "I wanted you to know how much I respect you. I'm sorry we got off on the wrong foot."

"That wasn't your fault," he insisted. "I felt awful needing this Project so Mandy could have the things she ought to. I reckon I took it out on you."

"Some of it *was* me. I was so nervous. Especially when you were set against letting Mandy join. I tried to cover it up, but I guess I came off kind of stiff."

"That's over and done with." He gently squeezed my shoulder. "I could see you were nervous. That didn't really bother me. Just seemed like you didn't approve of me. Guess I didn't have much use for you either," he said regretfully.

"She just seemed so young and you were so—" I felt myself blushing in the dark. "Well . . . you know . . . *old*—next to her."

"I am twice as old as she is. I guess I *am* her old man."

"You're a really good man," I blurted out. "I don't know how else to say it. You're very kind, and Mandy and Loretta are lucky to have you."

"Thank you kindly," he said formally. I could imagine him tipping his hat if he'd been wearing one.

"Not that my opinion counts for that much."

"It's worth a hell of a lot." He looked down. "It tore me up worse than buckshot to take charity for Mandy and the baby, but y'all did a good job here." He scuffed the gravel in the parking lot with his boot.

"Thank you, James. "I wish you and Mandy and Loretta, the very bes—"

"Laura, Nell told me about your daddy's heart attack," he broke in. I realized this was what he had wanted to say to me. "I hope he's better *real* soon. You're doing the right thing to be there for your folks," he said approvingly. "Of course it's what I'd expect you to do. You're a real special lady. Mandy and me won't forget you."

"But this isn't good-bye. I'm going to make it by to see Loretta."

"You'd be welcome any time, Laura." He rested his big hand on my shoulder. "But you're gonna be busy down there," he said sadly. "You won't have time to be running up here."

"Maybe not at first," I agreed, wondering when my life would be my own again and if I would see these families again.

He took my hand and shook it gently for such a big man. Then, in an instant, fast and light, so quick I almost couldn't be sure it was happening, he kissed me. On the cheek. Like a brother or an uncle setting off on a long journey. "Good night, Laura," he said. "You take good care."

When I came back inside, the cleaning-up was almost finished. Casseroles were covered, ready to be taken home. A couple of fathers were carrying out the trash. Someone had pushed the tables back against the walls. Chairs were being rearranged.

I said my good-byes, each one taking more out of me. I found myself held in many loving arms but couldn't bring myself to walk out for my last time. Then Susie helped me out.

"Laura, you got a lot on your mind," she said. "You want somebody else to carry me home?"

"It's no trouble, Susie. The car seat's already in my car. And it'll give us more time to talk."

"For the last time," she said bleakly.

"Don't say that," I answered automatically, still unable to face the separation. "I'll be back or maybe you'll bring Michelle to Atlanta to hear Steel Vulture," I said, momentarily buying into the dream, "and you'll bring her by to see me."

She looked away. "You'll forget all about us. In a few weeks you won't recognize me on the phone." The longing in her voice seemed worse than Nell's.

"That's not true. Besides, you'll be busy with your life."

"No, I won't. I'll be stuck here forever," she protested.

"Let's wait and talk in the car," I whispered. I handed her my car keys, wondering how I would comfort her. "I have a few more good-byes. You go ahead and get Michelle settled."

As they went out the door, Michelle woke and began to cry. "OK if I turn the radio on while we're waitin'?" Susie asked, rocking the baby in her arms. "That always calms her down."

"Sure. I'll be quick."

When I came out a few moments later, Susie was listening to Three Dog Night. She turned off the radio as soon as I got in. "You don't have to do that," I told her. "Play whatever you like."

She fiddled with the dial until she tuned in a local station. She turned it down to a very low volume as I pulled out on the highway. It was far too hilly to use bright lights so we progressed slowly. I wished someone would appear over the next hill to guide us, but no one did. It seemed we were in the only car in the world, driving off into unknown territory.

"You don't *really* believe you can't get away from here do you?" I asked, breaking the silence.

"Nowhere I want to go," she said sorrowfully.

"You don't know that," I challenged her, depressed by the defeated voice of someone with her entire life ahead of her.

"I been thinking," she continued hesitantly.

I looked at her, hoping with a sympathetic glance to encourage her.

"I haven't said it out loud yet, not even to Mama." Her voice trembled as she stared out the window. "But deep down, I've given up on Mickey. He won't marry me. It about broke my heart tonight seein' how proud James is of Mandy and their baby, and me knowing Mickey won't ever care for me that way. He cares about Steel Vulture more than he does about me and Michelle."

I was surprised she could face this cold truth after months spent defending Mickey, despite his erratic loyalty. A bouquet of flowers. A gold heart locket. An oversized box of Pampers. His few visits to the hospital had made up to her for his earlier desertion. She'd named her baby for him.

"Did y'all have a fight?"

"No. But Mickey can't handle anything serious. He changed his mind the first time, didn't he?" Not waiting for an answer, she admitted, "He's not gonna marry me. Even if he would, I couldn't count on him. If he ever does get a real job, he'll use his whole paycheck to cut another record or buy a better amplifier. He's not mean. He just don't think." She sat up very straight and sighed. "I figure there's only one way me and Michelle can make it."

"What's that?" I turned off on the road to Susie's house. It was so dark I hit a deep pothole in the blacktop. The car lurched precariously into a shallow ditch. "Damn!" I said, thinking we were going to be stuck. I tried to restart the car and it stalled. For a few seconds, we waited in silence, but on my second try the engine engaged and we slowly edged back onto the road.

"I'm sorry, Susie. Are you all right?" I looked back at Michelle, who was still sleeping angelically. I felt even more grateful for the Project's iron rule on car seats.

"I'm fine. I shoulda warned you. I forgot how bad that place is. Last year, this old man went clear off the shoulder all the way down that ravine. He got messed up real bad."

I shuddered and gripped the wheel tightly. "Anyhow, tell me what you've figured out for you and Michelle."

"I'm gonna get my G.E.D. I already called about it. They're sending me a book, and Mama says she'll watch Michelle when I start the classes."

"That's *great*. I know you'll do well." I hoped she could see me smiling in the dying light.

"I don't see why not." She smiled confidently, finally shaking her gloom. "Lots of people do it. Kind of like driving."

"How's that?" I asked, unable to follow her.

"It's like this, Laura," she explained. "I had trouble shifting when my daddy started teaching me to drive. I'd get real upset and start crying. Until one time Daddy said, 'Stop trying so hard. It's easy. Just think of all the idiots out there who drive every single day. If they can do it, so can you.'"

A car came out of nowhere and sped by us as if we were standing still. In seconds it was completely out of sight.

"What about after you get your diploma?"

"I may have to work nights at a Seven-Eleven, but I'm goin' back to school so I can get me a good job. Maybe key punch or court reporting. 'Cause they got some financial aid now. Mama and Ginger—she's my biggest little sister—remember? They're gonna help take care of Michelle if I have to take night courses. And I'm gonna make it, Laura. Me and Michelle are gonna do all right."

She sounded strong and so much wiser than the brokenhearted girl who'd been abandoned just before her wedding. Her determination recalled Nell's tiny voice standing up to her mother in front of the entire group, even if only to give her approval for Susan's rice salad.

I made a sharp turn onto the dirt road that ended at Susie's house. Michelle's eyes opened wide and she began to fuss.

"She can't be hungry," Susie said. "I just fed her." I couldn't see Susie's face clearly in the dark car, yet I knew her well enough to sense she was blushing. "Sometimes, I think she'll drink me dry." She reached over the back seat to feel the baby's diaper. "What is it sweetie? Tell Mama what's the matter." She smiled at me. "She's not wet or dirty. Maybe she's just upset about saying good-bye to you, too."

We drove on slowly. I didn't want to risk hitting another rut in the road. A few dogs barked as we passed by houses where every light was out. We seemed to be traveling through a deserted country. Michelle began to cry harder.

"Do you mind if I take her out of the car seat? Just this once? We're almost there, and I can't stand to hear her crying."

"Go ahead." I pulled over by the side of the road. We were almost in her yard. I didn't see what it could hurt. Susie cradled Michelle in her arms, cooing and stroking her, holding her close. But she cried almost without pausing for breath.

"Could you turn the radio up loud? She really loves it that way. Sometimes it's the only thing that helps when she gets like this."

I tuned the knob to a slightly higher setting and turned up the volume. Through all the static we heard a local DJ announce, "For everybody who loves the latest sound, here's the new single 'When Nighttime Shadows Fall' from Cherokee County's very own Mickey Osgood and Steel Vulture."

A burst of frenzied electronic sound, so loud I couldn't hear Michelle crying over it, was followed by a showy drum solo. Several dogs circled the car and barked, suspicious that we had stopped. I watched the pure excitement light up Susie's face, as we heard a ragged, wailing voice, which I assumed was Mickey's, roaring, "I need someone to love me, most every time of day. Someone who truly loves me, no matter what folks say. Just like a tiny baby when nighttime shadows fall, I need someone to love me more than anyone at all."

Michelle's small body relaxed as the loud music magically soothed her. She lay quietly in Susie's arms clutching her mother's shirt in her tiny hand.

"You just love music, don't you?" Susie asked the calm infant whose eyes had again closed. "I really love that song, too. Mickey said he thought of me when he wrote it." She wiped her eyes. "Especially this next part."

She sang along with Mickey's tortured voice, raising her own so that Michelle's eyes opened wide, and she listened mesmerized. "Someone who cares about me, who'll always take my side," she sang a little plaintively. But then as the crescendo came and the bass felt like it would pound through my car,

Susie shouted, as if she herself were the lead singer, "Won't let nobody curse me, 'less they want to step outside!"

I pulled up slowly to the small frame house on the hill. Michelle was silent, despite the relentless beat of the song. Susie had stopped singing, and I had run out of words, spoken or sung. I opened my window as if that might let some of our sadness escape the car.

Susie wiped her eyes on her sleeve. "Just like that song, Laura. It's all I ever wanted."

"What do you mean?"

"'Someone to love me.' And I thought Mickey was that person. That he'd stand by me no matter what, so nobody or nothin' could ever let me down." She cried softly, no longer even attempting to hold back her tears. "I was scared having a baby, but when he came to the hospital, I thought we were starting all over again. And that he wanted that, too." I could hear the tears coming back into her voice.

I squeezed her hand, trying to convey that I understood, even as I prepared to leave her. I handed her crumpled tissues from my purse.

"I'm sorry," she said, releasing my hand to wipe her eyes. "*I'm* acting like a baby again. I thought I was over it." She sounded put out and ashamed. "I'd do anything in the world for Michelle. But I wanted *him*. I really loved him. I guess I still do."

"We can't help who we love. That's nothing to be ashamed of."

"It is *now*. He doesn't want me."

"Susie, it's like the song says. You need somebody '. . . who'll always take my side.' Only this time it has to be someone who's ready to be in love, not just sing about it."

Michelle lurched forward in Susie's lap and batted at her mother's hair. She held on fiercely to one dark strand and looked up into her mother's eyes.

"It doesn't matter anyhow," Susie said impatiently. "I don't have time for love anyway. I got Michelle to think about."

"Maybe not right this minute. But you'll have time for love," I tried to convince her. "You're not even eighteen yet."

"But sometimes I feel so old, Laura." She spoke softly, rocking the baby, who rested against her. "Maybe you can't understand since you're not a mother." She spoke thoughtfully, trying hard to reach me.

"See, when you're a mother, all this weight piles up on you. Watchin' them. Feedin' them. Doin' for them. Bringin' them up right." She sighed. "I don't feel like a teenager anymore." She laughed gently. "Seems like I'm about a hundred years old. I might look the same. But deep down inside I'm different."

"You don't look any older. Certainly not a hundred," I teased playfully. "Not even twenty."

"Maybe not, but I don't think I'll ever *feel* young again. Not like those girls I went to school with who don't think about nothin' but boys and clothes and goin' to parties."

Then she hugged me close, yet very lightly so Michelle would not fret in her arms as she lay between us. I could feel Susie's own heart, beating as fast against me as a baby's.

"You want me to help carry your stuff in since she's asleep?" I whispered, noticing that Michelle's eyes were now tightly closed.

"Thanks, but I can manage all right. I better get used to it anyway," she said resignedly.

She rested the sleeping baby against her shoulder, gathered up her diaper bag, and skillfully eased herself out of the car without waking Michelle. She walked up the porch stairs, and in the harsh glow of the overhead light, I could see that she didn't look back. She stepped inside and closed the door.